The Tunnel

Robert Byrne, 1930-

The Tunnel

HARCOURT BRACE JOVANOVICH
NEW YORK AND LONDON

Printed in the United States of America

Library of Congress Cataloging in Publication Data

Byrne, Robert, 1930–
The tunnel.

I. Title.
PZ4.B99562Tu [PS3552.Y73] 813'.5'4 76–54585
ISBN 0–15–191385–4

First edition

B C D E

Contents

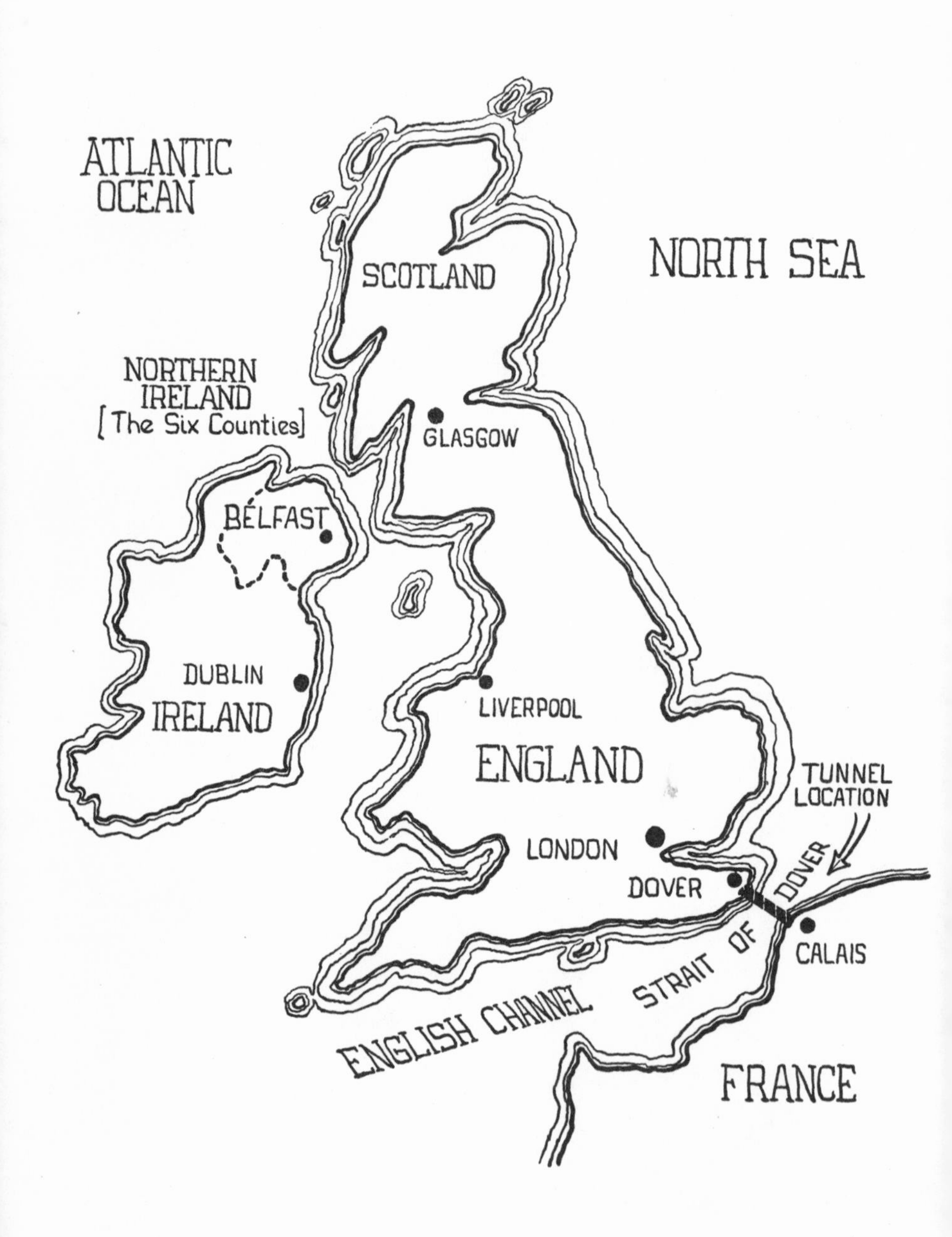
ATLANTIC OCEAN
NORTH SEA
SCOTLAND
NORTHERN IRELAND
[The Six Counties]
GLASGOW
BELFAST
DUBLIN
IRELAND
LIVERPOOL
ENGLAND
TUNNEL LOCATION
LONDON
DOVER
STRAIT OF DOVER
CALAIS
ENGLISH CHANNEL
FRANCE

Her Majesty the Queen of the United Kingdom of Great Britain and Northern Ireland, Head of the Commonwealth, acting in concert with the President of the French Republic;

CONFIDENT that a railway tunnel under the English Channel will greatly improve communications between the British Isles and the Continent of Europe;

DESIRING by this means to strengthen friendly relations between the United Kingdom and France;

CONVINCED that the tunnel will contribute to the expansion of trade between the signatory nations and the Member States of the European Economic Community;

HAVE DECIDED, therefore, to conclude a Treaty, and to this end have appointed their plenipotentiaries, who have agreed as follows: . . .

Article 4

(a) To make a final evaluation of economic, engineering, and environmental studies completed under terms of prior Agreements;

(b) To order the preparation of drawings, specifications, and contract documents for construction of the tunnel and its terminals;

(c) To invite, following approval of plans, tenders for construction on a worldwide basis;

(d) To seek ratification of this Treaty and related Agreements in the British Parliament and the French National Assembly, thus allowing contracts to be awarded and work to proceed.

[Treaty between Great Britain and France, November 1973]

Part One

The First Two Years

Chapter 1

Down a ruined street the young man ran, past barricaded entryways and the shells of burned-out buildings, his eyes burning with tears and his black, curly hair matted with drying blood. Sobbing, cursing, dizzy, his gait that of a drunk, Jamie Quinn tried to tear from his mind the picture of Maggie being killed by a bomb he had made himself. The plan had been to let the car roll silently down the hill into the sentry post. She was supposed to put it in neutral before jumping clear. Instead she left it in gear, and when the car lurched forward the door slammed on her coat. She was dragged to her death writhing like a fish on a hook, her screams cutting into him like shards of glass. The explosion sent her body spinning fifty feet across the pavement.

In his grief and rage, Quinn was running toward the headquarters of the Irish Republican Army's Belfast Brigade, the last place on earth he was supposed to go. He was going to make Kevin McCabe see that it was the policies of the Provisional Wing that led to Maggie's death. He would tell him that assassinations, revenge killings, and penny-ante terrorism weren't getting the job done. The Six Counties were as firmly trapped under England's heel as they ever were and the Protestants were yielding nothing. A dramatic act was needed, something spectacular that would force every nation in the world to hear the Irish cries for justice.

"Failure?!" McCabe shouted after listening to Quinn's outburst. "How dare you use the word? She died a hero's death and she'll get a hero's burial . . ."

They faced each other across the dining room table in McCabe's small Ballymurphy home: McCabe, a leathery veteran of revolution, and Quinn, whose childlike face was better suited to a choirboy than a gunman and bomber. Leaning against the wall with his arms crossed was Seamus Duggan, a powerful man with the shoulders of a plow horse. McCabe's wife Mary watched from the kitchen doorway, her fingers covering her mouth.

"What good will it do?" Quinn cut in. "A spread of pictures in *An Phoblact* about Margaret Maginnis, killed in action, and a funeral procession to show our strength. Is that why you dreamed up this crazy plan, so we could march to the graveyard again wearing our black armbands?"

"A crazy plan now, is it? Yesterday you thought it fine. A chance to eliminate ten British soldiers with one blow–"

"There's ten more to take their places, a hundred more, a thousand more! Six inches in the *Times,* that's all this blast will get. Maggie was thrown away for nothing."

"You threw her away. You let her drive–"

"We were the ones risking our necks, so we did what we thought best. When is the last time you heard the bullets fly? All I get from you is stories of the old days. Ancient history. Sniping, blowing up mailboxes and toilets, that's your idea of fighting a war. What has it got us? Twenty thousand British troops in our streets, three thousand of our best fighters in holes like Long Kesh rotting away like slabs of meat. We have to use teenage girls to drive loaded cars because with old men like you running things everybody else has been killed or locked up."

McCabe cursed Quinn then, calling him a puppy, a hothead, and a disgrace to his father's name, which brought the younger man to his feet with his fists flying. Before he could land a blow he was grabbed by Duggan and thrown back into his chair.

McCabe had not moved. He gazed evenly at Quinn, waiting a long time before speaking. His voice was tired. "Violating combat instructions. Breach of discipline. Insubordination. Assaulting an officer. I could have you shot. I *should* have you shot."

Quinn forced himself not to look at McCabe, afraid he would yield to an urge to fly at him again. He dug his fingernails into his palms to hold himself in check. Half an hour earlier, running down the street, he didn't care whether he lived or died. He half-hoped then he would be spotted by the army and police patrols that were fanning out across the city. He would have shot it out with them, as suicidal as that would have been. Now he wanted to live. He wanted to see McCabe stripped of power and humiliated, and a plan for bringing that about began forming in his mind.

"Against standing orders," McCabe said, "you came to this house even though you knew you were being hunted. We have God to thank that the Ulster Constabulary didn't follow you. The floorboards would be ripped up by now and the names and addresses of our members in their hands. Wouldn't that have been a fine thing?"

Quinn wasn't listening. He was telling himself that the reason the Irish revolution had accomplished so little was that its leaders lacked imagination. Men too small to think big. Men who didn't know how to get headlines and influence world opinion. He would show them. In one grand move he, James L. Quinn, would erase fifty years of I.R.A. futility. He was a hothead, was he? He would pick a target with care and plan an attack in the greatest detail. A big enough act of destruction with the threat of more to follow would force the British to release the Irish patriots they had held for so long. If he could set them free, whom would they support, McCabe and Duggan and the tough-talking relics in Dublin whose policies put them behind barbed wire in the first place? Or Quinn? Who would be first in the eyes of Ireland then?

He would need money and people he could trust. He glanced at Mary McCabe. Some wife she was, he thought, the easiest conquest he had ever made. She had once told him that she would do anything for him if only he would take her away from the nightmare her life in Belfast had become. He would find out how serious she was.

"Speak," McCabe was shouting. "Have you lost your hearing? What have you got to say in your own defense?"

Quinn's anger was gone, replaced by a feeling of certainty about what he had to do. His first task was to avoid getting shot.

"There is no defense I can make," he said. "Coming here was stupid. After the blast . . . I guess I couldn't think straight. I came looking for somebody to blame besides myself."

McCabe studied him, then looked at Duggan. "What should we do, Seamus?"

"Whatever you say."

"How old are you, Jamie?"

"Twenty-two."

"I'm forty-six. To you that's old. You won't think so when you're my age. Your father was fifty-five when he was cut down, and he was still one of the best fighters we ever had, not just with a gun but with his fists. When I look at you I keep hoping I'll begin to see him, and sometimes I think I can. I keep hoping you will come to know as he did the value of experience. We need youth in our struggle, yes, and we need vigor, but we need maturity and patience, too."

Quinn let him make his speech. It was a small enough price to pay for his life.

"I'm going to give you another chance. But to let you off as if nothing has happened wouldn't be fair to others who have broken rules and paid the price. You will spend three months on the farm in Donegal. You'll have plenty of time there to learn to control your temper and follow orders. In the mornings you can help with the chores. In the afternoons you can help train recruits. Seamus will take you there tonight in the truck."

Quinn nodded.

McCabe raised himself wearily to his feet. "If you were in my place, I wonder if you would be showing me the same mercy.

All right. We'll try to forget this day. In three months we'll begin again."

Mary McCabe turned away to hide her smile of relief.

Frank Kenward stepped off the elevator and walked down the carpeted corridor telling himself he must be nuts to come halfway around the world without knowing why. The company Cessna to Caracas, Pan Am to Los Angeles, Checker Cab to the Century Plaza, and Otis Elevator to the top floor. He should have told Ingram to go jump in the lake, which in his case would have been Lake Michigan. But you didn't say things like that to the president, chairman of the board, and sole owner of the William K. Ingram Construction Corporation, not unless you wanted a wild bull on your hands.

"Never mind why," the old man had shouted on the phone, "you just get your ass up to L.A."

"Goddammit, Bill, I'm trying to drive a tunnel. You're *paying* me to do it. I've got hot water in the heading, power failures every day, an outbreak of clap on the day shift . . ."

"I want to take you to dinner with a contractor who'll be here from England."

"Mail me his picture and a baked potato."

"*Be* there."

The line went dead. For a second, Kenward thought he saw and smelled cigar smoke curling up from the receiver.

After knocking on the door of Ingram's suite, Kenward gave himself a last-minute check in a wall mirror. Just as he thought. His suit not only felt tight, it *looked* tight. He unbuttoned the coat and patted his stomach, not the washboard it used to be. He'd better start working out again and cutting down on the booze. Either that or buy a new suit.

He tugged on his tie to straighten it, wishing he could do the same with his nose. That had been knocked permanently out of alignment, and the memory of how it happened still made him wince after twenty years. The first man through the line had been the blocking back, who stripped him of his helmet. Next came the ball carrier, who genuflected on his face with a two-hundred-pound knee. And so a promising sophomore linebacker was persuaded that career opportunities were more attractive in the field of engineering.

Now Ingram was drawing him inside, fixing him a drink, and introducing him to Sir Charles Crosley of Crosley and Black, Limited, London, England. Good old Ingram! Talk about a weight problem! He looked and walked like an overweight duck. The silver-haired Englishman could not have provided a greater contrast. Kenward, shaking his hand firmly, could more easily imagine him as a diplomat than as head of an engineering-construction firm.

"I am assured by your employer," Crosley said, "that what I have heard about you is true. When it comes to rotary tunneling machines you have no equal."

"He says things like that instead of cutting me in on the profits."

"Or the losses," Ingram said. "Enough chitchat. Let's get down to business. Frank, my boy, you are going to positively shit when you see what we've got up our sleeves. Positively *shit*. Sir Charley? Care to do the honors?"

Crosley laughed as the three men sat down next to the windows. "Not even my wife calls me Sir Charley," he said.

Nobody glanced at the view. To the north, a carpet of lights reached all the way to the Hollywood hills. Wilshire Boulevard was a glowing line angling westward toward the ocean. Crosley placed an attaché case before him and snapped it open. From a cloth bag he removed a piece of white rock the size of a golf ball and handed it to Kenward. "How would material like this be for tunneling? I don't mean lumps of it, I mean a stratum a hundred feet thick and thirty-two miles long, impervious and without so much as a hairline crack."

Kenward rolled it around in his fingers, estimating its density and hardness. With his thumbnail he was able to cut a groove across it. He drew the sample across the cuff of his jacket and left a white line. "Chalk," he said, handing it back to Crosley and brushing the mark off his sleeve, "a high grade of chalk. If the layer is dry and without fractures, it would be ideal for a rotary mole. Maybe even better than New Mexico sandstone."

"I was hoping that's what you'd say. I happen to know that the tunnels you drove for the Bureau of Reclamation in New Mexico set speed records that have never been surpassed."

"Anyone could have set records in that material," Kenward said with a shrug. "It was perfect . . . easy on cutting edges, consistent, and it stood by itself without support. Before we put in the concrete lining the bores looked like rifle barrels. I would guess that chalk would provide the same conditions. Where is it from?"

"Dover, England. To be specific, Shakespeare Cliff, the prominent one the photographers love. I know just how prominent it is, believe me. There are three hundred and ninety-eight wooden steps leading from the bottom to the top . . . I counted them because I thought each one would be my last. This pebble comes from the beach directly above the point where the English Channel Tunnel will cross the coastline on the way to France."

Kenward nodded slowly. "The Channel Tunnel. So that's the big secret."

"Big is right," Ingram said, lighting a cigar. "Low bid on the British half may run as high as one billion bucks. That's one dollar followed by nine zeros." He ejected a plume of smoke that spread across the table like a cloud of battlefield gas.

"Is it really going ahead this time? It's been delayed and shelved and restudied so many times I've more or less given up on it."

Crosley answered the question. "The French have already decided to construct their portion using government forces. In a few days there will be a worldwide call for bids on the British half. As soon as the low bidder is known, the House of Commons will vote to award the contract. We've surveyed every Member of Parliament. There will be no problem with the vote unless the proposals are totally unrealistic."

"The low bid won't be out of line," Ingram said to Kenward

with animation, "because you are going to be in charge of preparing it. The winner is going to be a joint venture of Ingram Construction Corporation and Crosley and Black, Limited, with maybe a few other cats and dogs thrown in to spread the risk. When work starts you will be the underground boss. How do you like that? Worth the trip from Venezuela, eh?" Before Kenward could answer, Ingram was rushing on. "Here's what you do. Go back to Maracaibo tomorrow and wind up your business there. Put Gilchrest in charge. Go to Dover and look over the site. Meet Charley's people and talk to the British Rail engineers. We can meet in New York or someplace a few weeks before the bid opening to put together the final figures. Charley brought along a set of condensed plans and specs that you can dig into on the plane . . ."

"Hang on a minute," Kenward said, raising his hand, "I didn't say I'd take the job."

"What? Of course you'll take the job. Are you kidding? It's perfect for you. It'll put Ingram on the map and it'll put you on the map."

"No, I'm not kidding. When Maracaibo holed through I was planning to take some time off. A vacation. A leave of absence."

"Take some time off, then. Take the whole weekend. Then roll up your sleeves and help us win the biggest project that ever came down the pike."

"I was thinking of more than a weekend. Maybe a few months. Or a few years. I haven't had my nose off the grindstone since we finished those Washington subway tunnels. Do you know what my wife said when she left me? That I was so married to my job I could be arrested for bigamy. I want to lie on a beach somewhere. Instead, you want to send me to the front lines for another five years of combat."

"For God's sakes," Ingram said in irritation. He went to the bar and began throwing ice cubes into a glass.

"I rather expected you to jump at the chance," Sir Charles said. "Opportunities like this don't come along often. I do hope we can persuade you to say yes. I was looking forward to having you as my underground superintendent."

"You'll be the project manager?"

"Yes. I was to retire next year, but for this I would delay it. The Channel Tunnel has been part of my life since early childhood. Advocacy of it in my family was practiced almost as a religion, and in my grandfather's family as well. It's more than just another large project. It's part of England's history; it's essential to England's future. I want my firm to be the builders. I want the men who do the work to be the best there are. That's why I invited Ingram Corporation to join us . . . to acquire your services."

The deal is sounding better, Kenward thought. It would be a pleasure working with a man of Crosley's stature, experience, and good manners. No more cursing contests with Ingram! It would almost *be* a vacation.

"There are other men who could do a good job for you," Kenward said. "Some of them on your own payroll."

"No one has your record of success."

"My record of success is mainly the result of pure, dumb luck. Mother Nature has been asleep on my jobs, that's all. She may be due to wake up."

Ingram returned and slammed a glass on the table. "Drink this," he said. "It might bring you to your fucking senses."

There were two glasses in front of Kenward now, a snifter of brandy Crosley had invited him to try and the tumbler Ingram had just brought, which appeared to be filled with straight Scotch. What a difference there was between the two men! It was hard to believe they were members of the same species, much less the same joint venture. Kenward took a deep breath. How could he refuse the challenge of the greatest job in history? If he did he could be declared legally insane. He picked up both drinks, one in each hand, and raised them in a toast.

"Okay," he said, "I accept. God save the Queen."

Chapter 2

"Following the opening of the bids, the House of Commons will ratify the treaty with France, which will, in effect, authorize the selling of the bonds and the awarding of the contract."

The speaker was the Minister for Transport, Stanley Markland, appearing on BBC's not-very-popular weekly feature *Domestic Issues*. He was a solid, self-assured man with a complexion so ruddy that when his face first appeared on the screen, owners of color television sets all over the British Isles reached out to make adjustments.

"Permit me to stress again," the Minister said, looking directly into the camera and, he hoped, into the hearts of his constituents, "that no new taxes are required. Funds for construction will come in the form of loans from the private sector to be repaid out of the income generated by tolls over the next fifty years."

The Minister smiled in a friendly fashion, pleased with how well the interview had gone so far. He had already disposed of two of the most frequently asked questions: why the portal was four miles down the coast from Dover (designers had to follow the course of the soundest chalk layer), and why vehicles were to be carried on trains instead of driven through directly (keeping such a long tunnel free of motor exhausts would be impossibly costly). Now he had made one of his most effective points—that the project would require no direct governmental expenditures. He dared not, however, let his guard down, for Cyril Jones, his interrogator, was not to be trusted. Jones projected an image of unwavering blandness, but behind the façade was thought to reside an anti-tunnel soul.

"Could you take a moment to explain to our viewers exactly what you propose to build? Provided Parliament approve?"

"Certainly, yes. Can your camera focus on the easel? Good. This is a plan view. The main yard, where cars and lorries will board the special trains, as you can see, is just outside Folkestone, with the portal at the tip of my pointer. The two parallel railway tunnels will run along the coast towards Dover, gaining depth as they go, always staying within what the geologists call the Lower Chalk. They curve under the sea here, at Shakespeare Cliff, and continue in almost a straight line to France. The next chart is an elevation view. Note how the tunnels slope downwards from the portals to just past the coastlines, then gradually rise to the midpoint of the Channel. The reason for the 'W' profile is to permit seepage, of which there will be very little, to drain by gravity to pumping stations near each coast. The final chart. Here we have the cross section showing the two twenty-six-foot-diameter tunnels fifty feet apart. The schedule calls for finishing the southerly bore first and using it to generate income while the second is under construction."

"I see." Off camera, Jones was drumming his fingers. "What would happen if income from tolls is insufficient?"

Markland shifted slightly in his seat. "Public money would be required then, yes, because the government is, in effect, guaranteeing the loans. But the chances of the tunnel generating too little revenue are almost nil. Demand for through-freight and passenger service to the Continent is very large and can be measured rather accurately. The project is viable even with the conservative traffic estimates we use in our planning."

"Some critics point out that income will also fall short if a catastrophe were to–"

The Minister had been warned that such questions might be asked, and he responded vigorously.

"The possibility of a catastrophe is extremely remote. A cave-in, for example, flooding the tunnel, which seems to be a popular fear, is scarcely conceivable in view of the geology of the Channel floor and the factor of safety designed into the reinforced concrete lining."

"I was not thinking so much of a natural disaster as a man-made one. The specter has been raised of terrorists destroying the tunnel with a bomb, thus leaving the British public holding the bag, as it were. You will forgive me, Mr. Markland, if I adopt an adversary position. Since announcing the subject of tonight's program, we've had a heavy mail, much of it raising the kinds of questions I am putting to you."

"I quite understand, and I appreciate having this opportunity to answer them. Much of the opposition, in my view, stems from a misunderstanding of the facts. Once people have the facts, they see by what a great margin the positive aspects outweigh the negative. To mention just one point, the tunnel will cut freight costs by at least fifteen percent. The refreshing effects of that will radiate through our entire economy. Now with regard to catastrophes and bombs and the like. They can't be ruled out with complete certainty, of course. Nothing that man has built or will ever build is invulnerable. But we are talking here about structures of tremendous strength and massiveness. A bomb, unless it were impossibly large, could do little more than interrupt traffic for a matter of hours or days. Those who worry unduly about bombings and earthquakes and so on are not being realistic. The same argument could be mounted against any human activity, indeed against leaving the house in the morning. Giving in to such fears would bring every human endeavor to a halt. No, the proper course is to assess the risks and take steps to make them insignificantly small. The rewards of pressing on are, after all, enormous . . ."

In County Donegal, Republic of Ireland, Jamie Quinn turned off the television set. The blurred image shrank to a pinpoint and disappeared. Reception had been terrible despite the antenna atop the chimney of the old farmhouse, but Quinn had heard enough to be convinced that the Channel Tunnel was the target he was looking for. He walked to the front porch and put his hands on the rough wooden railing. In the moonlight he could see nearly half a mile down the valley between the rounded, tree-studded hills. The air was cool and still, and above the chirping of crickets he could hear the snap of rifles from the firing range, where a platoon of volunteers was taking nighttime sniper practice. He tightened his lips in satisfaction. The Channel Tunnel . . . a symbol of pride and prestige for both Britain and France that would naturally capture the interest of the world press. An impossibly large bomb would be needed, is that what the pig had said? After completion, yes, but what about during construction? He knew enough about warfare to realize that the best time to strike was before the enemy had set up his defenses. During construction there would surely be a weak point, an Achilles' heel, and there would be more than enough confusion to cover the movements of saboteurs.

In his mind he began putting together the team he would need: a worker at the site to provide a description of the security system, someone with experience in tunnel construction, demolition experts who knew how to handle tons of explosives . . . All would have to be willing to risk their lives for the cause of Irish freedom. All would have to be willing to kill without hesitation or regrets.

Quinn needed candidates for martyrdom and he needed time. Ireland had plenty of both.

The most comfortable chairs in Sir Charles Crosley's Tudor home on the outskirts of London were in the library, so it was there that he and his wife and their American guest watched *Domestic Issues.*

"That's our Mr. Markland, Frank," Crosley said when it was over, closing the mahogany doors of the television cabinet, "what do you think of him?"

"He's not what you would call an electrifying speaker," Kenward said, "but he is forceful and he seems to have a good command of the subject."

"I should hope he has a good command of the subject. Lord knows British Rail and the Engineering Institute have spent enough time coaching him. The reason he is so important to us is that he carries the burden of Commons debates."

"He makes a better impression in person," Crosley's wife said. Lady Crosley was a tall, elegant woman, so thin as to appear almost frail. She spoke with such a marked accent that Frank had difficulty following her. "On television and on the floor of the House he is so frightfully stiff. I hope you can meet him while you are here. He has a perfectly delightful sense of humor."

"My wife is inclined to be overly generous. One of her many gifts is the ability to detect senses of humor that are invisible to others."

"A gift very much to your advantage," she laughed, "when you were courting me. Gentlemen, I'm going to say goodnight. Breakfast is at nine, Mr. Kenward, if you'd care to join us. When you are ready to go to bed, for heaven's sakes say so! Charles will keep you up all night talking about the tunnel if you let him."

"I'll be impolite if I have to."

"Good." She kissed her husband on the cheek and was gone.

Frank walked admiringly around the room. "I like your wife, your house, and your books," he said.

"Thank you. So do I. We all get on quite well together. The house and library have been in the family for generations. I am hardly more than their custodian."

"My God, you must have every book on engineering ever published."

"A good percentage of the older ones. My great-grandfather, who founded the firm of Crosley and Black, began the collection in the 1850s. The glass case on your right contains nothing but works by and about the Brunels, father and son. They're remembered mainly for railways, canals, and steamships, but they contributed a great deal to tunnel technology as well . . . the first shield, the first drive under a river, the first use of compressed air to keep a heading dry. One of the additions I've made is a section for plays and novels in which engineers play a prominent part. Such things are seldom written now, but they used to be quite common. Did you know how Goethe finally allowed Faust to find the total satisfaction he was seeking? By building a dike on a land reclamation project. My literary friends always seem to have forgotten that. Or Kafka in *The Castle*. The entire story concerns a man trying to confirm the fact that he has been given an important job as a land surveyor."

"What's this," Frank asked, running his eyes along a row of titles, "a whole shelf of books on the Channel Tunnel?"

"Quite a mass of material, isn't it? I believe it's the most complete in the country. The earliest item is a report presented to Napoleon in 1802 by a French mining engineer named Albert Mathieu, whose design called for chimneys protruding above the water so that horses galloping below on their way to invade England wouldn't suffocate. Then there are popular histories, *Hansard* transcriptions of Parliamentary discussions, magazine articles, brochures issued by various promoters along the way, even a scrapebook of newspaper clippings my wife keeps. Tell me something, Frank. You are the champion in the use of the rotary tunnel excavator. Have you any idea where it was invented?"

"I've a feeling you are going to say England."

Crosley nodded. "A hundred years ago. Beaumont was the gentleman's name, Colonel F. E. B. Beaumont. He drove a mile of tunnel with an air-powered mole of his own design, a remarkable machine fifty years ahead of its time. There's a model of it in the South Kensington Science Museum. His motive may surprise you. He was trying to demonstrate the feasibility of boring a tunnel between Britain and France. True! The spot he choose by instinct is only a few yards from where I picked up the piece of chalk I showed you."

Frank took one of the older volumes from the shelf and leafed through it, shaking his head. "I had no idea the project had such a literature. I'm going to read myself to sleep tonight."

"Excellent idea. I've done it many times myself."

Dotting the rolling green countryside of southeast England are hundreds of silolike structures called oast houses–bases of stone or brick topped by tall conical roofs. Many are still used for drying hops, as intended by the nineteenth-century farmers who designed and built them, some are abandoned and deteriorating, and a few are playing roles unrelated to their origins. Anne Reed, a commercial free-lance photographer, had converted one south of Canterbury into a studio using twenty gallons of whitewash and two glass skylights she had found in a waterfront salvage yard.

Although well known for her professional skill, Anne Reed was even better known as a defender of the natural environment. As president of SKAT–Surrey-Kent Against the Tunnel–she had invited to her studio home the most active members of the organization, a group that included the head of the seamen's union, the vice-president of an air cargo firm, a professor of botany, the director of the Cinque Ports Garden Clubs, Young Socialists who were against the tunnel simply because capitalists were for it, and a variety of housewives, retired schoolteachers, and country squires. Citizens normally unrelated to, uninterested in, and even at odds with one another were united on the issue of blocking construction of the Channel Tunnel.

"That's the enemy," Anne said, wrinkling her nose as if a foul odor were rising from the television set and touching the off button as she might a piece of garbage. "Have you ever seen a man so cold-blooded and unfair? He's supposed to represent all the people when in fact he speaks only for those who want to turn Kent into a railway yard. I hate to end our meeting on such a depressing note, but I think watching Mr. Markland will impress each of us with the power we are up against. We are, quite plainly, fighting the entire government and all the big corporations of the country. Our weapons are the facts, the same ones in many cases that Mr. Markland thinks support his point of view, and a good many more he seeks to conceal.

"Before we adjourn, I want to remind you that this battle was won more than once before and can be won again. It's going to take hard work in the few weeks we have left before the final vote. To review what we've decided today: The Seamen's and the Shipper's unions will urge their memberships to write, phone, or visit their Members of Parliament; student demonstrations will be held in London, Croyden, Canterbury, and Dover; and, let's see, what else? Oh, yes, those of us on the Media Committee will draft and send out as strong a plea for support as we can write to every newspaper and radio station in the country. For my part, I will take a series of photos of the Dover headlands in an effort to dramatize the beauty of the region the Tunnel will ruin. Anything else? Mr. Carberry?"

"I just want to say that in our campaign we should always make it clear that we are opposed to the tunnel for reasons that go beyond self-interest. It's one thing to win over a homeowner by saying, 'They are going to build a railway in the bottom of your garden and it's going to be ghastly,' and it's quite another to win over somebody in Wales or Scotland who isn't directly concerned. We must stress that the tunnel and the high-speed rail link to London will be terrible for everybody because of the way it will divert funds and attention away from more worthy goals."

"Good point. Mrs. Mott?"

An elderly woman rose to her feet and said in a wavering voice: "We should think of ourselves as a truth squad. Whenever we hear the words 'Channel Tunnel' we must say, 'Stinking fish! Stinking fish!' "

"With that war cry ringing in our ears," Anne said when the laughter had subsided, "I move we adjourn. We all have work to do and we had better get to it."

Chapter 3

Old Folkestone Road rose from Dover's docks and railroad yards, presenting ever more spectacular views of the old port city, and entered a shallow valley behind the coastal cliffs. Frank Kenward pulled his car onto the shoulder and opened a copy of the plans and specifications across the steering wheel. The designers had located the tunnel centerline beneath the depression in order to minimize the depth of a proposed vertical access shaft. Turning to the site map, he ran a fingertip to the point representing his present location, where the tunnel curved toward the sea. He smiled at a small x labeled "Old Folkestone Road Access Shaft–Contractor's Option." A shaft or some additional means of entry was essential, not optional. Anyone trying to drive the tunnel from the Folkestone portal alone would find the task impossible in the time allotted. They would need another adit here to allow two more headings to be worked, one advancing toward the Folkestone end, the other toward the union with the French crews under the center of the Channel.

It was hard to get used to the immensity of the job. Men would be working more than twelve miles from open air, requiring by far the longest lifeline in the history of underground construction. Twelve miles! Only astronauts had ventured farther from the safety of Earth's surface. And astronauts, Kenward thought, setting the plans aside and getting out of the car, didn't have to show a profit when the trip was over.

He turned up the collar of his corduroy jacket against a cold wind that was coming out of the northwest and began making his way up the wet, grassy slope. The sky was filled with black and white clouds that promised another day of alternating showers and sunshine.

Having the wind at his back helped in mounting the hill, but the shifting gusts were treacherous when he reached the edge of the precipice, and he dropped to one knee to guard against suddenly finding himself airborne. On a clear day, the desk clerk at his hotel had assured him, you can see the clock tower in Boulogne. Frank had no doubt of that, although Boulogne was hidden in haze at the moment. Calais was plainly visible, standing out like a button on the edge of a coat, and so were at least a dozen ships, those in the distance barely visible specks. The southwest face of Shakespeare Cliff towered above him on his left, a dull gray when shadowed by clouds, a brilliant white when reflecting the sun's direct rays. To the right was a long view of crumbling headlands, an indented line of chalk palisades ending in another promontory called Abbot's Cliff, beneath which the twin tracks of British Rail's Dover-Folkestone line disappeared into a tunnel.

Gazing across the shifting pattern of whitecaps at the thin line of land on the horizon, Frank found it easy to understand the fascination the Channel Tunnel had held for generations of engineers. There lay France, beckoning across a stormy strip of water. The Channel Tunnel—what a blend of engineering and science fiction its history was, what a comic opera! Those wonderfully Victorian schemes for long-legged rolling platforms and refloatable tubes . . . they could have come from the pens of H. G. Wells and Jules Verne. How laughably impractical they were, yet how expressive of the optimism of the times. Engineers were national heroes then and the purpose of life—at last it had been discovered!—was to make it easier to get from one place to another.

Behind Kenward was a rural valley glistening with new rain, before him was a majestic coastline. In his mind's eye the landscape gradually became filled with field offices, storage yards for equipment and supplies, trailer courts, and barracks for workers.

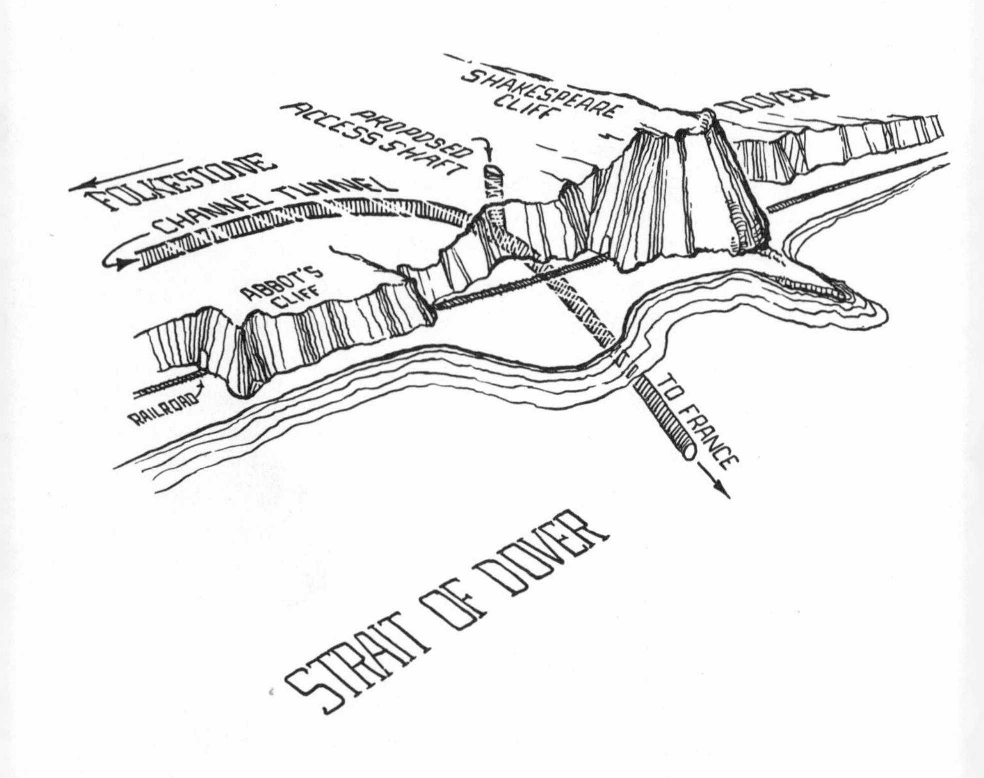
SHAKESPEARE CLIFF
DOVER
PROPOSED ACCESS SHAFT
FOLKESTONE
CHANNEL TUNNEL
ABBOT'S CLIFF
RAILROAD
TO FRANCE
STRAIT OF DOVER

The air carried the sounds of straining diesel engines as trucks labored with loads of tunnel spoil toward fill areas miles away. At the access shaft, he thought, it would probably be best to set up a couple of elevated loading hoppers to eliminate truck waiting time . . . or was there a better way? There was a flat piece of beach at the foot of the cliff, ten acres at least. Surely some use could be made of that. If British Rail could be induced to put in a spur track, materials could be unloaded there and perhaps carried to the main bore through an inclined tunnel . . . he would have to check the plans for relative positions.

So absorbed was he in his thoughts that he didn't notice the woman in the white turtleneck sweater who had set up a camera behind him and was peering through the viewfinder, twisting his image into focus . . .

Anne Reed had had a busy day, and her legs were trying to tell her to call it quits. She had gotten some wonderful early morning shots of the meadows as the fog was lifting, and by climbing a water tower she had found the perfect view of a stone bridge that was doomed if the terminal was built. Driving home, she was surprised when the sun broke through the cloud cover. She stopped the car and studied the sky; a patch of blue promised at least half an hour of sunshine, time enough to get a few shots of the coast. She shouldered the tripod and camera and trudged up the slope toward the sea.

When she reached the top and the distant views were opened before her, she paused to catch her breath. The wind was invigorating, and she let it send her black hair streaming behind her like a pennant. She noticed a man on one knee farther along the footpath. A good-looking fellow, she thought, despite the crooked nose. Probably dumb as an ox. The attractive ones almost always were, when they weren't married or queer. She considered taking his picture, hesitating because the scene was such a cliché: a man gazing into the distance atop a windy hill. Then again, perhaps just the thing for her booklet of photographs.

She quietly loaded a film pack into the adapter and pushed it into the back of her old Crown Graflex 4x5, an indestructible camera she always used in bad weather. Through the viewfinder the subject seemed separated from reality . . . a picture in a book, an image on a screen.

"Hey, what the hell . . ."

The image had sprung to life.

"I'm terribly sorry, I didn't mean to frighten you."

"Why did you sneak up on me, then? Jesus, lady, I almost jumped over the edge. It would have been the longest swan dive in history."

"You looked so picturesque perched there, I couldn't help—"

He burst into laughter. "Picturesque? That's the nicest thing I've ever been called."

At least he was good-natured, with an appealing vitality and directness. An American . . . odd to find one so far from a car.

"Would you mind taking a picture of the shore for me?" he asked abruptly, pointing downward. "A train is coming, it'll be below us in a minute. Could you snap it as it goes by?"

"I suppose so. It will cost you, though. It comes under the heading of 'special assignment.' I don't take pictures for my health, I do it to eat. Anne Reed, photographer, at your service. We never close. No job too small."

"Okay, Anne Reed, photographer, you've just been hired by Frank Kenward, picturesque photographer's model. Quick . . ."

She twisted the camera from its tripod mount and adjusted the settings as she moved to the cliff. "I don't think I can see the tracks from here," she said, peering over the edge.

"You can if you lean out. Go ahead, I'll hold you. Here it comes . . ."

His arm circled her waist. She pressed the camera to her cheek and leaned into space, wondering why she was so casually putting her life in the hands of a stranger.

"There's a flat section of the shore," he said, "get as much of that in as you can."

The train, a seven-car passenger run that had left Charing

Cross at noon, hurtled down the track at fifty miles an hour, already braking for Dover's Priory Station, and plunged into the darkness of the Shakespeare Cliff Tunnel.

The camera shutter clicked. "Got it," Anne said, and felt herself being hauled back to safety.

In her darkroom that night, Anne wondered if she were losing her touch. She had smiled at a man without stimulating the slightest response. Mr. Frank Kenward apparently had his mind set on only One Thing: climbing down to the beach before it started raining. No flattery, no lingering glances from him. When his arm was around her it had felt more like a steel railing than flesh and blood. Perhaps it was just as well. Getting interested in an American tourist was a useless thing to do.

She filled a tank with developing fluid. At least he paid. in advance. For that she would mail him the most compelling photograph of a train roof the world had ever seen. What on earth did he want it for? Maybe he was a fetishist with a flat lined with shots of trains plunging into tunnels.

The phone rang when she was halfway through developing the first batch of negatives. "Shit," she said aloud, "it never fails." There were ninety seconds left on the timer. "I'm busy," she called into the darkness. "Ring back later!"

Sitting on the edge of the bed in his Dover hotel room, Frank returned the telephone to the side table. He wasn't surprised that there had been no answer. It was wishful thinking, he thought, to imagine that a woman like her would be running around unentangled. She was probably out with her husband or one of her three dozen boyfriends. He dismissed from his mind the idea of sticking around to find out more about her and went back to his original schedule. Tomorrow he would leave for Venezuela. After a week or two there it would be a matter of shuttling back and forth between New York and London for meetings of the estimating teams. Then the big moment: the opening of the bids.

Chapter 4

Jamie found the old man just where he thought he would, sitting on a coil of rope at the end of a pier in Belfast's dockyards dangling a fishing line into the water. A short distance away a crew of men were stacking crates swung from the hold of a freighter by a derrick. It was illegal to fish from a privately owned pier, but who cared what an old man did if he didn't bother anybody? Certainly not the uniformed guard who stood watching the laborers, a Protestant who had no way of knowing that the old man was Eamonn Caldaigh, for twenty years one of the top strategists of the I.R.A.'s Official Wing. Jamie was surprised at how old his uncle looked. He had gone completely gray since he had seen him last. His eyebrows were like two puffs of cotton.

"Fish don't bite at this time of day, Uncle Eamonn," Jamie said.

"I know that," Caldaigh said in a coarse voice, not looking up. "I'm hoping I might snag one accidentally as it swims by. Fishing was good here before the ships took to flushing their bilges. Look at the water now . . . look at it! What could live in such muck? Reminds me of the chicken stew my sainted mother used to make, may her soul rest in peace, in the name of the Father and of the Son and of the Holy Ghost, amen." For the first time he turned his eyes. "Jamie Quinn, as I live and breathe! Why aren't you off with your Provo friends blowing up women and children? Ah, you're going to become a fisherman instead. Not as thrilling, my boy, not nearly as thrilling. Of course, there's always the chance you'll hook a boot filled with Spanish gold. No, I guess not. The Spanish never sailed to Belfast. I wonder why?" He waved a hand at the surrounding warehouses, the sagging wharves, the smoke hanging low over the line of factories across the water. "Has there ever been a more beautiful spot than this in God's green world?"

"We don't blow up women and children."

"Unless they get in the way." The old man turned his attention to the cork bobbing in the water.

"If I was the madman you think I am, I'd kill you for saying that."

"Your own flesh and blood? You've not sunk that low, have you now? I helped raise you, Jamie! I belted you when you spilled your pudding, I belted you when you wouldn't stop crying, I belted you when your mother and father got arm weary doing it themselves. It was for your own good, Jamie. Kept you out of jail, didn't it?" He laughed sourly.

Jamie sat down on the top of a low piling and rested his arms on his knees. "I'm leaving the Provos," he said.

Caldaigh looked at him suspiciously. "Leaving or getting kicked out? I heard McCabe sent you to the farm for taking a swing at him. I hope you hit him a good one."

"I thought the Officials didn't believe in violence."

"We do when the time is right. The time is always right to take a poke at Kevin McCabe."

"Well, I swung, but I missed. If I had hit him I suppose I'd be a dead man now."

"A dead *boy* you'd be. You're not a man yet, for all the killing you've done. You want to join the Officials, do you? All through with terrorism?"

"I'm through with McCabe's brand of it. I have a plan. I came here because I could use some help."

The old man widened his eyes and smiled. "You have a plan! That is grand news, Jamie. Its always nice to meet a young man with a plan, who has a *goal* in life. Let me guess what it is. You want me to loan you some money so you can go to Boston and become a policeman."

"Listen to me, Uncle Eamonn. I want to carry the war to England. I want to pull off something big that will force the Brits to empty the jails and call their troops back home. I have the perfect target. I need money to set things up and spring Maher and Carney from the Tobermore camp."

"Ah, sweet mother of God, I might have known. Jamie Quinn wants to carry the war to England. He wants to make a big splash. Maher and Carney . . . demolition experts, both of them. Tired of your little car bombs, are you? Now you want to blow up Buckingham Palace and Picadilly Circus. Forget it, Jamie. It's been thought of before. I've been at a hundred meetings at least where such things were proposed. Always they were voted down . . ."

"Because nobody had the nerve . . ."

"Plenty of people had the nerve, you young fool! They were voted down because they would do more harm than good. Killing a pile of Englishmen and destroying their beloved monuments, do you know what that would do? It would unite them in a bond of hate against us, it would silence the few supporters we have in Parliament, it would give the British Army the freedom to do anything it wants. There are a million Irish living in England. What would life become for them if wild-eyed Republicans started wrecking trains and strangling members of the royal family?"

"Threatening to destroy the target I have in mind will drive a wedge between the people and the government. When it is destroyed the government will be humiliated and the people will applaud . . ."

"There is no such target. Turn away from such ideas before you make things worse than they already are."

"How could they be worse? I have a plan that will put the Provos out of business and make the Officials number one again, and you won't even listen . . ."

"What do you mean, *again,*" said Eamonn Caldaigh, tightening his fists to contain a rush of anger. "We are still number one in the hearts of those who can see beyond their noses. The Provos are putting themselves out of business with their shootings and bombings. You're too soaked in blood to realize it. Not just the Protestants hate you, it's the majority of the Irish people as well. You should visit Dublin and the counties farther south. You'd find out what the people there think of your campaign of murder. They've had a bellyful of it. They fill the churches on Sunday praying for a stop. They don't want Ireland united if it's to be ruled by assassins."

"At least the Provos are *doing* something," Jamie said heatedly, "at least we're fighting."

"Keep your voice down or we'll have the guards and the dockers over here asking questions. Fighting, that's what you call what you're doing? Lenin had a better word for it: adventurism. Using force too soon, when you're overmatched, getting your best men killed for nothing. You've pushed the Six Counties to the bottom of the pit with your reprisals and revenge. You've changed the struggle from something political to something religious, which is the worst possible thing that could have happened. Northern Ireland has a million Protestants and only half a million Catholics. If Britain calls its soldiers home and civil war breaks out, who would win? McCabe counts on the Republic stepping in to turn the tide. He expects to be rescued and put in charge of a united Ireland by the gangsters in Dublin, as greedy a pack of capitalist pigs as you can imagine. There's only one path that's right, and that's to restructure the society . . ."

"Spare me the lecture . . ."

". . . so that the working classes in all parts of the country see that the enemy is not the men of the other faith but the man who gives him his pitiful wages. Eire is rotten, Jamie! It's backward, it's wrapped in religious superstition, it sucks at Britain's teat, it's ruled by hypocrites and thieves. Why do you want to deliver the Six Counties into hands such as those? If you want to join us you will first have to understand that the job that needs doing now is the political education of the masses. It will take many years . . ."

Jamie jumped to his feet. "I'm not waiting. It's true what I've heard about the Officials–you're all a bunch of Communists. Sit around and talk about classes and masses day and night. The Catholic workers and the Protestant workers are brothers who should join hands and overthrow the dirty bosses . . . what a stinking pile of dung! The Protestant workers hate our fucking guts, haven't you learned that yet? They'd kill us all if they could."

"That may be true at the moment, thanks mainly to the likes of you. It doesn't have to be true always. Not if we can teach them to see that–"

"Piss on teaching," Jamie said, kicking the old man's bucket of bait off the wharf into the water. "That's for women to do when the war is over. I came here with an idea that would put you and your cronies back in the driver's seat, and you don't even want to hear about it. All right, I'll do it myself."

"Don't go to England, Jamie. If you love Ireland, don't give the Ulstermen and the Army an excuse to bring down the iron fist."

"You make me sick." Jamie spat on the dock. "Talk, talk, talk. That's not for me. I'm going to make things happen."

Caldaigh watched him walk away, then looked at the bucket drifting on the ebbing tide. To fill it with worms had taken him half an hour on his hands and knees in the garden. Jamie shouldn't have kicked it in the water. Jamie was going to be very sorry he did that.

Quinn paced his flat waiting for darkness. Idiots! Fools! Cowards! He couldn't find strong enough words for the I.R.A. establishment. One faction was as bad as the other. The Provisionals couldn't rise above their rifles; the Officials wanted to turn Ireland into a classroom first and a battlefield second. He was better off rid of them both. He tried to think of people he could trust and who would follow him. There weren't many, but there were enough. Mary McCabe was one, dumb as she was. With information she could provide, he could loot the Provo treasury. Why take the risk of robbing a bank? He would finance his operation in a way that would cripple his rivals. It was Tuesday . . . Kevin would be at the weekly brigade meeting most of the night . . .

Ten o'clock found Quinn running along a deserted side street, stopping to crouch in shadows when a patrol car passed looking for curfew violators. Two-story stone houses stood shoulder to shoulder from one end of the block to the other like rows of old war veterans straining to hold themselves erect. There was no light in the McCabe home . . . apparently Mary was already in bed. She was going to get a surprise. He was not due back from the Donegal farm for another three weeks.

He let himself in with the key she had given him two years before and locked the door behind him. After watching the street for a minute to make sure he hadn't been followed, he slipped out of his shoes and carried them to the second floor. The bedroom door swung open silently. A street light outside the house made the two drawn windowshades on the far wall glow like paper lanterns. Quinn crossed to the side of the bed and in the pale light looked down at Mary, sleeping beneath a patchwork quilt. Slowly, very slowly he drew the bedclothes from her, letting them fall in a pile on the floor. As always when her husband was away she slept without the flannel nightgown he insisted on —her nakedness embarrassed him, he said, and turned his mind from more important matters. She was not a beautiful woman, but she was younger than her husband and far from unattractive, with a strong, ample body. She was another man's wife, Jamie thought, studying her, a man who thought she was his private property. When Quinn had taken her before, he was driven by sexual passion alone and was always left with the feeling that he had stolen something from a man he both feared and respected. There would be no pangs of guilt this time. Instead there would be the pleasure of humiliating a man he hated. She was lying on her side, her arms in front of her, one knee drawn up, her breasts resting one on the other, as round and full and soft as the pillows beneath her head.

The sound of Quinn's belt buckle and zipper brought Mary McCabe's head up. She could see the silhouette of a man against the light. "Kevin?" she said, stabbed by sudden fear. "Is that you?" As the bed sagged with additional weight she became aware that she was completely exposed. She sat up and began groping for the sheets and blankets as if they would offer protection against an intruder. Her heart began pounding wildly.

"Don't be afraid, Mary . . ."

"Jamie? My God, you've come back to me . . . You scared me half to death. You should have given me some warning."

The bedside light went on. She drew up her knees and covered her breasts with her arms in an involuntary reflex of modesty. "Don't cover yourself, Mary," he said, "I want to see you. It's been so long . . ."

"You shouldn't have come, there's not enough time . . . Don't look at me like that, you scare me . . ."

His hands moved up her arms to her shoulders and she felt herself drawn forward against him. "This is crazy," she said, turning her face to one side, "Kevin would kill us . . ."

"I'm sure he would." The prospect of McCabe bursting in on them excited Quinn. He pushed Mary down.

"Not so fast, Jamie . . . Jamie, please . . ."

Quinn pressed himself into her, ignoring her cry of pain.

"You're hurting me," she sobbed. "What's the matter with you?"

I want McCabe to open the door, Quinn thought, thrusting mindlessly, I want him to see me now . . . Using both hands he pushed her breasts together and upward and covered as much of them as he could with his mouth. I want him to see me doing this to his wife, her legs opened to me like garden gates . . . Oh, how I wish he could see this . . . he would put a bullet in my back, but it would be worth it to hear his scream of rage. I would gladly die if I knew he would spend the rest of his life with this picture burned into his brain.

Within seconds of his climax he withdrew and rolled away. He lay on his back breathing heavily, his gaze fixed on the ceiling. He couldn't think, and he had the feeling that he couldn't move. If the woman had turned to him with a knife in her hand and tried to slit his throat, he would have been powerless to prevent her. After a few minutes he realized that she was on her feet at the foot of the bed picking up the bed covers. He didn't look at her, even though he used to enjoy watching the way her breasts moved when she walked and turned and stooped. In the old days when McCabe traveled to Dublin and he and Mary could spend the whole day together they sometimes never put their clothes on. In the nude they would cook and eat and play cards, making love whenever her hand could coax his flesh into readiness, wherever they were in the house. Now his mind was blank and his strength was gone. It was cold in the room, he noticed for the first time, and he was glad when Mary spread the blankets over him. She turned the light out and returned to the bed, not touching him but lying close. When his breathing returned to normal and the room was very quiet, he felt her fingertips move lightly across his chest.

"Jamie," she said, "I . . . I didn't . . . enjoy that very much. You made me feel like . . . a clump of sod. You . . . you used to try to please me." She spoke as softly as she could, afraid of angering him and turning him once again into the animal she had just seen. "Have you forgotten how to be gentle? You mustn't forget. I'll help you remember, if you'll let me."

Quinn's self-control gradually returned to him, and he realized how important she was to the success of his plans. The lies came easily to his lips. "I'm sorry, Mary. I've been cooped up on that damned farm for so long I'm like a caged lion. I've not forgotten." He embraced her and softly kissed her eyes and lips.

"Oh, that feels good. We could be so happy together . . ." Her voice broke and she turned away. In a half-whisper not intended for his ears she said, "Mother of God, forgive me for loving this man."

"Mary, I came to tell you something. I'm leaving Ireland. Not because Kevin will be looking for me when he hears I've skipped the farm. Because I'm sick of the war. I want to go away forever and start a new life. In Canada. Will you come with me?"

She gasped and drew herself up on one elbow, facing him in the darkness. "Do you mean it? You know how I hate it here."

"I mean it. Will you?"

"Yes! Yes! Now?"

"No, no . . . we need money."

"I have a little . . . a couple of hundred hidden in the kitchen, a couple of hundred more in the bank."

"We need far more than that. False papers and passports, plane fare to British Columbia, enough to live on for a year or two until our trail gets cold. Your loving husband will send his gunmen looking for us, you know, and I want to be beyond their reach. I know how we can get all the money we need, enough to fix us up for life. Before I went away the Army Council had decided to buy a load of Czech arms. Have they collected the money yet?"

"Brian has been making speeches in the United States for the last two weeks. Contributions are coming in. Kevin says they'll need a hundred thousand American dollars at least. Jamie, there's no way we can get it. If we tried we'd never get out of the country alive."

"We won't steal it here. Where will the payoff be made?"

She told him what she knew. The men had spent night after night at her dining room table going through the glossy pages of the Omnipol arms plant catalog picking out rifles, submachine guns, hand guns, ammunition, bazookas, plastic explosives, and grenades–five tons in all, to be packed in two hundred wooden crates. A chartered plane would leave from Prague and land at one of the major airports on the Continent. At the last minute somebody from the Belfast Brigade would be given the money and sent to take possession, giving the money to an American middleman who was arranging the deal. The crates would be trucked to the coast and transferred to fishing boats. That's all that had been decided so far.

"Keep your eyes and ears open," Jamie told her. "I'm leaving for England tomorrow. I'll call you next Tuesday night and give you my phone number. The minute you know the time and place of the pickup, let me know and I'll do the rest. When I've got the money I'll call you and you can slip away and meet me at Heathrow."

"It sounds so dangerous. I don't think it will work . . ."

"It will work. In a month or two we'll be far away and safe."

Jamie's words made her feel dizzy, and she pressed the back of her fist to her forehead. "I'm almost afraid to let myself believe you," she said in a trembling voice.

He took her hand and drew it between his legs, closing her fingers around his sex. Minutes later they were interlocked again, making love the old way, the slow way, the way that left Mary's eyes glistening with tears of joy.

Chapter 5

Placing a phone call would make him a few minutes late for the meeting of the estimating committee, but . . . "Hello, is Mr. Reed there?"

"There is no Mr. Reed. This is Anne Reed."

"Good! I was afraid there might be a Mr. Reed to contend with."

"Who is this?"

"Frank Kenward. Remember me?"

"Of course! I sent you a photo on Monday. Did you get it?"

"I did, and it's beautiful. It could be framed and hung on a wall."

"Thank you. Where are you calling from?"

"Direct from the Hilton Hotel in New York, New York."

"Why on earth . . . Have you an assignment for me that can't wait and for which you will pay any price?"

"In a sense, yes. I want you to go to dinner with me two weeks from tomorrow. I figured you could hardly refuse an invitation made on a transatlantic call. How about seven o'clock?"

Not all of the men seated at the conference table were cost estimators; also on hand were specialists in construction contract law, insurance, financing, labor relations, and scheduling. Sir Charles Crosley, without rising from his chair, speaking in a conversational tone, addressed the group. Kenward, he noted, who had rushed in late, was the only one present not wearing a tie, although he was otherwise presentable.

"Bill and I thought it would be useful to get the team together one last time to make sure we all understand one another and aren't working at cross-purposes. Bids will be opened one week from today, leaving us with about one-tenth the time we could profitably use. Let me apologize in advance for the sleep we must do without between now and then. We did try to persuade the government to delay the bidding for a month, arguing that lower estimates might well result, without success. Stanley Markland, the Minister for Transport, whom I talked to just before leaving London, said that the bid opening has already been delayed one hundred years.

"Several matters have been decided in the last few weeks. Our bid will be submitted under the name Channel Tunnel Constructors. The joint venture will comprise Crosley and Black, Limited, sponsor, with an interest of forty percent, Ingram Construction Corporation, with an interest of thirty percent and a share of job management, H. J. Beckstead Associates, Limited, and Cardovan Enterprises, Limited, who will share the remainder as an investment only. I shall serve as project manager at the site. In charge underground will be Frank Kenward.

"There are over one hundred bid items in the contract. The key to winning the job rests on items 11, 17, 34, 41, and 79, namely, excavation, lining, lining installation, muck disposal, and trackwork. If our total figure is to be below those submitted by the competition, our bids on those five items must be as low as we can make them, consistent with safety and profitability."

"Can I stick a word in here, Charley?" William Ingram said, clearing his throat. "We don't know who exactly we're up against. We know that a hundred sets of plans and specs were sold at two hundred bucks a pop, but the bid list shows that most of them went to subcontractors and suppliers. Of course, some of those may be fronting for big boys who don't want us to know they're in the race. I'd be surprised if more than four envelopes are on the table when Tuesday noon rolls around. The Germans will be there, you can bet on it. And the Japs. Don't count the Japs out. They tell me that the beach around Dover has been crawling with German and Jap engineers, snooping around, looking under rocks, and so on. If we knew who exactly we were bidding against, we'd have some idea of how close we have to figure. Since we don't, we just have to bid the job and not the competition, is the point I'm trying to make. Excuse me, Charley."

"That's quite all right," Sir Charles said, resuming. "Item number one on the bid document, mobilization, is still pegged at five million pounds and will not be raised. As we agreed at our last meeting, I explained to the appropriate people in the government that the figure was absurdly small for a project of this scope, especially one in which many months will go by before the major pay items are reached. I pointed out that shifting an extra financial load onto the contractor is bad economics, insofar as the government can borrow money at lower rates than can a private firm. They were unyielding, I am sorry to say. There is a political problem involved. To those who are unfamiliar with how large government works projects are financed, the payment of even five million pounds to the contractor before any work is done appears to be a giveaway. A larger figure would be much too hard to explain. Bill?"

"So we are going to have to unbalance the bids to get more early money," Ingram said. "Fred, Tom, the rest of you who are working on the estimates for the early items, site clearing and access roads and so on, don't faint when you see the figures we actually submit. They'll be pumped up. We'll compensate by cutting back on the estimates for the electrification and cleanup items at the end."

Crosley asked for a comment from Earl Whitehead, who was in charge of financing. Whitehead, portly, balding, and gloomy, spoke in a monotone. "With the mobilization money, with unbalancing, with the cash the partners are willing to put in the pot, we shall still have to borrow in the neighborhood of twenty-five million pounds—say, forty-two million dollars. Financing charges are going to be a major cost. Whoever finds the lowest interest rate is going to win the job."

One of the British estimators asked a question. *"At least* twenty-five million or *as much as* twenty-five million?"

"At least," Whitehead replied. "Once the mole gets going and the per-foot-of-advance payments are coming in, we'll be all right. If it breaks down or there is a labor strike or something else interrupts production, we'll have a cash crisis in a big hurry."

"That's the pessimistic view," Crosley said. "It's also true that if things go smoothly the profits will be very substantial."

Whitehead shrugged. "What job this big ever went smoothly?"

Crosley couldn't surpress a smile. "I want you to know," he said, glancing around the room, "that I made a special point of having Mr. Whitehead with us today. I knew he would be a sobering influence should there be an outbreak of enthusiasm." He paused for a sip of tea. "Gentlemen, enthusiasm may well break out when you hear what Frank Kenward has to say. His ideas for attacking the work put us in a strong bidding position. Frank, suppose you tell the group what you told me last night?"

Frank's remarks were confined to three areas that seemed to him to offer the greatest opportunities for cost savings: the Dover adit, the mole, and the disposal of muck from the seaward drive. As he talked, William Ingram beamed, at one point nodding to Crosley as if to say, "Didn't I tell you he was the right man for the job?"

Frank unfolded a map of the job site on the center of the table. "In my opinion," he said, "we should forget the vertical shaft at Dover proposed by the designers and use two inclined access tunnels instead. That way we could make use of a flat section of beach for part of our construction plant. Look at the geometry. . ." He placed the point of a pencil on the map. "If we start from Old Folkestone Road behind Shakespeare Cliff and drive a tunnel three hundred eighty-five meters long downward at a ten-

SHAKESPEARE CLIFF
CONSTRUCTION OFFICES
UPPER ACCESS TUNNEL
OLD BEAUMONT TUNNEL
[UnKnown Depth]
LOWER ACCESS TUNNEL
1ST BORE
2ND BORE
CHANNEL TUNNEL

to-one slope–I've labeled it 'upper access tunnel'–we would come out near the bottom of the cliff right here. A ramp could carry traffic the rest of the way down to the shore, which is wide enough for a railroad spur, a concrete plant, maybe a precasting setup for the concrete liner. Call that area the 'lower yard.' From there we drive another bore–the 'lower access tunnel' –three hundred fifty meters long at a downward slope of seven to one, intersecting the centerline of the main tunnel right here . . ." He made a checkmark on the map. "From that point we can start two headings. One will advance toward Folkestone using mining equipment, the other will head toward France as soon as the mole arrives. See the advantages? We'll be able to drive trucks right into the main tunnel without having to rehandle everything at the top and bottom of a shaft. A rail spur will cut the cost of–"

"Just a minute," said Fred Conroy, one of the members of the British estimating team. "Are you sure the foreshore is big enough for a spur and a marshaling yard? That map is not to scale for the waterline."

"It's big enough," Frank answered. "When I got the idea I could hardly wait to pace it off. I climbed down Aker's Steps in the rain to do it. It's about seventy-five meters wide and five hundred meters long."

"Mud or sand or what?" Conroy persisted.

"Good rocky material. Here's a shot of it from above," Frank said, reaching into his briefcase. "I had a photographer take it just as a train was going into the Shakespeare Cliff tunnel so you would have a comparison of size."

Conroy took the photograph in both hands and studied it, frowning.

"What's wrong," Crosley asked, "don't you like the idea?"

Frederick L. Conroy, for fifteen years in charge of construction cost estimating for Crosley and Black, Ltd., looked at his employer. "I think it's an excellent idea," he said, still frowning. "I just wish to ruddy hell I had thought of it myself." He turned to Kenward: "Congratulations. You have just cut our costs I don't know how many millions of pounds."

"It'll cost more at the beginning," Earl Whitehead put in, finding a dark side. "Not enough front money is already the problem."

Ingram dismissed the point with a wave of his hand. "Borrowing will be a cinch with this plan. Even a banker will be able to see the advantages of it. What about the mole?"

"It's got to be the best ever built," Frank replied. "You don't need a computer and a scheduling network to know that the seaward drive is going to be critical. Delay that and the job is delayed. Downtime on the mole would kill us. I think we should try for a modular design. If something breaks down we would be able to switch in an entire assembly instead of trying to fix it on the spot. The whole rig has got to be at least partly collapsible so we can drag it back to the portal after meeting the French crews in the middle of the Channel. It's got to be well enough made so that it's ready to go another twelve miles in the second tunnel. It's got to be equipped with secondary drills so we can probe ahead at least fifty meters. If the sea is waiting for us in a fissure, we want to know about it while we can still save our skins. We've got to have pinpoint accuracy, so we'll need the most precise laser guidance system ever devised." Frank leaned forward. "I hope we're all agreed that there must be no corner-cutting on the mole. It's got to be as close to perfect as we can make it, no matter what the cost. The whole job depends on it."

"I don't think there is any question about that," Crosley said. "We need reliability, and we are simply going to have to pay for it. Have you got a manufacturer in mind?"

"Seville Steel in Pittsburgh. They charge an arm and a leg, but nobody does better work. If we get the job, I'll sit down with Joe Seville and I won't let him get up until he understands the kind of machine we've got to have."

"Jesus," said Ingram, "you'll have to watch him like a hawk. Turn your back and Seville will put turning indicators and backup lights on the goddam thing and add ten thousand bucks to the bill. Is the mole really all that important? Seems to me muck removal is what's going to hold us back. Once we get six, seven miles in, the mole is going to be waiting for empty muck trains. I can see the crews at the face sitting around with their thumbs up their asses."

"I was coming to that. At about the five-mile mark I think we should consider using a slurry system. The chalk will peel off the face in fairly small particles, just right for mixing with water and–"

"Aw, God, Frank," Ingram cut in, shaking his head, "you've been trying to sell me on that for years. Other people have tried it and it never works. First you have to pump water all the way to the face, then you have to pump it all the way back out–always you got to be screwing around extending the pipelines. By the time you're done, a gang of coolies could walk the stuff out in laundry baskets."

"Who said anything about pumping water to the face?" Frank said. "We've got the whole English Channel a hundred meters over our heads. We'll use that. We'll hire an offshore oil rig to drill a series of holes, say one a mile, along the route. After we mix the slurry we'll use the same holes to get rid of it. Send it straight up and let it settle on the ocean floor."

There was a moment's silence, broken only by someone's low whistle.

"Even if it can't be done," Sir Charles said, "it's a splendid idea."

Conroy shook his head dubiously. "Straight up? That would be a terrible head to pump against."

"I have in mind a closed system," Frank countered, "that would make use of the pressure of the incoming water. The heads would balance each other."

"But the cost of developing a new system . . ."

"What about the cost of hauling six million tons of muck an average distance of six miles? The cost of slowing the mole down to wait for trains?"

"The environmentalists won't like it," Crosley said.

"Why not? They'd rather have a few valleys in Kent filled in?"

"They won't like it, Frank, because . . . well, because it would muddy the water. It's the English Channel, you know. It runs through English veins along with blood."

"Storms muddy the water, too."

"But you can't file a lawsuit against God. You can against us. You know how environmentalists are. They get excited by all sorts of things."

Conroy had the last word. "It's worth looking into, I'll say that. But there is no way in the world it can be researched and priced out in the few days we have left, not if we had ten times the estimators we've already got."

The point was indisputable. After a lengthy discussion it was agreed that the job would be bid on the assumption that a conventional train-haul system would be used for spoil removal. If the bid were successful, Conroy would assign several men to work with Kenward on the feasibility of the slurry proposal. They would have several months before having to reach a decision.

For six hours the men sat without a break. Twice calls were made to London for pieces of information. When adjournment finally came, at ten minutes to midnight, there was a general feeling of confidence that the winning tender would be submitted by Channel Tunnel Constructors. Frank was congratulated several times for his plan of attack, the two-tunnel access and the water-level staging area being singled out for special praise.

Jamie Quinn would like those features, too. For him they would represent the Achilles' heel he was looking for.

Chapter 6

Chief Inspector Penton of the Criminal Investigation Department gazed across his green metal desk at the only interesting thing in his office, a hand-carved Victorian coat rack he had salvaged from the old building. The fluted central shaft was divided at the bottom into three legs, each of which ended in a lion's head the size of a fist. The mouths were open, the teeth bared, the eyebrows arched. Often, in some uncanny way, the beasts mirrored his emotions. God knows they had been watching him for enough years to know how he was feeling.

He wished the Yard had never moved. His office in the old, turreted headquarters on the Thames was too hot in the summer, too cold in the winter, too small in all seasons, and a four-minute walk to the gents' room, which was also too hot, too cold, and too small. There was something nice about the place, all the same. The clutter, the file folders stacked on the floor because there was no room for more cabinets, the kettle hissing in the corner against regulations, the balky intercom system . . . these things made him feel warm and comfortable. They had reminded him, in fact, of home. His study at home was messy and crowded in the same way. There was a hissing kettle there too to keep him company, and his wife, like his secretary, could be fetched only by repeated shouts. All of that was missing from the dreadful glass towers of New Scotland Yard at Number 10 Broadway. He was surrounded now by so much plastic and efficiency it was hard to get anything done at all. His feelings of privacy and coziness were gone. Through the glass partitions he could keep an eye on his colleagues and they could do the same to him.

The coat rack stood out in welcome relief from the general sterility. He got some of his best ideas while studying the grain of the wood and tracing the sensuous curves of the arms and legs. When he stared at it long enough it sometimes seemed to come alive. He perceived it then either as a dancing, many-limbed Hindu goddess of fertility or as six strips of bacon writhing in a Teflon pan.

The thought of bacon reminded Chief Inspector Penton that he had arrived at the next item on the day's agenda: the eating of lunch. From a briefcase he removed a series of wax paper packages and unfolded them on his desk, nodding in approval at the contents. A hard-boiled egg. A sandwich on white. A small apple. A paper packet of salt substitute. A celery stalk filled with peanut butter. Once again his wife had done her job well, following his instructions to the letter. The thing he disliked most about retirement–now just two years away–was that he would have to make his own lunch. He could hardly expect his wife . . .

Something made him look up. What he saw through the glass partition made him curse under his breath. The lion heads recoiled in sympathy and seemed to say, "Oh, no!" Making his way between rows of desks was Inspector Kenneth Greene, waving his hand as if to say, "Good day, Mr. Chief Inspector, sir," and "Stay where you are, I have something to tell you." Penton could guess what it was. Another unlikely conspiracy theory. Another suggestion for restructuring the department. Another request for permission to fly in the dead of night to Paris or Madrid. Permission denied. Confound it, why couldn't Greene stick to his duties, which were clearly defined in the *Manual,* instead of forever mucking about where he didn't belong? Look at the young fool, walking with that exaggerated bounce in his step. He does that just to irritate me. What makes him think he has the right to bound into my office without an appointment just because Mrs. Wheeler is away from her desk?

"Hello, Mr. Chief Inspector, sir. I had a thought I wanted to pass along. You were so busy this morning I decided to wait until you weren't doing anything." Greene sat down without an invitation.

"Not doing anything? This isn't evidence I'm sifting through, it's food. I was preparing to eat it."

"The Provos are raising money in the States," Greene said, nodding and smiling briefly as he talked to show that he had heard the Chief Inspector's remarks and agreed they were amusing. "Naturally, they are saying it's to help people widowed and orphaned by the dastardly British. I have a feeling it will go to buy guns and bombs to create still more widows and orphans."

"I was also about to work out some problems in my mind, for which I need a period of quiet reflection, such as the noon hour."

"This will only take a minute. I think it would be well worth the time spent to follow the course of the money. Keep tabs on how much is raised, trace it as best we can when it comes back to Ireland. Find out how it's really used."

The problem to which Penton had intended to address himself was the relocation of his compost heap. Moving it to the other side of the garden would involve a great deal of hard labor, but once done would afford years of pleasure. Such things were best begun far in advance of retirement. He had seen too many colleagues very nearly killed by the shock of converting suddenly from full-time police work to full-time gardening. A smooth transition, that was the key.

"Assuming it is intended for arms," Greene went on, narrowing his eyes, "we could possibly disrupt the deal. After all, how many sources are there? I mean, for heavy goods?" He began counting them on his fingers. "Libya. Russia. Czechoslovakia. The U.S. by way of Latin America . . ."

Penton peeled back the top slice of bread. Chicken salad. He distinctly remembered telling his wife salami. He rested his hands on the edge of the desk and looked at his junior officer with an expression intended to convey both indifference and loathing. "No," he said.

"No, what? I haven't asked for anything yet. What I was going to propose is that I be assigned several men with information sources in Northern Ireland. Together we'll follow the money. You can bet the Provos wouldn't have gone to the trouble of raising it if they didn't need to replenish their stocks or if they weren't planning an offensive of some sort."

"No. You will not chase a wild goose while under my direction. You will pursue your present duties, which, if properly carried out, will more than fill your day. I know you want to become involved in something less routine than liaison with the Army. It will come, in time . . . as a reward for dependable service. Permit me to give you a piece of advice. You will be miles ahead in the long run if you find a way to curb your natural ebullience."

"But surely, sir, you agree that the money could lead us to–"

"Inspector Greene. One of the things you haven't yet learned to appreciate is the comprehensiveness of the Yard's operations. Keeping track of suspicious money is standard practice. We have specialists for that. It takes years of training to do it well. Please, go back to your desk and give us some credit for knowing what we're doing."

Greene shrugged, then stood up. "It seemed worth getting your opinion. In case you wanted to take some action." Was there sarcasm in Greene's voice? Penton couldn't be sure. "I may keep an eye on the money in my spare time," Greene added.

"What you do after hours is entirely your affair."

Penton watched him leave, noting that there was less spring in his step. Following the course of the money, he had to admit, was an interesting suggestion. He wondered if the Yard really did have specialists in that area. Gradually his mind drifted back to the compost heap, and he nearly let time run out for the current item on his agenda, namely, the eating of lunch. The lion heads reminded him of it. He noticed that their mouths were agape as if ready to snap shut on stalks of celery.

Chapter 7

W. Mitchell Hargrave-Mott, Principal Engineer of the Ministry of Works, walked to the microphone at the center of the stage. A dolly-mounted camera rolled alongside and closed in on him as he spoke. Another camera panned the spare scene behind him: a long table that supported the folded hands and notebooks of officials and recording secretaries from the Ministry of Transportation, the Ministry of Works, the Department of the Environment, and the British Railways Board. On the left stood two flags, the Union Jack and, to underscore the purpose of the occasion, the Tricolor of France. On a small side table was a stack of six manila envelopes. At the right was a blackboard.

Mr. Hargrave-Mott squinted in the unfamiliar glare of the television lights and apologized for the crowded conditions in the auditorium, a private facility normally used for concerts and lectures and the largest that could be engaged on short notice. The original intention was to open the bids at British Rail's headquarters on Marylebone, he explained, but it quickly became obvious that the main meeting room there was not going to be adequate. The government hadn't anticipated that a crowd of more than a thousand people would materialize. The huge turnout, he suggested, reflected the realization on the part of the public of the importance of the English Channel Tunnel to the nation's future and, indeed, to the future of Europe as a whole. Because his remarks were being sent over the airwaves, recorded on tape, and taken down in shorthand, he didn't mention what he knew to be the case, that the audience was made up largely of those with a commercial or professional interest in the project, primarily the merchants of construction equipment, supplies, and services. As soon as the home address of the winning bidder was known a veritable siege army of salesmen would be on the march.

The press contingent alone numbered nearly a hundred, with representatives on hand from the wire services, radio and television networks, daily newspapers, and the trade, technical, and business press. In the balcony was a delegation of twenty engineers from the People's Republic of China who were touring the country under the auspices of the Federation of Civil Engineering Contractors as part of an exchange program. They were being told through an interpreter that the competitive bid system in the construction industry was free enterprise in its purest form.

"Unless someone comes rushing down the aisle with an envelope in the next three minutes," said Hargrave-Mott, gesturing toward a wall clock, "it would seem that we shall have six contenders for the project. Let me explain that at precisely noon no further bids will be accepted. The project has been divided into one hundred twenty-one categories, not just for the purposes of bidding, but for payment to the contractor as progress is made. As the project moves forward, our field engineers will keep careful track of the amounts of earth moved, steel erected, concrete placed, and so on, so that monthly payments can be made based on the prices per cubic yard, per pound, and per ton as they appear on the bidding documents."

He glanced at the clock again before continuing. "Our purpose today is to determine which group of contractors has submitted the lowest total bid, that is, the lowest summation of his estimated unit prices times our estimated quantities. According to law, since this is a public bidding, the estimates of all bidders on every item must be read aloud. However, we don't intend to subject everyone to the hour or two of droning that will take. To begin with we shall read only the total figure so that we shall all know promptly who the winner is. A ten-minute recess will then permit those of you who wish to leave to do so. A bank of telephones has been set up in the lobby, and I am told that taxicabs are waiting for those who wish to return to their offices. Anyone wishing to stay for the detailed reading of the unit bids is, of course, welcome.

"I must caution you that before the contract can be awarded, the low bidder's proposal must be gone over to make sure it is fully responsive and free of errors. The bidder himself must be matched against our criteria for financial and technical competence. Finally, Parliament must vote approval of the contract. Only then can work begin on what many of us have been involved in for . . . well, it seems like most of our lives."

He turned to a woman seated at the end of the table behind him who was holding a telephone to her ear. "Mrs. Baker, it seems to be twelve o'clock. Does Greenwich agree? Good. Ladies and gentlemen, the bidding period is officially closed. The moment we've been waiting for has arrived."

With a nervous glance and smile at the camera, he took the first envelope, ripped it open, and withdrew the bid form, a collection of fifteen mimeographed sheets with filled-in blanks bound between cardboard covers. He read from the first page: "Tunnel Construction Associates, a joint venture sponsored by T. and J. Sasaki, Incorporated, and including Kubo Steel Corporation and Ogata International, all of Tokyo, Japan." He turned to the last page. "Total bid, five hundred twenty-three million, six hundred twelve thousand pounds. That's five, two, three, six, one, two."

There was a rush of whispering in the hall and the sound of hundreds of pencils and pens moving across notebooks. The reading of the Sasaki offer had a special impact on two groups of men, the representatives of the firms submitting higher bids. With only one bid opened they already knew they were out of the running, having wasted months of costly planning.

Mrs. Baker entered the bid on the top of the blackboard, writing in bold strokes:

Sasaki, Tokyo £523,612,000

"Cross Channel Builders," said Hargrave-Mott, "a joint venture of Morrison-Knudsen Company, Incorporated, of Boise, Idaho, Peter Kiewit Sons' Company of Omaha, Nebraska, and Guy F. Atkinson Company of South San Francisco, California. Total bid, five hundred twenty-two million, seven hundred one thousand pounds. Five, two, two, seven, zero, one."

"So much for the Japs," whispered William Ingram to Frank Kenward and Sir Charles Crosley. The three were sitting near the left aisle with a group from Crosley's London office. Frank gestured with his eyes to the Japanese, who were sitting several rows away. They were crestfallen, and one had lowered his face into his hands, "The poor bastards," Frank said, watching the figures go onto the blackboard, "imagine losing a job this big by less than a thousand pounds."

Sasaki, Tokyo	£523,612,000
M-K, U.S.A.	522,701,000

Ingram nodded happily. "And so much for M-K, Kiewit, and Uncle Guy," he said, thinking of his own bid. "They don't have the ballpark to themselves any more."

"Too early for congratulations," said Sir Charles, though he couldn't help showing relief at hearing the figures of the Japanese and American groups, which contained some of the biggest and most experienced construction organizations in the world.

Mrs. Baker held her piece of chalk in readiness as Hargrave-Mott opened the third envelope. "Channel Tunnel, Limited, a joint venture. Johnson Dunkley, London, sponsor, with Blackwood Enterprises, Liverpool, and Davis, Bartels, and Cross, Limited, London. Total bid, five hundred sixty million, one hundred eleven thousand pounds. Five, six, zero, one, one, one."

Sasaki, Tokyo	£523,612,000
M-K, U.S.A.	522,701,000
Dunkley, London	560,111,000

"And so much for the limeys," Sir Charles said quietly.

Three envelopes were left.

"Dover Strait, Limited," announced Hargrave-Mott, "a consortium of Impreglia and Sons, Rome, Italy, Piero Bellugi Construction Company, Milan, Italy, and Zilfi-Shaqra, of Riyadh, Saudi Arabia."

"Guess who's bankrolling that bunch," Frank said.

His companions didn't smile. They had heard rumors that an Italian group backed by a Middle East oil country was in the race, and it worried them. "They might offer to build the bloody thing for tuppence," Crosley had said, "just to rub our noses in their money."

The numbers came over the loudspeaker: "Five hundred seventy-one million, seven hundred thousand pounds. Five, seven, one, seven, zero, zero."

Sasaki, Tokyo	£523,612,000
M-K, U.S.A.	522,701,000
Dunkley, London	560,111,000
Impreglia, Rome	571,700,000

"How do you like that!" Ingram said excitedly, slapping the arm of his chair and raising his voice to be heard above the buzz of reaction from the audience. "Five seventy-one! Those goddam Arabs! Did they think they could get the job for that? They must think we're all idiots."

Hargrave-Mott opened the fifth envelope and waited a moment for the noise to subside. "This is the tender submitted by Channel Tunnel Constructors, a joint venture comprised of Crosley and Black, Limited, of London, sponsor, Ingram Construction Corporation, of Chicago, Illinois, H. J. Beckstead Associates, Limited, London, and Cardovan Enterprises, Limited, Birmingham."

Frank leaned toward Ingram and whispered, "Sounds like a fly-by-night outfit to me."

"Total bid: four hundred ninety-eight million, nine hundred ninety-nine thousand pounds. Four, nine, eight, nine, nine, nine. That's the lowest so far." During the wave of whispering and rustling that greeted the surprisingly low offer, Hargrave-Mott smiled into the camera again, plainly pleased that the new leader was a group sponsored by a British firm. The BBC director turned to an aide and pointed out the location of Sir Charles. Several newspaper reporters and technical journal editors who knew the eminent English engineer took up positions along the left-hand wall, ready to close in for interviews if the bid held up.

Sasaki, Tokyo	£523,612,000
M-K, U.S.A.	522,701,000
Dunkley, London	560,111,000
Impreglia, Rome	571,700,000
Crosley, London	498,999,000

Frank was stunned by the figure. "Four ninety-eight? Is that our bid? I thought we agreed on five-seventeen . . ."

"Charley and I got together last night and decided to shave off a few more percent."

"Christ, Bill, five-seventeen was already too low. We can't possibly turn a profit at four ninety-eight, especially if there are any problems."

"If there are problems," Ingram replied, "you will solve them. Solving problems is your hobby as well as your job."

Frank turned to Crosley. "You shouldn't have let him talk you into it."

"If anything, I talked *him* into it. I was afraid five-seventeen wouldn't be low enough to win against this kind of competition. I want this job . . ."

Hargrave-Mott was asking for attention by waving the last envelope over his head. "The last proposal," he said. He withdrew the booklet and turned the cover.

Frank tensed himself in apprehension, half-hoping that the final bidder was even hungrier for work than Ingram and Crosley. Four ninety-eight! Getting the job at that price would create a tremendous pressure to cut corners and take chances. He was irritated, not because he hadn't been consulted on the last-minute price cutting, but because he suspected that Ingram was taking for granted that he would work around the clock and give in to compromises. "No matter how low we bid," he could imagine Ingram assuring Crosley, "Frank will bring the job in beneath it. He'll bust his ass to show he can do it." If that's what Ingram was counting on, he was in for a surprise. The Channel Tunnel project was not going to be the scene of penny pinching, Frank vowed, not with so much water overhead.

"Ladies and gentlemen, the final offer is from a consortium of Swedish companies headed by Sandsvall-Sotrsryd–I hope I'm pronouncing that right–and including Lokker Construction Corporation and Olaf Olafson, Incorporated, all of Stockholm."

"Where are the Germans?" Ingram whispered. "Where are the French?"

Frank shook his head. "Chickened out. Maybe they saw something everybody else missed." Already he was feeling the standard fear of the low bidder: What did we overlook?

W. Mitchell Hargrave-Mott broke into a broad smile as he read the Swedish total: "Five hundred twelve million, five hundred forty-five thousand pounds. Five, one, two, five, four, five. The winner, it would appear, subject to double-checking, is the group sponsored by Crosley and Black, a fine old British concern if there ever was one." His next words were almost lost in the rising hum of conversation, foot shuffling, and scattered applause. "A ten-minute break before we start on the units . . ."

Mrs. Baker's chalk broke as she underlined the winning bidder:

Sasaki, Tokyo	£523,612,000
M-K, U.S.A.	522,701,000
Dunkley, London	560,111,000
Impreglia, Rome	571,700,000
Crosley, London	498,999,000
Sandsvall, Stockholm	512,545,000

Sir Charles turned to Frank. "You see? At five-seventeen the Swedes would have beaten us." He extended his hand in congratulation.

Frank took it without enthusiasm. "Then the Swedes would

have been stuck with an impossible task instead of us. My God, we left thirteen million pounds on the table."

"A mere trifle," said Ingram, lighting a ceremonial cigar, "we can easily make that up."

Frank shrugged. "If you two want to go broke, that's your business. All I can say is that I hope you shaved the profit margin rather than the contingency fund. Because if anything goes wrong . . ."

"The project will be adequately funded," Crosley assured him. "Now please remove the gloomy expression. It will have a depressing effect on the television audience." He turned to meet the oncoming reporters.

Chapter 8

"Well, so much for my social life," Frank muttered to himself, sitting in his parked car outside Anne's cottage. He watched her going from window to window snapping the drapes shut. What a transformation! What a temper! He had talked to her several times on the phone before coming to pick her up for what he had hoped would be the first of many evenings together and was struck by how friendly and easygoing she was. She was salty and unconventional, too, so much so that his mind had begun to dance with visions of joint housekeeping. Two minutes after he presented himself at her front door he knew it was all over. She had found out who he was and launched immediately into a tirade against the tunnel. His efforts to refute her criticisms infuriated her and within ten minutes they were shouting at each other. "A rapist," she had called him, "a professional despoiler."

"I don't represent the whole goddam engineering profession," he remembered saying at one point, just before calling her a narrow-minded birdwatcher more concerned about insects and weeds than people.

"Why don't you go back where you came from?" she said. "Aren't there any streams left for you to pollute in your big, rotten country?" He had grabbed his coat then and stomped out in a high dudgeon, which was more dignified than getting chased out with a meat cleaver.

Frank switched on the ignition and sighed at the thought of what might have been. Now he had only a bad taste in his mouth. He should have told her who he was right at the start to avoid trouble. Now it would be terribly hard to repair the damage. Damn that woman! She probably would never speak to him again, much less invite him into her bed. He should have told her she was cute when she was mad. Too late for that, so he did the only thing he could think of for a parting comment: he spun his wheels in her gravel.

In a corner of an Irish pub in Manchester's industrial district, Jamie Quinn sat talking with a stocky, square-faced, sometime construction worker named Tanner Eagan. The room was crowded and the air was heavy with the smell of tobacco smoke, ale, and sweat.

"I'm glad you're not a copper," Eagan said, smiling. The gaps in his teeth were souvenirs of drunken brawls. "It took you only three days to find me. The law has been looking three years."

"I had an edge on the poor lads. I knew what you looked like and I knew you liked your pints at night. It amazes me that you're the only one left from the old Midlands Brigade that hasn't been nabbed, the way you live."

"I'm a new man, Jamie, haven't you heard? I don't drink myself blind anymore. I haven't even lost my temper lately. My motto is stay out of trouble and stay out of jail. After the Birmingham blast I stayed on my job as if nothing had happened. Everybody else went on the run."

"There'll be no running or hiding after the tunnel operation. We'll go back to Ireland as heroes."

"Maybe. I like the idea of pulling off something really big, but how are we going to spring Maher and Carney from Tobermore? Where are we going to get enough money to live on while a gang–"

"We want no gang. The four of us can take care of the tunnel if we're patient. As for money, forty thousand pounds will be plenty."

"I hope to God it'll be plenty! Where are we going to find

forty thousand pounds? We can't go on a fucking lecture tour of the States like McCabe and his pals."

"No, but we can grab the money they collect. There's a phone booth outside. Follow me and I'll show you how."

The repeated ringing brought Mary McCabe out of a troubled sleep. She fumbled for the bedside light and switched it on, squinting at the electric clock. It was after midnight. Kevin was still not back from the weekly Army meeting.

"Hello?"

"Mary? Can you talk?"

"Jamie! I've been so worried . . . I thought you'd call before this."

"Everything is fine. Any news?"

"Yes. The planeload of guns will be landing in Amsterdam in a fortnight."

"Who's taking the money to pay for it?"

"Duggan. The Czechs want it in cash. Duggan's to take it to a downtown hotel by taxi." In a hushed, hurried voice she told him what she had been able to find out. Duggan would be traveling alone with the payment in a metal case handcuffed to his wrist. To get through Customs he would have false papers identifying him as a bank courier. The money might be hidden behind a false lining or inside hollowed-out reels of computer tape—the details were still being argued about. She saw no way Quinn could get his hands on the money without getting killed. Duggan was a powerful man, she reminded Quinn, and he would be on his guard.

"I'll think of something," Quinn said, "and I'll call you in a week. There might be some way you can help."

Mary's voice broke. "Seamus Duggan . . . he has such a fine family. If he doesn't come back to them because of this I'll never forgive myself."

"He'll come back. I might have to give him a tap on the head. He'll have a hangover, that's all. He's used to that."

"When it's over you'll tell me where to meet you, won't you,

Jamie? I'll be packed and ready to leave. Don't go back on your word. I'm older than you, I know, but we'll have a good life together. I'll make you happy . . ."

"Will you stop worrying, love? Everything's going to be fine."

Quinn kept the receiver angled away from his ear so Eagan could listen in. When the call was over Eagan howled in delight and danced in a circle on the sidewalk. "McCabe's own wife!" he said, his voice pitched high in disbelief. "McCabe's own wife robbing him blind and planning to flee the coop! How did you ever set her up for this? How in the name of Jesus did you ever get her to do it?"

Quinn put his arm around Eagan's shoulders as they walked back to the pub. "It was easy," he said. "She is crazy about my prick. That woman can't get enough of my big, lovely prick."

Their laughter echoed down the dark street.

Joe Seville, wiry and remarkably energetic for his sixty-five years, leaped to his feet and walked quickly to the front of his desk with his hand extended. "Frank Kenward, by golly, how are you? Welcome to Pittsburgh. Sit down, sit down . . ."

The office was at the second floor level of the hangarlike main building of Seville Steel and Manufacturing Company. Two large windows looked onto the factory floor, where arrays of cylinders, tanks, and boilers were in various stages of fabrication. The blue haze in the distance was punctuated by the flashes of welding torches and the spark showers of grinding tools.

"Joe, you look great. How do you do it?"

"I'll give you the secret of my beauty and my health," Seville said, returning to his chair and waving at the scene behind him. "I never breathe anything but fumes from the foundry and paint shop, and I never eat anything that's not dusted with stack emissions. To tell the truth, ever since this town cleaned up its air I haven't felt so hot."

"Well, you look like a million bucks."

"No, *you* look like a million bucks. *Three* million bucks. When you came through the door I said to myself, 'Here comes three million bucks.' Because that, my friend, is what I'm going to charge you for the mole."

"A little more than I wanted to spend," Frank said with pretended pain. "Have you got anything for, say, two million nine hundred thousand?"

"Six million would be more like it. Three million is a steal. The Channel Tunnel is a prestige project. Having it depend on one of my rigs is worth something in advertising, which is why I'm quoting such a ridiculously low price. The reliability you want, the reserve power, the speed, the forward probe capability, the laser guidance system, all that costs money. What I propose to build is something special. It'll knock the tunneling world on its ass." He took two hardhats from a shelf. "Come on, let's take a walk."

Frank had a naturally fast stride, but he had to hurry to keep up. Good old Joe Seville. Everything he did, from going down the stairs to taking a drink of water and a salt tablet, was with the air of a man racing to beat a deadline.

"Lots of changes around here since your last visit," Seville said, gesturing as they walked between the presses, benders, and shears of the sheet metal shop. "Especially in warehousing and inventory. Electronics. I can find out how much of any stock we have on hand just by punching a keyboard in my office. I used to have to go out on the floor and punch a foreman. Ha! We even have computers that reorder toilet paper when we get low. Sometimes I wonder why I come to work in the morning. Do you realize I've earned four years of vacation? I guess I want to be here when all this fancy new equipment breaks down so I can say, 'See? You can't get along without me after all.' No such luck so far. The machines have been doing a fantastic job. They cost a fortune, but not one of them has ever caught a cold, asked to go to a funeral, or walked out on strike."

"Joe, that's terrific, but I want to talk about tunneling. Let's go back to your office and–"

"Not till you've seen my baby. That's it in the corner. What do you think it is?"

They had walked the full length of the assembly area and were standing before a large steel structure covered with tubular scaffolding. On each side welders were attaching what appeared to be short wings.

"It's either a flying locomotive or a submarine."

"It's a submarine," Seville said proudly, spreading his arms wide. "OSARV. Ocean Salvage and Research Vessel. Look at the gauge of the hull steel! She'll be able to work five miles down. She'll have lights that'll make the Marianas Trench look like Times Square. Remember when SAC dropped an A-bomb into the drink off the coast of Spain? It took them months to find it because they didn't have the right kind of equipment. I called the Navy and I said, 'Look, let me build you something that won't make people die laughing.' They bought the idea. This is the fifth rig I've put together for them and by far the best."

"Good. I'm happy for you. Now about the mole . . ."

"The indents along the bottom–telescoping outriggers come out of there to stabilize the thing on the ocean floor. On the front will be grappling arms with circular saws, cutting torches, and clamshells strong enough to crush a Volkswagen down to the size of an alarm clock. The oceans, Frank! The new frontier! Get out of tunnels and into the oceans . . . that's where the future lies!"

"No, thanks. Oceans get up my nose."

"There's not just the military market, you know. Soon there'll be farming in the sea, building in the sea, mining in the sea–"

"Goddammit, Joe, will you knock it off about the sea? I hate water. I came here to talk about a tunnel machine. If you don't want to, I'll take my money across the street."

"Okay, let's talk about your tunnel machine. Look behind you and you'll see it."

Frank turned around and saw a steel cylinder towering twenty-five feet over his head. He had noticed it before but assumed it was one of the many storage and pressure vessels Seville was constructing for the petrochemical industry, the kind

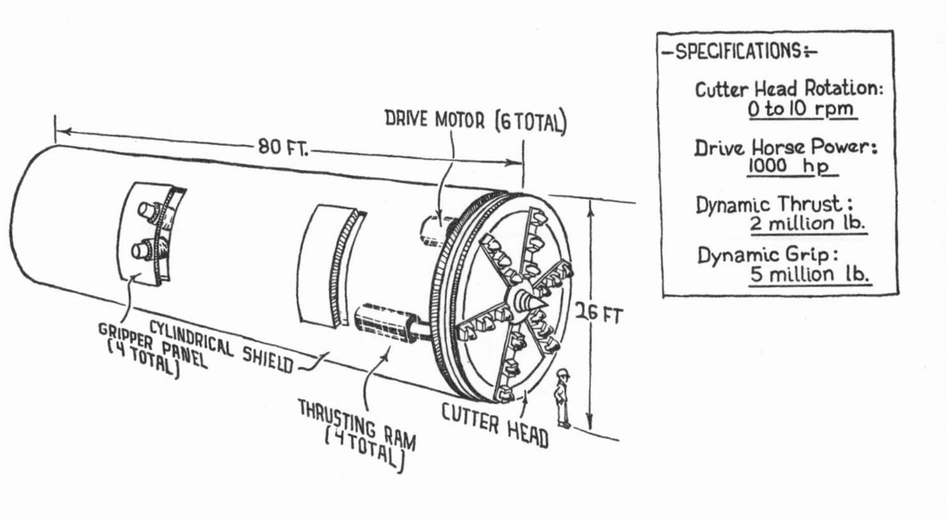

—SPECIFICATIONS:—
Cutter Head Rotation: 0 to 10 rpm
Drive Horse Power: 1000 hp
Dynamic Thrust: 2 million lb.
Dynamic Grip: 5 million lb.
80 FT.
DRIVE MOTOR (6 TOTAL)
26 FT
CYLINDRICAL SHIELD
GRIPPER PANEL (4 TOTAL)
THRUSTING RAM (4 TOTAL)
CUTTER HEAD

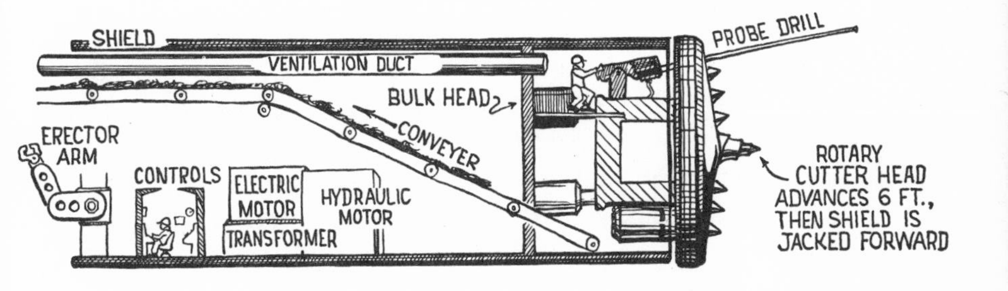

SHIELD
VENTILATION DUCT
PROBE DRILL
BULK HEAD
CONVEYER
ERECTOR ARM
CONTROLS
ELECTRIC MOTOR
HYDRAULIC MOTOR
TRANSFORMER
ROTARY CUTTER HEAD ADVANCES 6 FT., THEN SHIELD IS JACKED FORWARD

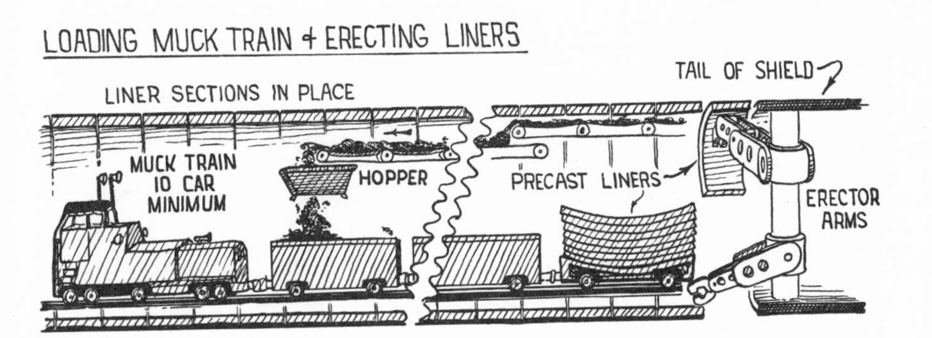

LOADING MUCK TRAIN & ERECTING LINERS
TAIL OF SHIELD
LINER SECTIONS IN PLACE
MUCK TRAIN 10 CAR MINIMUM
HOPPER
PRECAST LINERS
ERECTOR ARMS

of thing that made up the bulk of his business. "What do you mean, 'I'll see it'?"

"You're looking at the cutterhead shield for the Channel Tunnel mole. Behind it is one of the rings for the expandable gripper shoes. On your left is one of the main thrusting rams."

Frank's mouth opened. "You mean you started building the thing before the job was let? Before you knew who the low bidder was or what he'd want?"

"I haven't finished it, as you can see. I've only put together what I knew would be needed. I figured by getting a head start I could lock up the business by being able to deliver the goods six months ahead of anybody else. What risk did I take? All we have left to do is decide on the details and refinements."

"I'll tell you what risk you took. Parliament can turn the whole job down. Where will that leave you?"

Seville shrugged. "That will leave me with the world's largest rat-proof corncrib. Let's go up to the office."

Kenward slapped him on the shoulder. "By God, Joe, I admire your gambling spirit. You should have been a contractor."

Dressed in the white coveralls worn by the janitors at Amsterdam's Schiphol Airport, Quinn and Eagan crossed the central concourse and climbed the stairway to the duty-free area. Seamus Duggan would be arriving soon from Glasgow, where he had an hour-long layover for a change of planes. Quinn was carrying a square of cardboard on which "Out of Order" was written in five languages.

Eagan was worried about the confrontation. "Anybody but him," he said to Quinn. "Duggan could kill us both in a fair fight with his hands tied behind his back."

"It won't be a fair fight, though, will it? What can he do sitting on a crapper with his britches around his feet? Let's make sure we've got it straight. When the plane lands, you put the sign on the gents' room door. Let people leave, but if anybody tries to go in, block the way and point to the sign. The place should be empty after ten or fifteen minutes. When I see that Duggan has cleared through Customs, I'll give you a nod and you take the sign down. Once he's inside, the sign goes back up, we both go in, we kick open the door to his stall, and . . ."

"What if he didn't eat the lunch in Glasgow that McCabe's wife packed for him? What if she didn't put the stuff in the food? What if she did and it works too soon? He might do his shitting on the plane and head straight for a taxi."

"Duggan sticks to plans. Mary can be trusted and so can the chemist who sold me the powder. The strongest known to man, he said it was. Two hours after you swallow it, the shit starts flying in all directions, and it *keeps* flying. So what if he gets in a taxi? We follow him into the back seat like we talked about and let him have it there. The driver will be no problem with a gun stuck in his ear."

Quinn fingered the length of steel pipe in his pocket and hoped that was all he'd need.

The public-address system crackled with an announcement in Dutch, then in English: "Passengers on flight 847 from Glasgow, British Caledonia Airways, are now arriving in the international zone, central concourse, second level." Wide double doors swung open and a crowd of passengers carrying coats and packages came through. Quinn spotted Duggan at once, not only because he was six inches taller than anyone else but because he was desperately elbowing his way to the front of the column. Once in the clear, he broke into a run, swinging wildly the metal case and raincoat he was carrying.

With his collar torn open and his face covered with sweat and full of panic, Duggan rushed past Quinn without recognizing him, blind to everything but the arrows indicating the location of the rest rooms. Eagan was still peeling tape from the edges of the sign when Duggan was around the corner and upon him. He shouldered Eagan aside and threw himself against the door as if he were afraid it might be locked.

Quinn helped Eagan secure the sign again, listening to a stall door slam and a bolt lock shoot into place. The two men removed the pipe sections from their pockets, made sure no one was approaching, and pushed their way inside.

A young man stood at the sinks flossing his teeth, a pack of camping equipment on his back. From the nearest stall came the explosive sounds of Duggan's labor and a stream of curses: "Jesus Christ Almighty! Holy Mother of God!" The young man smiled, glanced in the mirror, and said something in Dutch. Quinn and Eagan turned uncertainly toward the urinals.

"We'll have to kill that bastard, too," Eagan whispered.

"Wait," Quinn said, looking over his shoulder. "I think he's leaving."

The youth put his roll of floss into a pocket of his jeans. Leaning close to the mirror, he bared his teeth and examined them closely. After several minutes he was satisfied, and with a few parting glances at himself moved to the door. Tossing his head toward Duggan's stall, he addressed another comment to Quinn and Eagan. He shrugged at the cold stares he got in response and said something in an insulting tone. As he left there was the sound of a toilet flushing and a bolt lock being undone.

Coming out of the stall, Duggan caught a split-second reflection of the figures lunging toward him. It was all the warning he needed. He took the first blows on upraised arms, then brought the metal case down on Eagan's head, bringing a knee sharply upward into Quinn's stomach. With a roar of rage, he seized Eagan as he would a sack of potatoes and used him to shove Quinn against the wall. Eagan, trying to twist free, found himself hurled in the opposite direction, coming to rest on the floor near the urinals and feeling blood on the side of his head. Quinn made a move toward his gun, but with the wind knocked from him he was far too slow. Duggan caught his wrist and twisted his arm behind him brutally. Now Quinn's gun was in Duggan's hand.

"Don't make a move," Duggan ordered, backing toward the

door and groping for the knob with his free hand. The metal case, dangling from a small chain, clattered against the wall. He recognized one of his assailants. "Quinn! Quinn! How did you . . . you rotten bastard! You bloody, thieving traitor . . ."

As Duggan trained the gun to fire, the door behind him burst open against his back. The shot went wild, shattering mirrors above the sinks and reverberating deafeningly. Eagan sprang forward from a crouch, swinging his piece of pipe with savage force into Duggan's forehead. The big man's knees sagged and he crumpled awkwardly to the floor. The building engineer who had opened the door to investigate the ruckus stood paralyzed with shock; before he could react, Eagan pulled him inside and sent him down with a chopping blow.

Quinn was already rolling Duggan over. "Jesus Christ, he's done for. You caved in his skull. The money . . . the fucking money is locked to his wrist. There must be a key . . ."

The two men, breathing heavily, went through Duggan's pockets.

"Could be anywhere," Eagan said, "in a shoe, taped to his body somewhere . . ." Blood from the cut that had been opened alongside his ear was dripping onto his white coveralls.

"He might have swallowed it . . . he might have mailed it ahead . . ."

"Shoot the chain off."

"Looks too tough. I have a better idea. Stand back . . ." Quinn stepped on Duggan's hand to hold it in place on the tile floor. Carefully he pressed the muzzle of his pistol against the bones of the wrist . . .

Eagan was in the bathroom groaning and tending to his wound when Quinn placed a call to Belfast from their Amsterdam hotel room. Spread out on the bed was a hundred thousand dollars in American ten-, twenty-, and fifty-dollar bills . . . a beautiful green blanket of money.

"Kevin McCabe speaking."

Quinn disguised his voice by speaking hoarsely. "Your wife has been making a fool of you. Ask her why she has a suitcase packed. Ask her why there's a one-way plane ticket to London in her purse."

He couldn't help smiling as he hung up. It wasn't often a man could arrange to have his dirty work done by his worst enemy.

Chapter 9

The final debate and vote on the Channel Tunnel Bill began with long-established ritual. Sir Oswald Stone, Sergeant-at-Arms and Principal Doorkeeper for the House of Commons, impressively dressed in frock coat, white gloves, knee breeches, and silk stockings, carrying the ceremonial golden mace on his shoulder, entered the cathedral-like Central Lobby of the Palace of Westminster followed by the Speaker of the House, in black robe and gray wig, the Train-bearer, Secretary, and Chaplain. Past the lines of visitors Sir Oswald grandly strode, past the statues of Lord Granville, Mr. Gladstone, Lord Russell, and the Earl of Iddesleigh, down a broad corridor and through an archway. The procession arrived in the Chamber of the House just as Big Ben was sounding 2:30 P.M.

The speaker bowed to the assembled Members–not an empty seat could be seen on this occasion–while the Sergeant-at-Arms placed the mace on the central table to signify that the seven-hundred-year-old "mother of parliaments" was officially in session, took a position in front of the canopied Speaker's chair–a gift from the government of Australia–and lowered his eyes for the prayer. When the Chaplain had finished and had retired from the hall, a team of shorthand reporters in the balcony began to compile a verbatim record of the day's proceedings . . .

The Minister for Transport (Mr. Stanley Markland): I beg to move, That the Channel Tunnel Bill now be read a third time.

The call for construction bids produced a low bid that was nearly twenty-five million pounds below the estimate made by British Rail's technical consultants. Thus the predictions made by several hon. Members that construction costs would render the development unfeasible need no longer concern us. The Bill before us has the effect of accepting the bid and authorizing construction to start. We recommend passage with a new argument in favor of it, namely, that we have been offered a bargain price.

Mr. Peter Clarkson (Romney and Dymchurch): Are we to understand that the right hon. Gentleman advocates buying a piece of goods because it has been marked down? Even if it is not needed, or, worse, is harmful to health? France could offer to build the entire thing herself and present it to us as a gift and still I would vote against it.

Mr. Markland: Since the hon. and gallant Member for Romney and Dymchurch has expressed himself at length and on numerous occasions, and because he seems proud of his immunity to new facts or conditions, I fail to see how the further articulation of his views illuminate the debate.

Mr. Clarkson: Consistency, I see, is now being characterized as vice. I should remind the Minister for Transport that his opinion and his votes coincided with mine when he was on the Opposition side of the Chamber. Only upon ascending to the lofty post he now occupies did he begin to see things in a different light. I congratulate him on the grace with which he has learned to stand on his head.

Mr. John Strand (Liverpool, North): Ralph Waldo Emerson said that "Consistency is the hobgoblin of little minds, adored by little statesmen and philosophers and divines."

Mr. P. N. Carberry (York): And Gandhi said it was a sign of weakness—

Mr. Clarkson: Emerson was talking about a *foolish* consistency. Mine is hardly—

Hon. Members: Point of order! Point of order!

Mr. Speaker (Mr. Thompson Smith): the hon. Members will permit the Minister for Transport to complete his statement.

Mr. Markland: A man should not remain trapped by opinions formed in infancy. The Labour Party has never been opposed to the principle of the tunnel, I should point out. Indeed, the basic agreements to explore its possibility are still those of 1966, made by my right hon. Friend the Prime Minister and by my right hon. Friend the Secretary of State for Social Services, who was then Minister of Industrial Affairs. I am hopeful that today we can dispense with the restatement of arguments we have each of us made before and proceed directly to the Division. Surely it has been established beyond serious question that the advantages of the tunnel far outweigh the disadvantages, especially now that we have a firm and very attractive bid before us.

Mr. Clarkson: If the advantages to Britain were so great, France would not be such an enthusiastic supporter of the scheme.

Mr. Markland: Of all the utterances I have suffered from the hon. and gallant Member for Romney and Dymchurch, that is indisputably the most myopic.

Mrs. Margaret Blakely (Royal Tunbridge Wells): It is understandable that the Minister for Transport wishes to cut off debate. He can see as well as anybody that several Members who may be counted on to enter the "no" lobby are not yet in attendance. When the tunnel was last taken up by the House the fear was expressed that the whole of Kent would become a lorry park. That fear still exists and is well founded. I should like to mention another fear, that we are entranced with projects of national prestige that do not contribute very much to real economic growth. Even if the Channel Tunnel were to have the multiplier effect that is claimed for it, the benefits will accrue mainly in the Southeast, already one of the most developed areas of the country, instead of in the Southwest or in Scotland, where growth is needed.

Mr. Ian Field (Glasgow): Hear, hear!

Mr. Markland: We are faced with a stubborn fact of geography, which is that the Strait of Dover is at Dover and not at Edinburgh. Would the hon. Member from Glasgow and his fellow

Glaswegians support the project if it were relocated to run under the vast expanse of the North Sea between his constituency and, say, Helsinki?

Mr. G. Caldwell Morestock (Plymouth and Devonport): The right hon. Gentleman, the Minister for Transport, who speaks well and who has apparently read many books, urges us to approve the Channel Tunnel Bill without delay. I recommend the greatest caution. We should be on our guard against any proposal that bears the universal approval of the multinational corporations, the international banking fraternity, and the Civil Service. When those elements are united in favor of a plan, the only force left to prevent its imposition on the British people is the House of Commons.

The main reason I am opposed to the project relates to national defense. It is simply untrue that technology has altered the basic principles which govern our military strategy. The nuclear deterrent has become so incredible that conventional warfare becomes increasingly likely, and when it comes it will be of the lightning strike variety. With the existence of the tunnel our main natural defense will be breached. It would be feasible for a force of parachutists and commandos to seize the tunnel head and hold it for a long enough period for an invader to pass through and thus completely bypass the barrier that has protected us for thousands of years. I ask the hon. Members not to treat this matter lightly. History offers a plethora of examples of successful lightning strikes–Rotterdam, Nijmegen, and Corinth from the last war alone.

When I speak of defense I refer not to sabotage, blackmail, hijacking, or individual acts of lunacy or terrorism, but to the larger defense of the entire British Isles. I urge that the Bill before us be withdrawn and rewritten to include provisions for a fail-safe method of demolishing the tunnel instantly should the need arise, a method not controlled locally but from a military post well inland.

Mr. Gerald Avery (Prescott, East): How nostalgic to hear the military argument raised after so many years. If the hon. Member will forgive me, that was disposed of after the First World War and rightly so. The Royal Air Force could easily handle any demolition that was required. As for blowing up the tunnel from a military post, if I were going on a Continental holiday and I knew that such a system existed, I should skip the tunnel and take the steamer out of Southampton.

Mr. Jamison Brendt (Cotswold, East): Thank you, Mr. Speaker. I was wondering if I would ever be recognized to speak again. My legs are worn out from popping up and down. During the Second Reading of this Bill I was not given a chance to reply to my hon. Friend from Chipping Camden when he said that any imperfections in it could be corrected when it came before the House of Lords. Allowing that body to play *any* role in the legislative affairs of this nation is an insult to the very name of democracy. Far from relying on it to make up for our shortcomings, we should abolish it entirely.

(Interruption, unidentified): And the Queen should be made a bus conductress!

Mr. Speaker: The Chair regrets having given the hon. Gentleman from Cotswold, East, yet another opportunity to air his views on the Upper House, which he has done so many times and at such tiresome length. Many Members wish to speak on the Channel Tunnel Bill. Please confine your remarks to the points at issue.

Sir William Harlow (Oxford): The military argument should not be dismissed as a kind of stale joke. Many people are genuinely concerned about it. I myself have a terrible apprehension that the words of Alice Duer Miller, penned in 1940, will one day come back to haunt us if the tunnel goes through . . .

> I have loved England dearly and deeply
> Since that first morning, shining and pure,
> The white cliffs of Dover I saw rising steeply
> Out of the sea that once made her secure.

I trust the poet would approve, in view of the circumstances, the emphasis I gave to the last line.

The debate continued for three more hours. At 10:08 P.M. the question was put and the House divided. Ayes 305, Noes 295. Construction accordingly was ordered to proceed.

Chapter 10

For the first few months following the start of construction, Frank rose at dawn and worked until midnight, and so did Sir Charles and the other members of the supervisory staff. Their offices were in a one-story prefabricated structure perched on the edge of the cliff that gave them views of both the upper marshaling yard and the lower worksite on the shore two hundred sixty feet below. Weekly meetings were held with the joint-venture principals, which William Ingram usually attended via telephone from Chicago, and with British Rail's engineers and consultants, who were sometimes accompanied by government officials down from London on inspection tours.

While Frank depended mainly on Crosley and Black's director of personnel for the assembly of production crews, he insisted on men he knew for certain critical jobs. For master mechanic he was able to lure Henry Stiles out of retirement, a mechanical genius who had gotten his start under Frank Crowe at Hoover Dam in the 1930s and who still drove a car he had bought second-hand in Nevada at the time. Chet Benzalek agreed to take a leave of absence from the Los Angeles Department of Water and Power to serve as safety engineer. From Kiewit's Mangrum Dam project in New Zealand Frank managed to steal Gene Stearns as concrete superintendent. It was said of Stearns that his favorite midnight snack was a sandwich of sand, aggregate, and cement, with a swallow of bentonite slurry to wash it down.

"They ought to be good," Crosley said during a lunch break after listening to Frank brag about his growing staff, "for the salaries they're getting. Have you noticed what our payroll is already? We're likely to be eaten to death by the check-writing machine."

"They're worth it," Frank said, pouring a cup of steaming black coffee from a thermos. He had tried getting used to tea, but had given up. "We're going to have the best management team ever put together. All the top people want to work for us. Years ago in the States you were nowhere unless you could say, 'I was at Coulee,' or 'I was at Hoover.' From now on the password is going to be, 'I was on the Channel Tunnel."

"Provided we don't go broke."

"Yes, I know, or make a wrong turn and end up in Portugal. There'll be no wrong turns. As for the money, I'm not as worried about our bid price as I was at the beginning. The morale around here, the enthusiasm . . . I've never seen anything like it. You watch, this is going to go down as the best-run, smoothest, and safest major job in history. It'll be in all the trade journals and textbooks as a classic example of how things should be done."

"I hope so. It will be nice to have something to read in debtors' prison."

Despite his remarks, Crosley, too, was confident that the project would be a success in every sense of the term. The spirit of cooperation he met on every hand was most comforting. Even the labor unions were conciliatory, apparently hoping to stimulate industrial investment in other segments of the economy. After only three weeks of negotiating, signatures had gone onto a no-strike master contract. The contractor had had to agree to a costly package of benefits as well as a clause providing for wage increases tied to a cost-of-living index, but it was a small price to pay for a guarantee of labor peace.

Crosley and Kenward were for a time the most sought-after engineers in the world, having the power to determine how several hundred million dollars were to be spent. Venders, brokers, manufacturers' agents, and even company presidents came to Dover to present their sales pitches.

A number of visitors wanted the Channel Tunnel project to be the testing ground for ideas on the fringes of technology. From the University of Montana came a professor of mining engineering who had conducted tests for Anaconda on the electrical resistivity of rock. He had found that current tends to seek natural planes of weakness and cause shattering through differential heat expansion. Frank told him it was an interesting concept and he would consider it as soon as the professor had some test results with samples larger than one cubic inch.

A French engineer who had already been rebuffed by the French Channel Tunnel Company insisted that he could melt rock economically with a plasma jet in a process similar to arc welding. The only thing lacking: a means of protecting the human operators from the toxic fumes, the heat, and the creeping lava.

A German scientist claimed that the tunnel could be drilled neatly with light rays, and to prove it he conducted a demonstration using a small ruby laser of his own design. Wearing welding goggles, Frank and Dr. Heinrich Kunz of the University of Stuttgart watched a brilliant, string-thin red beam burn a hole in a dime (Frank's), discolor but fail to split a pebble, and raise a blister on the side of the telephone. It took Frank only two minutes with his pocket calculator to discover a drawback: A laser big enough to cut a hole the size of the tunnel would consume more electrical power than the City of London.

The most bizarre proposal of all, but one which had a kind of crazy logic to it, came from an English inventor named Miles Watney, a cousin of Sir Charles's whom Frank agreed to see only at his insistence. Watney, a small, intense man with penetrating eyes, wanted to encase an atomic reactor inside a ten-meter-diameter sphere of tungsten. The fission process would heat the metal to a temperature above the melting point of rock, which would enable the device, surrounded by a layer of liquid rock, to be drawn by gravity into the Earth's crust like a red-hot rivet sinking through a tub of butter. As he explained the concept, he leafed through a portfolio of crowded drawings. With certain "adjustments," the sphere could be made to leave an open shaft behind it with walls of ceramic hardness, eliminating the need for further lining. Two problems remained, he said, putting his drawings away before they could be examined too closely. One was a guidance system to make the vessel travel horizontally instead of straight down to the planet's core of molten nickel. The other was the acquisition of an atomic pile, which, he hinted darkly, might be possible through "certain connections" he had in the Communist bloc. The man would not leave until Frank promised to lay the proposal before his board of directors and "the highest councils of government." When he was gone, Crosley appeared in the doorway shaking with laughter. "Now you know," he said, dabbing at his eyes with a handkerchief, "what the family has been going through for so many years."

Frank had seen Sir Charles laugh out loud only once before. The older man had a cheerful disposition, but apparently felt that open laughter was a breach of decorum. The other occasion was when Crosley saw the photo on the cover of Anne Reed's booklet of photographs. The project was still in its first days when Sir Charles, grinning, had tossed the publication on his assistant's desk.

"Am I losing my mind," Crosley said, "or is that my underground superintendent?"

Frank frowned at the photo. There he was on one knee, Shakespeare Cliff and a dramatic sky behind him. "What the hell is this?"

"It's a set of photos SKAT circulated just before the Commons vote. The captions imply that the tunnel will wreck everything in Kent that's fine and good. Cost us a few votes, I dare say."

"It's me, all right. By God, I think I'll sue."

"At least donate your model's fee to the miners' pension fund."

Frank described his early meeting with Anne. "Remember the photo of the foreshore I passed around at the meeting in New York? I had to hold her over the edge of the cliff to get that."

Crosley's eyes widened. "You held the Joseph Goebbels of the environmentalists over the edge of a cliff," he said, giving way to wholehearted laughter, "and you didn't drop her? I thought you had better judgment than that."

Unlike the near-disaster at the Amsterdam airport, the Tobermore breakout was calculated down to the smallest detail and carried out without a hitch. The exercise yard of the detention camp was bounded on the south side by a ten-foot-high electrified wire fence. Beyond a dirt road parallel to the fence was deep grass lining a grove of trees. At precisely two o'clock on a Sunday afternoon a car bomb exploded outside the main gate, followed by another fifteen seconds later. John Maher and Robert Carney were the only ones in the camp not taken by surprise. They had managed to detach themselves from the central group of prisoners and were standing at the extreme southern end of the compound next to a corrugated metal storage shed. In the confusion caused by the blasts, they darted behind the shed, picked up two pairs of shears with insulated handles that had been thrown there during the night, and went to work cutting a hole in the fence. Only one guard, stationed in a low wooden watchtower, was in a position to see them. He was cut down by rifle fire from outside the yard before he could sound an alarm.

Within forty seconds, Carney and Maher were sprinting across the road, leaving smoke, sirens, and shouting behind them. Quinn was waiting in the trees with motorbikes. Four minutes later, in a meadow out of sight of the camp, they emerged from the woods just as a helicopter was touching down.

The project progressed swiftly. A fleet of scrapers, graders, and crawler tractors arrived by rail and took only a week to level the work area below Shakespeare Cliff. A second fleet of earth-moving machines prepared the terminal site at the Folkestone portal. Truck-mounted excavators with rotary cutters on the end of telescoping booms were used to drive the two access tunnels, one from Old Folkestone Road behind Shakespeare Cliff to the lower work area, the other from near the water's edge downward to the level of the main tunnel a hundred feet below sea level. The mobile excavators performed so well on the access tunnels that the decision was made to use them for driving the entire five miles between Dover and Folkestone. With crews advancing toward each other from both cities, the so-called landward drive would hole through well before the mole, starting six months later, would complete its twelve-mile run from the coast to the meeting with the French under the middle of the Channel.

Construction began at once on steel buildings for the air compressors that would ventilate the underground workings, the generators that would supply electrical power, the warehouse for parts and supplies, and the changing house with showers and lockers for tunneling crews. Structural steel was swung into place by truck cranes for a concrete batch plant next to the portal of the lower access tunnel. The upper work area was the location of a two-acre paved parking lot for employees, a storage yard for material arriving by truck, and a two-hundred-unit mobile home park. At the end of three months the overall scene was not far different from what Frank imagined it would be when he first saw the site, departing from his early vision in that it was vaster and more complex than he thought it would be.

Walking through the equipment yard or initialing the daily sheaf of purchase orders he had to approve, Frank was impressed by how international the heavy-construction industry had become. The Channel Tunnel project was drawing on the resources and expertise of the entire world. The bulk of the equipment, materials, and manpower was supplied from Great Britain, but by no means all of it: Atlas Copco compressors from Sweden, timber lagging from Norway, reinforcing steel from Japan made from Australian iron ore and American coal, Caterpillar earthmovers from the U.S. giant's several European plants, Poclain hydraulic cranes from France, wire and tubing spun in West Germany from Chilean copper–the list went on and on. The nations of the world, whatever their differences, were entangled in a closely woven web of trade and technology. The internationalism even showed up in the project's mess hall. The cook was Indian, the manager British, the waitresses and tablecloths Irish, the busboys Pakistani and Algerian, and the coffee Brazilian. Coming to work in the morning was like visiting the United Nations.

Fortunately, the project was functioning better than the United Nations, with scarcely a serious disagreement or setback. In the early months, out of hundreds of decisions made and problems solved, only two didn't work out to Frank's full satisfaction. One was the location of the casting yard for the concrete liner segments. He wanted it located on the lower work area, as close as possible to the point of use. British Rail, however, which had its way, insisted on having the segments manufactured at Ashford, twenty miles away, to help alleviate unemployment in that area.

The other defeat, if it could be called that, was his disastrous evening with Anne. Never before had he struck out with a woman so emphatically. He couldn't put her out of his mind, partly because her name kept popping up in the course of his work. Her organization of nature lovers hadn't dissolved as predicted when the project was authorized. Now SKAT was starting legal actions to force the contractor to cover earthmoving trucks with canvas so that no dirt would be spilled on roads, to confine hauling to daylight hours only, and to replace Aker's Steps with something the public could use. British Rail's plans to rebuild the rail line between the portal and London were under heavy attack on the grounds that the public had been insufficiently consulted on the design. For personal as well as professional reasons, Frank Kenward would have to risk another call on Anne Reed. Surely she had cooled off by now.

Chapter 11

Rain had been falling on the city of Maidstone for almost three days without letup and the cold air and dampness seemed to penetrate every corner of the three-room flat. Quinn, Maher, and Carney were sitting at the kitchen table wearing sweaters and jackets, as close as they could get to the gas stove that provided the only heat. Complaining to the landlord or moving to better quarters would be too great a risk, as only a month had passed since the breakout. Eagan was already living in Dover, where he had been taken on by the contractor as a member of the equipment maintenance crew on the early morning shift. Eagan got the job despite the number of men applying for every opening. He had compiled a good record on previous tunnel projects, which was why Quinn had approached him in the first place.

There was a pencil in Quinn's hand, and he was making a rough sketch of the Dover headlands. "What they call the lower access tunnel," he said, starts at the shore and runs down to the main bore. The old Beaumont tunnel, from what I've been able to figure out, starts a mile or so away, goes along the coast, turns toward the sea about here, and passes underneath the access tunnel." He drew a line across the paper. "It seems to me that a big enough blast in the old tunnel would open a trench across the beach for the sea to come in and flood the whole works. The lower access tunnel would act like a funnel."

"Of all the schemes you've described," Maher said, concentrating on the orange he was peeling with a pocket knife, "this is the only one that stands a chance of working. It depends on exactly how deep the old tunnel is and where it crosses the shoreline." Maher was a man with a solemn face and voice that never varied in pitch or quality. At fifty he was by far the oldest member of the group. He didn't like taking orders from someone as young as Quinn, but he was grateful to him for his freedom and had agreed to help destroy the Channel Tunnel by way of repayment.

"If it's too deep," said Bob Carney, "we'd need an H-bomb to blast through to the surface." He snapped a lid off a bottle of ale. "And if I *had* an H-bomb, I wouldn't waste it on Dover. I'd pick London." In his late twenties, Carney was short and overweight, with a round face and a restless manner. His words came in rushes, like bursts from a jackhammer.

"What I like about the idea," Maher said, "is that we could take our time planting the charge and not have to breach the project security system. Can we get a look at the old tunnel?"

"There's an old watchman who takes people in," Quinn said. "He works for British Rail. They don't want to be bothered with tourists, so we'll have to make up a reason for wanting to see it."

"Well," said Carney, "we have a good reason, don't we? We want to blow the fucking thing up."

Frank walked resolutely up the gravel path to the cottage, took a deep breath, and rang the doorbell. The worst thing she can do, he thought, is slam the door again. He cautioned himself to keep his nose and fingers out of the way.

There was the sound of approaching footsteps. The door was pulled open, and there was Anne, dressed in slacks and smock stained with chemicals. She greeted him cheerfully.

"You're smiling," he said. "Is this a trap?"

"I'm surprised to see you, that's all. Did you come to use my phone or beat me up or what?"

"I came to . . . to suggest that we, ah, give it one more try."

She studied him for a moment, then stepped aside. "Would you care to step into my office and discuss this further?"

Anne fixed two drinks and waved Frank to a seat at one end of a couch. She sat at the other, tucking her legs beneath her. "I'm sorry I called you an ugly American. When I found out you were in the enemy camp I lost my self-control. What I should have done is stayed calm and started in on the job of correcting your education. My spies tell me you are quite reasonable. I think I could change your point of view."

"I have the same feeling about you. I don't think you are as mean and vicious as British Rail paints you."

Anne narrowed her eyes. "Were you sent here by your depraved employers to flatter me and see if you could get SKAT to back off from its demands?"

"My depraved employers would never let me take such a risk. Right now I feel like a commando who has dropped behind enemy lines. I was wondering, in fact, if you'd been ordered to be nice to me in the hope of wringing some concessions from our side."

"I have a suggestion. Let's not talk about the tunnel for a while."

"Good idea," Frank agreed. "Until we get to know each other better we'll stick to safe subjects like religion, politics, and sex."

They smiled and clinked their glasses together.

Nearly two thousand people showed up for a Channel Tunnel Open House arranged for the press, local residents, and job personnel and their families. Visitors looking self-conscious in hardhats walked in and out of the access tunnels in groups of ten, ushered by British Rail construction inspectors. Photographs were taken of children at the controls of cranes and trucks. A front-end loader decorated with pennants moved slowly through the crowds, its bucket filled with crushed ice and soft drinks.

The Seville Rotary Tunnel Excavator was the center of attention; it was next to its massive, circular cutterhead that a grandstand and speakers' platform had been erected. Fully assembled, the mole stretched across the lower work area like a beached sea serpent, three stories high and as long as a football field.

"It reminds me of a worm," Anne said to Frank, partly to irritate him. She had first seen it after a winter squall when its curved steel skin was dripping with water. "A horrible, slimy creature you might find under a rock. If it doesn't soon wiggle into the mud, a bird might swoop down and snap it up."

"You poor thing," Frank said with pity in his voice. "Your mind has been so twisted by SKAT you can't appreciate magnificence when you see it."

For the machine was magnificent. Beautiful, in its way . . . an enormously powerful and sophisticated device that was the result of hundreds of years of evolving tunnel technology. It was aimed at the mouth of the lower access tunnel, into which it would soon be eased on steel rails. Three days would be needed to move its entire length underground, a sword-swallowing act on a gigantic scale. Despite its size, it did seem somehow vulnerable in the open air, though at five hundred tons it would have taken quite a bird to snap it up. Without surrounding walls of rock to bear against it was, like a submarine in drydock, utterly impotent. Lacking leverage and traction, it couldn't propel itself in any direction as much as an inch. Underground, locked in the grip of the Earth's crust and chewing its way relentlessly forward, it would show its strength and speed.

"What did you expect?" Joe Seville said when Frank complimented him on the near-perfection of the design and craftsmanship. "You paid our price, so we gave you a lovely hunk of iron."

Stanley Markland, Minister for Transport, was on hand for the day and was the first to stand before the microphone. Speaking beneath flags of Britain and France that were being rippled so vigorously by the wind that they threatened to tear loose from their mountings, he characterized the project as "an unparalleled example of the vision of an entire people."

Philippe Tristant, chief engineer on the French side, said that the tunnel across the Channel could be thought of as "a wedding ring between our two countries."

British Rail's Clerk of the Works, Clement Hendricks, summarized progress to date. After only nine months of effort, the Dover and Folkestone headings had advanced to within two kilometers of each other. Now that the mole was ready to go, hole-through on the twenty-kilometer seaward drive could come in as little as eleven months.

Sir Charles Crosley explained to the audience that the ponderous tunnel machine that dominated the scene was the outgrowth of two key advances in heavy-construction technology, both of which took place in Britain. The first was the shield built by Marc Isambard Brunel for the first tunnel under the Thames in 1825. The second was the rotary tunneler invented by Colonel Frederick Beaumont for an early Channel-crossing scheme. "It may surprise many of you to know," Sir Charles said, "that the demonstration bore the Colonel drove a hundred years ago passes directly beneath our feet." He concluded his remarks with a word about safety. "There used to be a rule of thumb in the construction industry that you should expect one fatality for every million pounds in the contract. Modern methods have consigned that precept to the dustbin of history. We fully intend to complete our work here without the loss of a single man. God willing, we will succeed in that aim."

Sir Charles stepped aside amid a warm round of applause from the audience, the younger members of which had already drifted away in search of the loader with the soft drinks. Tanner Eagan, standing at one end of the grandstand, applauded with the rest to avoid attracting attention. He looked upward to the edge of the cliff where a short time before he had spotted Quinn, Maher, and Carney. He couldn't see them now. They probably had had enough of the cold wind, and had gone back to Maidstone to finish moving out of the flat and into the new digs in Dover. He turned up his collar and buried his hands in his pockets. He would stick it out. His job was to learn as much about the construction operation as he could.

Kenward, the last speaker on the program, stepped before the microphone and began describing the mole. His task wasn't made any easier by Anne Reed, who sat huddled in an upper corner of the bleachers pretending to vomit whenever he looked in her direction. Signaling to an operator inside the mole, he demonstrated the machine's moving parts. The cutterhead with its radial pattern of teeth began to rotate, quickly reaching its maximum speed of ten revolutions per minute and just as quickly gliding to a stop. Steel gripper shoes along the sides of the cylindrical shield that would anchor the machine in place were extended and retracted. Segments of the cutterhead were folded back under smooth hydraulic control, a feature that would allow workmen easy access to the face if obstructions were encountered. Smaller panels swung open to reveal what appeared to be the muzzles of machine guns: these were the pneumatic drills that would probe ahead in a search for water.

Just behind the cutterhead was a continuous bucket-wheel that would scoop up the excavated chalk, carry it to the crown, and drop it on a conveyor that would send it to muck cars two hundred twenty feet away. Only the forward eighty feet of the mole was a continuous steel shield; the rest was a series of rings supporting the conveyor, under which the muck trains would be positioned for loading.

When the day was over, Anne announced to Frank that she had developed a new theory. "Men go into construction," she said, "because they haven't grown up. They want to go on playing with their little trucks and shovels and this is the only way they can do it without being locked up."

"I think you're right," Frank said. I'm just a big, overgrown kid. But how do you like the mole? It's one hell of a toy, isn't it?"

Chapter 12

Kevin McCabe unlocked the door of the Belfast Brigade's basement headquarters and admitted a man in a dark sweater and cloth cap. They nodded wordlessly. The man sat down heavily, peeled off his leather gloves, and rubbed his eyes with his fingertips. He had spent most of the night driving from Dublin on back-country roads.

"Finally had some results on the Carney phone tap," the man said. "Bob called his mother from England last night. He's up to something, all right. He said it was big and would get his picture in the papers. Operation Bluebird, he called it."

"Did you get an address? Who is he with?" McCabe's voice was marked with tension. The tap had been maintained day and night for months without results, and he was on the verge of ordering it abandoned. At last there was a break in the search for the renegades.

"No address. The call came from Maidstone. He said he was working with a young fellow the world would be hearing about."

"Jamie Quinn," McCabe said. "Now we're on his track." He walked across the room and back. Quinn was planning a blast of some kind, he was sure. Hostages, ransom demands, lots of publicity, a bid for control of the movement . . . all paid for with stolen Provo money. "Have we got any people in Maidstone?"

"A few," the man said.

"Send them pictures. Tell them who we're after. I don't care about Maher and Carney." McCabe's fists tightened to whiteness. "Quinn's the one I want."

Like all men born and raised in Northern Ireland, John Maher's accent was closer to Scottish than Irish. It was not hard for him to pose as a professor of geology from the University of Edinburgh. Accompanied by Quinn and Carney, he presented himself at a small house with a well-kept garden behind Abbot's Cliff. They were welcomed by Adam Hempstead, semiretired Inspector of the Line for British Rail's Southern District, who was covered from head to foot in yellow rubber rain gear. In his hands were four electric lanterns, which he passed our during the introductions.

"You must be the professor . . . How do you do, how do you do. Right on time! Good! I've been waiting for you."

"These are the two post-graduate students I told you about on the phone. Mr. Peters and Mr. Blake."

There were handshakes all around.

"We'll take my van," Hempstead announced. "Four-wheel drive will come in handy on a day like this. Sure you want to wear those brand-new raincoats underground? Might get them scuffed a bit. I'll get you some oilskins from the shed down below. Boots, too. It's dry once you get into the hill, but you have to wade through a bit of slop first."

He's an old man, Quinn thought, climbing into the rear of the van, over eighty at least, judging from the lines in his face. He was in excellent shape, with quick movements and a nonstop line of chatter. After only five minutes with him, Quinn and his two companions had learned that he had lived in the house all his life, as had his father and grandfather before him. All had been local railroad men. His grandfather, in fact, had been an employee of Sir Edward Watkin on the old South-Eastern Railway and as a young man worked in the old tunnel they were about to visit "under the direct supervision of Colonel Beaumont himself. He was quite a man, my grandfather was. The stories he could tell!"

Hempstead pulled off the paved road and followed two ruts across the grassland to the edge of the cliff, where he got out of the van and unlocked a flimsy gate. Quinn made a silent note of the padlock, a standard type that would be easy to pick.

"I'm long past retirement age," Hempstead said when the van was under way again and lurching down the steep path toward the shore. "They tried to get rid of me for the first time fifteen years ago, but it didn't work. I know more than anybody else about the old workings, and I'm handy, living right on the scene, so they pay me a few peppercorns to conduct guided tours. Tradition plays a part. There's always been a Hempstead working on the Folkestone-Dover line. What did you say you were professor of?"

"Geology," Maher replied. "Peters and Blake here are writing a paper on the chalk deposits, so we—"

"Excuse me, professor, but that pile of scrap iron we're passing on the left is what's left of the Whitaker machine that bored a tunnel four hundred feet long back in 1923. I suppose the promoters are still waiting for the green light." He laughed good-naturedly. "We've never had any shortage of people around here who want to burrow their way to France."

"The Beaumont tunnel," Maher said, "do you know where it goes in relation to the construction site at Shakespeare Cliff?"

"Of course I know where it goes. There isn't anything about that tunnel I don't know. They've been after me for years to put my brains on paper, but I won't do it. If what I knew about this stretch of coastline was all written down, they wouldn't need me, would they?"

The van stopped at the end of a high concrete seawall. Hempstead disappeared into a toolshed, emerging after a few minutes of rummaging with an armload of yellow slickers and rubber boots. "Put these on," he said. "Geologists, that's what you gents are? You came to the right place. Look at that cliff! From out at sea it looks as smooth and clean as a bar of soap. Up close it's different. Gulleys, furrows, valleys. Something happening all the time. Slides. Slipouts. Falling rocks."

The old man clambered spryly up a series of steel rungs set into the concrete of the seawall, then leaned down to give the others a hand as they followed him. They walked single-file along a narrow ribbon of concrete. The tide was out, leaving a drop of ten feet to the water. Even so, an occasional wind-driven breaker sent a splash of salt spray higher than their heads. Quinn, Maher, and Carney concentrated on their footing while Hempstead strolled as unconcernedly as if he were walking down a country lane.

"The worst slide was probably the one in 1915," Hempstead said to no one in particular. "My father was in charge around here then. He noticed whole sections of the cliff moving. Cracks got wider before his very eyes. He flagged down a passenger train as it came out of the Abbot's Cliff tunnel and told the driver to forget about going to Dover, that the hill was about to come down. They didn't want to believe him, but they had to when he pointed to the track ahead, which was pushed all out of alignment. Back the train through the tunnel, my father told them, because where it was it was a sitting duck. Oh, no, we can't back through the tunnel. 'Why the hell not?' my father said. If you knew him you would know how mad he could get. Because it was against regulations! A train could not be put in reverse on the main line without the permission of the district dispatcher. 'Get the blighter on the phone, then!' my father shouted. I was just a lad then, but I can remember the thunder in his voice. While the engineer and the conductor went off looking for a phone box, my father emptied the train. Told the people to walk to Folkestone along the beach. Nothing in the rule book against people walking on the beach. Well! The dispatcher couldn't be reached by phone and do you know why? It was Sunday morning and he was in church! In church, he was! Couldn't be disturbed till services were over!" Hempstead whirled to face his followers, who had to stop suddenly to avoid colliding with each other. The old man, his eyes filled with mirth, raised his arms and brought them down like the conductor of an orchestra. "Then the whole cliff collapsed! Buried the bloody train from one end to the other. I'll never forget the sight. Even after all these years I sometimes have to look twice because I think I see it still. Just the end of the brake-van was peeping through. My father lived on until 1934."

He turned and jumped lightly to the ground a few feet below the landward side of the seawall, pushed his way through some low shrubs to the gravel embankment that carried the two sets of railroad tracks, and waited at the base of the cliff, into which was set a dark, wooden door. The Irishmen followed as best they could, having a difficult time with the slippery footing. Behind them an unusually large wave crashed into the seawall and sent a broad geyser of water high in the air.

"No need to look each way before crossing the tracks," Hempstead laughed, holding up a gold pocket watch. "The 1:33 isn't due for ten minutes yet. All right. Here we are. I don't know if you noticed doorways like this one when we were on the wall. There's one every fifty feet. Drainage galleries. Try to keep the cliffs free of water, we do, so they'll stay put. This one intersects the Beaumont tunnel." From his coat pocket Hempstead took a large wrench and applied it to a nut on the side of the door. "The tunnel was actually driven from a shaft up above, but that was filled up in the 1890s. This is the only way in now. Give me a hand, will you, son?" Quinn took hold of a steel ring and helped the old man pull the heavy door open. Inside, a rectangular passageway receded into blackness.

The four men switched on their lanterns and entered one behind the other, crouching slightly to keep their heads below the rotting beams that spanned from wall to wall. The floor was bare and saturated with water. A few two-by-twelve planks had been laid end to end to provide patches of firm footing.

"It gets better further in," Hempstead said, his voice and footsteps magnified and distorted in the close quarters, "not so wet and more headroom."

The men trudged forward, accompanied by the dancing shadows thrown up by their lights. The air became staler and staler as they went until, so it seemed to Quinn, it became nearly unfit to breathe. He looked over his shoulder. In the far distance was a small square of pale white–the doorway through which they had entered. If the wind were to blow the door closed, if a few boulders were to fall into place, they would be entombed like pharaohs in a pyramid. Carney, directly ahead, looked at him with misery on his face and sweat on his forehead. "Jesus, Jamie . . ." he began to say.

"Peters is the name," Quinn hissed, jabbing Carney in the back with his lantern. "Keep going."

They arrived at a circular cross-tunnel at right angles to the drainage gallery. "This is it," Hempstead said, casting his beam about, "this is where history was made a hundred years ago. The Beaumont tunnel. Look how smooth and straight this bore is, professor! Seven feet in diameter and more than two miles long. Or should I convert that to kilometers and be right up to date? You can see the grooves cut by the teeth of the Colonel's machine. This is as far as we go, because down the line are some wet spots and cave-ins."

Maher asked again about the construction site. Hempstead explained that another access shaft, which was also filled in in the 1890s, was located at the spot where the contractor had erected his batch plant, adjacent to the mouth of the lower access tunnel. The Beaumont tunnel was about fifty feet below the surface at that point, he estimated. Quinn asked if the tunnel ended there.

"No, it makes a swing to the right and starts sloping downhill to get beneath the Channel. The heading is flooded about a hundred yards beyond the shoreline. Was, anyway, last time I went that far, which was about ten years ago. Nothing you can see at that end you can't see here. Well, there is one interesting thing . . ."

"Do you get a lot of people wanting to come here?" Quinn asked.

"Eh? Not any more. A while back when they were designing the new tunnel every engineer in Britain wanted a look. They wanted to see how the chalk was standing up after a hundred years of exposure. There was so much bloody measuring equipment where we're standing it looked like a hardware shop. But I was telling you about the other end. There's a chamber down there where Watkin used to have parties for M.P.'s and the royal family. He was quite a promoter. Hauled them down from London, he did, in private railway cars and lowered them into the shaft six at a time in iron skips. I have a diary my grandfather kept. He saw the Duke of Cambridge, the Archbishop of Canterbury, the Lord Mayor of London, almost anybody you could name. Not from a distance, but right up close, shoulder to shoulder the way we are now. He pushed Gladstone to the face once in a tram car. I am telling the truth. I have it written in my grandfather's hand."

Quinn was smiling in satisfaction. The means of destruction was in his hands. From the rubble that marked the old shaft under the contractor's yard to the edge of the sea, that was the critical section. He and the others would come back at night and push their way to the end. If the way was blocked they would dig their way through. If there were sections that had to be shored up, Eagan would show them how to do it. A tremendous pile of explosives would be needed, probably tons and tons of it. Maher and Carney would figure out how much. They would need a lot of time, but there was no shortage of that. According to Eagan, the scheduled meeting with the French under the center of the Channel was still ten months away. Hempstead . . . Hempstead might notice something and get suspicious. So what? When a man his age is found dead nobody thinks a thing about it.

He tugged on Carney's shirt. "Let's get out of here," he said. "I've seen enough."

Chapter 13

After months of effort, Fred Conroy, Crosley and Black's chief cost estimator, completed his study of Kenward's slurry-pumping idea—hydraulic spoil disposal, as it came to be called in government hearings. According to Conroy's analysis, which drew on coal slurry pipeline experience in several countries, the method would be twenty percent cheaper than the use of muck trains.

A pumpable mixture required a particle size no greater than one-quarter inch. Frank saw no problem there. If necessary, muck conveyed to the tail of the shield could be fed through vibrating screens with a quarter-inch mesh, the oversize shunted through a crusher. Connections drilled between the tunnel and the sea bed from floating platforms would be far more expensive than he had thought—nearly five hundred thousand dollars per hole—which meant that they would have to be spaced at least two miles apart. The two thousand horsepower needed for milling and pumping would generate a great deal of heat, but that could be dissipated by making use of the relatively low temperature of the incoming seawater.

Except for Anne Reed the plan might have won an early okay. When she heard about it she leaped immediately into the saddle of her war-horse. Frank had made the mistake of casually mentioning it while they were driving to Canterbury after an evening of theater in London.

"Is this the same crazy idea you told me about back in the

beginning?" she asked, her voice taking on a sharp edge. "Pumping clouds of grit into the Channel?"

"More or less."

"Don't more or less me, you faker! It's the same thing exactly! SKAT won't let you do it."

"Now, Anne, don't get excited. Nothing's going to happen to your precious fish."

"Not just *my* precious fish, they're *your* precious fish, too. Everybody's precious fish."

"They're in no danger."

"How do you know? There are spawning beds all over the Channel."

"The report deals with the environmental impact, which would be minimal."

"Who wrote the report?"

When Frank admitted that it had been written by a group within Crosley and Black, Anne held her sides and laughed with pointed sarcasm. "That's terribly funny," she said. "I can imagine how objective it is."

"There will be some turbidity, yes," Frank said in exasperation, "but it would be temporary, and it would be a thousand times less than that caused by even a minor storm."

"That's your opinion."

"That's not my opinion, goddammit, those are the facts!"

"*Your* facts. Wait till you hear *our* facts."

The ensuing blitz of lobbying and propaganda forced the Department of the Environment to hold a public hearing on the matter. SKAT's facts were forcefully presented by Percival Rawley, professor of marine biology at Cambridge. The amount of damage to spawning grounds, he said, would depend on the shape and density of the "discharge plume" formed by the slurry. When the tide is running, he said, illustrating his remarks with large drawings, the plume would be long and broad and the resulting sedimentation in any one area would be negligibly light. Under some current conditions, however, the plume could be narrowed and bent back upon itself, with lethal consequences for flora and fauna alike. "If a school of fish were to be engulfed by the cloud," the professor said, closing his presentation with a phrase calculated to be taken down by every journalist present, "the evidence of the disaster on the beaches of Thanet would be both visual and olfactory."

Sir Charles Crosley was scheduled to be heard from next. He intended to make clear that the tidal conditions hypothesized by Professor Rawley were so unlikely as to be almost fanciful. In any event, the shape of the plume could be broadened by discharging the slurry through a long perforated pipe instead of from a single orifice. Furthermore, studies of oil spills and red tides showed that birds, fish, and plant life almost always re-established themselves quickly after being decimated by what seems at the time to be a "disaster." However, remarks made by the chairman of the government committee, a Member of Parliament from Wales who obviously had been coached by the environmentalists, made it plain to Sir Charles that the battle was already lost. More facts were needed, the chairman said. A technical study was in order. Not enough was known about the habits of fish schools, the location of the spawning beds, and the nature of the currents at the proposed discharge points. Dispersion patterns of chalk slurry in seawater, he had been assured, could be determined through a program of scale model testing in a laboratory. Currents could be charted with dyes and radioactive tracers.

Crosley nodded imperceptibly, realizing he was beaten. How could he rise and state for the record that more information was not needed? He couldn't, not in the climate of public outrage that SKAT had created with rumors that the Channel was to be turned the color of milk. Pausing now for studies that were sure to run many months rendered the case moot. If a rail system for hauling muck was going to be used, it would have to be ordered now or it wouldn't be ready in time.

"I was impressed by Professor Rawley's statement," Sir Charles said when he was called on and introduced. "He has plainly spent a good deal of time studying the possible consequences of hydraulic spoil disposal, and he raised some points that were not dealt with thoroughly enough in our preliminary studies. Speaking for the companies involved in the construction of the tunnel, which will be of such great value to Great Britain for so many years to come, and agreeing with those who wish to protect the integrity of the marine environment of our island nation, I hereby withdraw our request to make use of the Channel floor for chalk disposal. I wish to thank the members of the committee for taking the time to . . ."

His words were drowned in applause and cheering from the gallery, filled to overflowing with members of SKAT.

"Oh, that Crosley is smooth," Anne said to Frank over dinner. "I have to admire the way he shifted gears when he saw the situation was hopeless. He even fooled me for a minute. I'm afraid some of the reporters left the hearing room with the idea that he was a defender of the environment instead of its foremost despoiler."

Frank groaned. "God, how you exaggerate. You could teach a college course in it. Principles of Advanced Exaggeration. Prerequisites: failing grades in Logic and Fair Play. Charley is not despoiling anything, certainly not the English Channel. I'll tell you something. The tunnel is going to be the best thing that ever happened to the Channel for the simple reason that it will cut down on shipping." He raised a glass of wine. "Here's to the shipping industry, number-one polluter of the world's oceans and SKAT's main source of financial support. Those drunken stevedores in the maritime union are interested only in saving their own jobs. You think they give a shit about nature's delicate balance?"

"And you," Anne said, refusing to join in the toast, "could teach a course in Twisting the Knife."

William Ingram paced back and forth across his office trailing the wires of his telephone. The fumes from his cigar were drifting into an air-conditioning vent in the ceiling, but not quickly enough for his secretary, who kept a perfumed handkerchief pressed to her nose while waiting for him to resume dictation. His voice was loud, as it always was on a long-distance call or when money was worrying him. As he talked to Sir Charles Crosley in London, he kept his eyes on the jagged skyline of Chicago's Loop, which reminded him of a crosscut saw, perfectly designed for ripping and tearing.

"I don't get it," he said. "You gave up without a fight?"

The Englishman's voice was faint but clear. "There was no point in fighting. The government were going to demand a study of everything under the sun. I could do nothing but concede the battle as gracefully as possible."

"While a million bucks flew out the window."

"They were gone in any event. The study would have taken months, then months of arguing over it, then very likely a decision against us in the end. I did what had to be done. We'll proceed with a train-haul system."

"I'd like to know where the money is going to come from. The job's a year old and we're still in red ink. That goddam mole better start picking up speed or we're sunk."

"I have every confidence that—"

"Don't expect the Ingram Corporation to bail everybody out! We're sucking air in Venezuela and we've got a terrible mess on our hands on the New York water tunnels. I've got three cases going to court this month trying to get more cash from jobs already done, and if we don't win at least two of those I'm going to be doing stoop labor in Fresno. What does Frank think? The slurry idea was his in the first place. I'll bet he's hopping mad."

"He took it very calmly. I think his girlfriend had him convinced that the slurry would damage the Channel."

"His *girlfriend!* You mean he's still fooling around with that posyplucker?"

"I'm afraid so. Every weekend they disappear together."

"Fire him then! Consorting with the enemy! She's obviously in the pay of the shippers and airlines to get into his pants and fuck up his judgment. Kenward! My God, I can't believe it!"

"We don't have to fire him quite yet," Crosley said. "In some ways his involvement with her helps us. I'm almost sure that SKAT has modified some of its more absurd demands because Frank talked some sense into her head. It works both ways. She's the one who's likely to lose her job."

"A conservationist! A daisy sniffer! A complete kook, from what I hear. What the hell is wrong with him? What do they do with their time? They can't screw constantly."

"From what Frank tells me," Crosley said, "they argue a good deal."

Chapter 14

Twenty-three months after the job had begun, when the mole had been working for ten months, Crosley was at his desk going over the weekly computer printouts from the accounting department, devoting part of his attention to the messages being exchanged over the intercom loudspeakers. Frank was giving a series of orders in a tone of voice that made Crosley lay down his pen. The American's normal style was casual; he *asked* his superintendents to do things, he didn't *tell* them. Frank had apparently received a telephone message from the seaward face, which was now sixteen kilometers from shore and nearing the center of the Channel. The message must have been upsetting, judging from the way he was shouting at Barnes, the muck-train dispatcher.

"I don't care how many cars you still have to unload, put them on the back shunt and out of the way. Disconnect the locomotive and have it waiting for me. I'll be there in four minutes. Sidetrack all other traffic to give me a clear run to the heading."

"Righto. No need to get mad."

"Two to five, two to five," Frank said.

"This is Benzalek."

"I'm on my way to the heading, Chet. We might need Horatio, so stand by. I'll phone you from the heading when I've had a look."

Crosley's throat tightened. Horatio was a code word for an

underground emergency calling for an evacuation of the tunnel and the notification of medical and rescue personnel.

Next to be paged was Stiles, the master mechanic.

"Two to four, come in, Hank."

"Hank's on the crapper, Mr. Kenward. This is Clark."

"Goddammit . . . listen, Clark, I want to know how we are fixed for pumps. Run a quick inventory on every pump we can lay our hands on. I'll call back in twenty minutes. Tell Hank to wipe his ass and get busy."

Crosley's phone rang. It was Frank with news he didn't want coming over every loudspeaker on the project intercom system.

"Yes, Frank. Trouble?"

"Looks like it. Malone just called from the face. Two of the probe holes are showing mud. He says it's oozing around the drill steel like toothpaste. Could be really bad, could be just an isolated wet spot. I'm leaving for the face now. Better notify Hendricks. If we've hit a major fissure, British Rail might want to dust off its plans for getting across the Channel on a bridge."

Crosley swiveled his chair to the window. He watched Frank's car come out of the upper access tunnel, race down the ramp to the batch plant at the water's edge, make the turn, and disappear into the mouth of the lower access tunnel. He could imagine him sounding the horn with one hand and waving with the other to clear the way in front, skidding to a stop at the bottom, and jumping onto a mine locomotive for what could be a one-way trip to oblivion.

Sir Charles turned back to his desk and stared blankly at the wall. Mud was squeezing out of the probe holes, was it? Could be a minor wet spot, yes, or . . . Or the Channel Tunnel might go into the history books as another Lötschberg, only a hundred times worse. If the drills had struck a crevasse, the entire North Sea was waiting to carry the Channel floor's mud and silt into the tunnel. Saint Gotthard, Simplon, Tanna, San Fernando . . . if the stories of those blood-soaked tunnels were better known, the wages of men who worked underground would be even higher than they were. Crosley knew the stories well. He had studied them more than once in an effort to find out what factors had combined to produce disaster. Lötschberg was the worst of all. The way the miners there met their deaths made Crosley's flesh crawl: they were engulfed by sand that surged through a ruptured face and moved down the tunnel faster than they could run. When it happened the miners had reached a point nearly seven hundred feet beneath the River Kander, north of Switzerland's Rhone Valley, protected, they thought, by hundreds of feet of solid rock. In fact, they had hit a wide vein of saturated sand and gravel that reached all the way to the surface. Witnesses on top reported seeing a vast whirlpool form in the river and cracks opening on each side of the valley. The tremendous pressure forced a million cubic feet of material into the tunnel, filling it for a distance of a mile from the face and burying every man in its path, twenty-five in all. The bodies were never recovered, for every shovelful of sand removed by rescuers was replaced by a new surge from the depths of the mountain.

Could such a disaster befall the Channel Tunnel? Impossible. The chalk strata had been blanketed with test borings in the most comprehensive soil survey ever made. There was not the slightest evidence of faults or cracks. And yet . . .

Crosley relayed the news to Hendricks and asked him to review the survey data for the present location of the mole. If the tunnel were approaching a break in the chalk, he wanted to know how it could have escaped detection.

A phone call came through from Malone at the face.

"Malone, what the devil is happening down there?"

"We've got water," the veteran miner said. "Holes B and C are like firehoses. We hit mud at eighty feet. That lasted ten minutes, now it's water."

"Eighty feet of protection should be more than enough to hold the face. Tell the men that anyone who wants to leave the heading is free to do so, but that Kenward is on his way and may need their help."

"Nobody's leaving."

"Is the drill steel still in position? Don't try to withdraw it, and for God's sake don't let anybody near the face where they might get hurt."

Crosley rang off and radioed Benzalek, the director of safety. "We're getting water now," he told him. "Better declare Horatio."

At the medical trailer in the upper yard a light began to flash. The doctor on duty, a nurse, and the ambulance driver boarded a panel truck with Red Cross markings and headed for the access tunnel.

Hurtling down the track at the controls of a locomotive Frank saw the red warning lights go on and heard the blasts of the alarm horn, distorted by the Doppler effect as he sped past them. The heavy machine was built for power rather than speed, and no amount of urging would make it go faster than twenty miles an hour, a speed that seemed three times greater in the confines of the tunnel. He leaned into the wind that streamed against his face and kept his eyes on the tracks ahead, which converged at a distant point along with the air and water lines and the row of overhead lights. The wheels roared and vibrated against the track, and the curved walls raced by on all sides so swiftly that it seemed as if he were falling down an open shaft. He passed Marker Thirteen–thirteen kilometers from the Shakespeare Cliff adit–the lowest point in the tunnel. The grade gradually changed from downhill to uphill, although the transition could hardly be noticed. He remembered the relief he and the other men had felt when the mole began its upslope climb to the center of the Channel. Driving a tunnel downhill is dangerous because water breaking in behind you flows toward the face, which can be flooded at high pressure. Uphill, that's the way tunnels are driven whenever possible. Seepage then flows by gravity to the portal.

Twice he slowed down for siding switches, where crews assigned to trackwork and grouting were boarding trains in response to the evacuation signal. He hoped the sight of him traveling *toward* the heading would convince them that nothing was seriously wrong. Panic was the last thing that was needed.

At Marker Fifteen, less than a kilometer from the face, he noticed water between the rails reflecting the dim glow of the crown lights. Water was coming in. No doubt about it now–the emergency was legitimate.

Malone was probably happy, Frank thought. He had been complaining that the job had become too routine. Malone was a man who believed that tunneling was meant to be war, something for heroes, not technicians. He liked the smell of sweat, the chatter of drill bits hammering into hard rock, the sight of an old-fashioned mucking machine clawing at a pile of blasted rubble. Mother Nature was supposed to fight and twist and scream, not lie there as if she enjoyed it. Tunneling with a mole that was more than a match for the material was, to him, like working in a factory. Frank had stood with him a few weeks earlier watching the operation. Over their heads the conveyor was carrying chalk debris to the rear. Every forty-five seconds the muck train lurched as another empty car was positioned under the discharge point. The precast liner segments were swung into place by two hydraulic hoists and secured to the tunnel walls by a crew of five men who knew their jobs so thoroughly that their movements were almost automatic. The mole driver sat at his controls watching the loading of cars on a television screen, touching levers that kept the cutterhead pressed evenly against the face, and keeping an eye on the red beam of the surveying laser to make sure it was centered on its target. Added to the sound of the conveyor and the high-pitched whine of the axivane motors in the ventilating ducts was the grinding rumble of the cutterhead as it relentlessly peeled off layer after layer of chalk. Frank thought that there was enough noise and activity to satisfy even Malone, but he was wrong.

"Do you know what you've done, Mr. Kenward," Malone had said after several minutes of observing the routine, "you and men like you? You've taken the joy out of tunneling."

Frank slowed his speed to a crawl and eased the locomotive under the end of the conveyor. Ahead he could see the lights at the rear of the mole and Malone standing with a dozen of his men. The water was a full-fledged stream reaching nearly to the top of the rails. A man seemed to be hurt. The only sound was a steady rushing noise from the face.

In London, Inspector Greene of Scotland Yard laid on the desk of his superior a summary of circumstantial evidence suggesting that recent thefts of explosives in the South East were perpetrated by a single gang, the same gang that had looted the Provo treasury by waylaying a courier in Amsterdam and had later sprung two bombers from Tobermore. "They've got something big in mind," Greene said, "and we may be running out of time to stop them. We've got to start a manhunt now." Penton, finding the evidence unpersuasive, admonished his junior officer to keep his imagination in check. Greene turned red with anger and slammed the door as hard as he could on the way out. "One of these days," he said to a startled Mrs. Wheeler in the outer office, shaking his fists, "I'm going to find a piece of proof so obvious that even that blind bastard can see it."

A small radio filled a garage in Dover with the tinny strains of popular music. Thus serenaded, four men went about the task of attaching axles and bicycle wheels to stolen shopping carts, forming vehicles that would be ideal for carrying hundred-pound loads of dynamite along the rough floor of a hundred-year-old tunnel. The dynamite was stacked against a wall and hidden under a tarpaulin—two thousand sticks, each one an inch-and-a-quarter in diameter and eight inches long, packed in shredded paper, ten to a carton. The musical program was interrupted by a news bulletin. An emergency had been declared on the Channel Tunnel project. Details were still sketchy, the announcer said, but apparently water had been struck and the tunnel had been evacuated except for emergency crews. More news would be relayed as it came in.

The men looked at each other, wondering if the English Channel was going to destroy their target before they could do it themselves.

Chapter 15

At the first appearance of water draining from the probe holes, Malone thought of trying to stanch the flow by sending a quick-set chemical grout through the hollow, eighty-foot long strings of drill steel. Before the grout pump could be moved into position and connected, the flow had increased so much it was obvious the effort would be futile. When the jets had reached firehose force, Malone waved the men to relative safety behind the steel bulkhead that confined chalk dust to the forward section of the mole. One man was knocked down when he was struck on the legs by a section of drill steel that was hurled from its hole with the force of a javelin. His broken ankle was the only injury, Malone told Frank as they waded through knee-deep water. All eight access panels in the cutterhead had been folded back for the forward drilling operation, and it was through one of these at the invert that the two men squeezed to inspect the face. To make himself heard over the thunder of the water hitting the bulkhead, the foreman had to cup his hands and shout directly into Frank's ear.

They stood in front of the cutterhead casting flashlight beams upward through sheets of falling water. Frank caught glimpses of the jets in the upper left quadrant. They looked like two quivering silver poles suspended between the face and the bulkhead twenty feet to the rear.

"They must be six inches in diameter now," Malone shouted.

Frank nodded. Even though the holes were rapidly being scoured larger, the trajectories of the jets showed hardly any sag, an indication of the great pressure behind them. At eye level was one of the cutterhead teeth, deflected water pouring from it as if it were a broken faucet. Frank moved his face close to it and sniffed. The water was odorless. He touched his lips to the stream, felt its coldness, then filled his mouth, swishing the liquid from side to side before spitting it out. He turned to Malone with a grin.

"Our worries are over," he said, slapping him on the back. "This stuff is delicious."

Crosley picked up the phone before it completed its first ring. As he hoped, it was a report from the heading.

"We've got a couple of real gushers down here," he heard his superintendent say. "Too bad it's not oil."

"Frank, for God's sake . . ."

"It's fresh, Sir Charles. We haven't found the sea at all, unless the Channel is filled with pure Rocky Mountain spring water."

"Fresh?"

"We must have hit a pocket of water trapped millions of years ago when these strata were formed. It tastes better than the swill I've been drinking. What did the borings show for this location?"

"Nothing unusual, Hendricks says. The spacing where you are was about five hundred meters."

"Christ, they didn't waste any money, did they? You could hide Carlsbad Caverns in five hundred meters. Here's what I think we should do: nothing. See if it drains by itself. If it doesn't calm down in a few days, we can try freezing it by drilling holes from here or from a barge on the surface. I've moved the cutterhead against the face and extended all the gripper shoes. If the face tries to cave in, it will have a five-hundred-ton cork to contend with. Set up all the pumps we have at Marker Thirteen, that's where the puddle is going to form. Hard to estimate the flow, must be ten or fifteen thousand gallons a minute right now. I think it's beginning to slack off a bit already."

"Are you sure you are safe? Maybe you should get out of there while you can."

"Nothing to worry about. The water's only up to my hips. You should see the look of happiness on Malone's face . . . you'd think he was at a party."

William G. Ingram slammed the phone down. The news had reached him in the middle of the night, and he was sitting on his bed in his pajama bottoms. Tight gray curls covered his chest and spread across the curved expanse of his stomach. He started to light a cigar, then noticed that in his first spasm of alarm he had crushed it in his fist. He threw the remains against the wall and began stomping around the room, cursing, not caring if he woke his wife, asleep in the next room.

"Of all the no-good, rotten fucking luck," he said, bobbing his head and snapping the words.

His mind spun as he calculated the effects of a two-week delay, a four-week delay, a six-week . . . no, six weeks would be too long. The Ingram Construction Corporation couldn't stand six weeks. It wasn't so much the cost of the cleanup that was going to hurt as it was the suspension of progress payments. And things had been going so *well*. The mole was setting one new mark after another–835 feet a week, 880 feet, 920 feet . . . Black ink was just around the corner. Ten miles of steady progress without so much as a blown fuse, and now this.

"God *damn* it!" he said, sitting down on the bed again and jamming another cigar in his mouth. He made no move to coax a flame from his lighter. He sat woodenly, staring straight ahead.

I'll need a loan, and the bank isn't going to be thrilled with the idea. What happened to the last loan? what's-his-name will ask, the goddam, milk-sop sonofabitch. I'll call my lawyers in the morning. Hitting underground water will have to be classified as changed conditions. File a claim for additional money. If only contractors could sue for mental anguish! For pain and suffering! He'd tell the idiot at the bank that the British will have to fork over plenty eventually because of the changed conditions. Yes, the bank should lend him a few million on the basis of that. How could they refuse? He had a piece of the action on seven projects around the world totaling two billion dollars! He was *big!* And if they demanded to see his books? Well, then they would find out that he was likely to lose his ass on every contract. If the Channel Tunnel turned sour, it was all over. The octopus he had built over the years would roll belly-up and spit out no more than ten cents on the dollar.

He lay back on the bed and stared at the ceiling. The cigar clenched between his teeth was like a dead tree waiting to be struck by lightning. He would talk to Kenward and tell him to step on it. Take a few chances. Open up that cookie cutter of his and see what it will do. A thousand feet a week? Try for two thousand. He lit the cigar and closed his eyes.

The French. Sure would be nice if those pricks ran into some trouble. They had bad ground at the beginning, but were coming along fast now. The crews didn't have to meet in the middle. If one side bogged down, then the other side could go right by the midpoint and collect for the extra footage. Why couldn't it have been the *frogs* that hit an underground lake? Why us? Maybe France would be crippled by a general strike . . . yes, he would pray for that.

Clara Ingram walked lightly across the carpet and stood looking down at her husband, who had drifted off into a fitful sleep. Before turning off the bedside light she disengaged the cigar from his teeth. She didn't want him rolling face down and burning a hole in the sheets.

The mole resumed its advance three-and-a-half weeks after shutdown. The water jets had begun to sag twelve hours after appearing, their points of contact on the bulkhead dropping lower and lower, and after forty-eight hours the flow had stopped entirely. Aside from some electrical components and circuitry that had to be replaced and a build-up of chalk in its lower sections, the mole escaped serious damage. Further down the line silting was extensive. When the pumps had completed their work at the tunnel low point, the sediment was found to be two feet deep, and half a mile away in both directions it was still deep enough to cover the railroad tracks. The cleanup operation was speeded by the special tools and attachments devised by Stiles and his welders and mechanics, most notably buckets for the front-end loaders that were shaped to match to tunnel floor, one with cutouts for the rails.

The cavity that had been encountered turned out to be lens-shaped, several hundred feet in diameter and up to ten feet thick. A team of scientists took samples of the walls and of the water remaining in small pools, but since cave-ins were a constant threat they did not stray far from the forward shield of the mole. Denied was a request received from the Thanet Association of Spelunkers to explore the outermost reaches of the cavern. Exploratory drilling showed that the floor of the cavern was in no place lower than the floor of the tunnel, which meant there was no gap to be bridged. The chalk immediately ahead, though showing a higher-than-normal moisture content, was sound and more than cohesive enough to support the weight of the mole.

A small navy of research vessels from both Britain and France converged on the center of the Channel. Using radar, sonar, test borings, and seismic analysis, they determined that the tunnel would not encounter any more hidden reservoirs. "While the unknowns cannot be reduced to zero," read a statement released to the press, "the chances are extremely high that the remaining six kilometers that separate the tunnel crews will be traversed without further serious delays. The historic union under the center of the Channel could take place in as little as four weeks. A suitable ceremony is planned."

Part Two

The Last Seven Days

Chapter 16

"Aha!" Adam Hempstead said aloud, slapping the steering wheel. "I was right! Something funny *is* going on around here, and I'm going to jolly well find out what it is."

His headlights had revealed that the gate across the Folkestone Warren road had been unlocked and propped open with a stone. For months the old railroad inspector had noticed puzzling signs that something was afoot—tire tracks and deep footprints on the beach, half-heard and dimly remembered sounds of a vehicle coming and going while he slept. Several times he had awakened in the morning with a nagging question in his mind: Did I hear a car on the road last night or was I dreaming?

He eased his foot off the brake pedal, allowing the truck to roll forward silently. He hadn't been on this road in the middle of the night since his days as a warden in World War II. The truck he had in those days was worse, but his eyes were better then, not to mention his reflexes. As the truck bounced down the slope toward the beach he gripped the wheel tightly and peered into the light mist that clung to the headlands.

Parked at the toolshed was a vaguely familiar gray van. No sign of a beach party with a bonfire and young people singing, which is what he half-expected to find. Rain the day before had erased all footprints except for a freshly made trail leading to the end of the seawall. Hempstead remembered then where he had seen the van: it was the professor's, the one from Scotland with the two students who had taken a look at the old tunnel six or eight months before. He couldn't recall the names. Geology, yes, he was a professor of geology and the two lads were writing a paper on the chalk, that was it. What the devil are they up to now in the middle of the night? Some sort of measurements or tests? Why didn't they ask his permission, then, instead of picking locks and creeping around like burglars?

"Professorrrr . . ." he called into the blackness, his hands cupped beside his mouth. The only sound was the lapping of water at the base of the wall and an echo of his voice from the cliffs that rose gloomily into the mists above him. He shouted twice more without response.

The van was locked. By standing on the rear bumper and shining a light through the two small windows he could see that it was empty except for a dozen cartons filled with . . . what? Looked like warning flares of some kind.

The old man climbed the ladder at the end of the wall, the corroded iron rungs feeling rough and cold against his hands. Winter weather didn't agree with him; it made his nose run and his joints stiffen. When he had turned seventy-five seven years before he had given some thought of accepting his grandson's offer of retiring in Florida. He turned it down. Lying in the sun all day would turn him soft. He'd go to seed before his time. Better if life is a bit difficult. Keeps a man tough and alert. He stepped off the wall and worked his way up the embankment to the railroad tracks. Walking briskly to stimulate his circulation, he listened for sounds of the intruders and kept an eye out for any light they might cast up.

After a few minutes the beam from his flashlight fell on something that made his jaw drop in astonishment. The door to the Beaumont drainage gallery was standing open! What in the name of God Almighty . . .

Hempstead directed his light inside. The mud on the invert was covered with footprints that looked as if they had just been made. He stepped through the opening and trudged toward the intersection with the old tunnel. The walls were dripping with moisture and the planks he had laid across soft spots years before made sucking sounds when he put his weight on them.

He tried to remember what he could about the three men he had escorted this way so many months ago. A ribby lot, he had concluded after they were gone. Hardly said a word all the time he was with them. Asked no questions proper geologists would ask. All they wanted to know was if the tunnel led under the construction yard at Shakespeare Cliff. He would have a word with the professor, he would, if such he was.

At the junction he turned his light both ways. There were no signs of activity to the left. Pools of shallow water. A new roof failure since last he'd been there had formed a muck pile three feet high. He'd have to report that. To the right . . . to the right fresh chalk had been spread on the invert and there were so many footprints that a path had been worn smooth. A short distance away a rockfall that had for years partially blocked the passage was no longer there. Someone had gone to the trouble of shoveling it up and down the line to improve the footing. He shone his light against the crown. The gaping cavity from which the material had dropped no longer could be seen. The tunnel for a distance of fifteen feet was now lined with fresh lumber. Anger rose in Hempstead's veins as he pushed deeper and deeper into the hill. The nerve of that "professor"! Doing all this work right under my nose! Invading my territory night after night without so much as a by-your-leave!

After advancing a hundred feet he found the entire tunnel blocked by a steeply sloped pile of chalk. There was something odd about it. It seemed to rise more steeply than its natural angle of repose, and . . . and the footprints and what appeared to be the tracks of thin tires proceeded right under it. Was it some sort of camouflaged door? Yes, there was a steel ring at the toe . . .

Hempstead heard voices, more than one, and footsteps, and the creaking of metal carts. He switched off his flashlight. In the dark the pile of chalk was outlined by the flickering beams of flashlights approaching from the other side. Fear replaced the anger Hempstead had felt a moment earlier. He backed away, his mouth opening and closing, then turned and ran. Behind him he heard the groan of hinges and the sound of voices suddenly louder. Random flashes of light brought the curved walls of the tunnel beside him into uncertain view.

At the mouth of the drainage gallery he fell. He'd never make it to the outside without being spotted, he realized . . . he hardly had the strength to get back on his feet. On his hands and knees he crawled past the intersection and pulled himself behind a heap of rubble. He lay still, trying not to breathe, ignoring the coldness of the wet ground against his cheek. His heart was leaping like a fish in his chest. All his life he had hardly known his heart existed, but in the last few years whenever he had tired or excited himself he could feel it, even hear it, pounding. It was pounding now, filling his body and especially his arms with an ominous discomfort.

"A few more cartons in the lorry and that's the end of it. When that stuff goes off they'll think it's the blitz all over again."

The men were only a few feet away. Hempstead closed his eyes and hoped for the best.

"How long do you want to wait, Quinn? I'm awful sick of this fucking hole."

They turned the corner and their voices became too muffled to be understood. Hempstead raised himself to a kneeling position. The realization came over him that he was still not safe . . . the men would see his truck and come back looking for him. He managed to stand up, steadying himself against the ancient timbers that outlined the opening of the drainage gallery. He made his way slowly to the portal. The door was still open. Cautiously, he stepped outside.

The mist had retreated to the upper reaches of the cliffs, but the night was still very dark. Thirty feet away, standing on the tracks with his arms folded, was the man called Quinn, apparently waiting for his companions to return with the rest of what Hempstead now guessed was dynamite. He remembered Quinn as the youngest of the three, a fine-looking lad with black curly hair, a mouth that never smiled, and a voice that was strangely hard.

He turned to the cliff and began climbing one of the many steep trails that led to the top. Whether he could make it all the way he didn't know, not having tried it for thirty years and never in the dark. The trails had a way of becoming impassable with slides and debris and his strength might not be up to it in any event, not with his breath so short and his heart acting up the way it was. But he couldn't stay where he was . . . they'd find him sure. He began the ascent, making every move as quietly as he could.

He had managed to climb about twenty-five feet when he saw approaching lights bobbing along the seawall and heard shouts.

"The old man's lorry is here . . . He must be hiding somewhere . . ."

Hempstead pushed himself higher and higher with his legs, trying not to dislodge any rocks or pebbles. When he was forty feet above the bottom the men held an excited conference directly below him.

"The lids were up on some of the cartons. He probably saw the dynamite."

"He might be running up the road," said the man who had stayed behind.

"There are no footprints anywhere. He came this way. We saw where he jumped off the wall and climbed to the tracks."

They aren't disguising their accents now, Hempstead thought. They aren't from Scotland at all. No wonder they didn't do much talking when they were with him. They didn't want him to know they were from Northern Ireland. West Belfast, more than likely.

Hempstead was working his way up a narrow gulley with rounded shoulders of chalk protecting him on either side. How far have I gone, he wondered, seventy or eighty feet? Another hundred and fifty to go. At the top I can cross the meadow to the road and be less than a mile from my cottage . . . but I'll never make it . . . too steep, too slippery, no shrubs or roots to hang onto, just the smooth, gray slope.

He knew he was doomed when he put out his hand and felt a blank wall. He lifted his head and saw a vast expanse of chalk rising vertically. In his panic at the bottom, in the darkness, he had chosen a dead end.

"There! There he is!"

The men had spread out for the search and at last a beam of light had fallen on him. He rolled onto his back and gazed toward the invisible sea. He wished for the dawn and a last look at the hills and coast that had been his life. In the distance he saw a slowly moving cluster of lights, no doubt a ship in the inshore lane reserved for traffic bound for the mouth of the Thames.

"Come down, Hempstead, or I'll shoot . . ."

He'll shoot, he says. Well now! They have an eighty-two-year-old man trapped like a rat in a tree and he wants to shoot! A brave bunch of lads they are.

"No shooting," he heard Quinn hiss. "A bullet in his body will put the law on our trail."

"We could dump him in the tunnel . . ."

"Then they'll come hunting for him. This has got to look like an accident. Hempstead! Come down! Come down or I'll climb up there and throw you down!"

He was finding it harder and harder to breathe. Was he now to have an asthma attack on top of everything else? The pain in his arms . . . he should have known he couldn't climb the cliff at his age. Below him he heard the sound of scrambling, of breaking twigs, of curses, as one of the Irishmen climbed toward him. Hempstead dragged the heel of his boot back and forth on the ground, sending a cascade of pebbles and grit onto his pursuer. With a final effort he raised his flashlight to his waist and aimed it at the lights on the sea. His thumb pushed the on-off switch back and forth–three longs, three shorts, three longs, three shorts . . .

The first mate, standing in the darkened bridge of the container ship *Golden Star,* lowered his cup of coffee and stared at the coast of Kent, one mile distant. A pinpoint of light was winking the international signal of distress.

"Captain, look there. Am I seeing things or is that an SOS?"

His superior officer and the pilot who had come aboard at Folkestone moved to his side.

"You are right," the captain said. He turned to check the radar screen, enclosed in a brass fixture on the navigation table. The sweep of the green scanner showed that there was nothing between the *Golden Star* and the coast. He faced the window again and watched the barely visible flash for a moment more. "Fix our position," he said quietly. "Take a bearing on the South Foreland light. Call the Dover Strait Coast Guard on VHF 16. They may want to have a look."

"Looks like it's about halfway up the cliff," said the first mate. "Definitely on land. Uh-oh, it's stopped."

The men stood side by side peering into the night for several minutes. The flashes did not reappear.

"Whoever it is has given up," the captain said. "Could be a prank."

He looked at his watch. It was 4:00 A.M. They'd be passing Deal soon . . . plenty of time for a nap before docking at Gravesend.

Quinn saw Hempstead's flashlight coming, its beam whirling crazily as it caromed down the cliff, and he covered his head with his arms. It struck him a glancing blow on the shoulder before careening to the bottom and smashing to pieces at the feet of Maher and Carney.

"You bastard," Quinn shouted, "if you throw any more shit on me I'll wring your neck." He could see the soles of the old man's boots above him. He wasn't kicking or squirming anymore . . . apparently he was simply waiting for his fate. How had the old sonofabitch climbed so high, Quinn wondered, working his way from handhold to handhold. He was having a hard time keeping from losing his grip and sliding all the way to the bottom. The old fool . . . he had to go poking his fucking English nose around . . .

When he was close enough he reached up and closed his fingers around Hempstead's ankle, which was so thin it felt like a broomstick wrapped in cloth. "Let go," Quinn demanded through clenched teeth, "it's all over."

"Quinn!" Maher called. "Have you got him? What's the matter?"

From high on the cliff Quinn's voice came floating down. "He's . . . he's not breathing. I think he's dead . . ."

Chapter 17

"The Inspector is on his way in." The flawless intercom brought Mrs. Wheeler's voice to the corner of the Chief Inspector's desk with such fidelity that he jumped in fright, seized for a second with the mad notion that she had sneaked up on him as a joke. Then he remembered that he had asked her to fetch Greene.

"Those lion heads," Penton said as his visitor was sitting down, "on the coat rack. What do you suppose they are doing, roaring in anger?"

"In frustration, I would guess, sir," replied Greene, "this being the Special Branch."

"Wrong," said Penton, smiling indulgently at the man who was thirty years his junior. "They are gasping in surprise. If I were a man who displayed his emotions, as you are, that's what I would be doing, and that's what you will be doing in a moment. An amazing thing happened to me this morning. In all the time I've been assigned to the Irish troubles, I've never heard the like of it. I doubt if such a thing has happened in the entire history of this division, which goes back to 1884. Do you know why the Special Branch was formed in the first place? To combat the Fenians in London. It was called the Special Irish Branch."

"Yes, sir, I know."

"It was only later that we were given protection of VIPs and national security matters."

"I know."

"You are young and clever, Greene. You work hard and you have an attractive wife."

"Thank you, sir."

"With luck you could make it all the way to Commissioner of Metropolitan Police."

"You are full of fun today, sir. What happened to you this morning?"

"But like so many of the young fellows, you tend to overlook the background. You are thin on the long view and the perspective. That will come in time, I suppose. Let me tell you what happened to me this morning, just an hour ago. When I got on the underground on my way to the office, an old man got on with me. I hardly noticed him until he took the seat beside me. Before I could unfold the *Times* he was tugging at my sleeve. I turned and looked him squarely in the face. It was Eamonn Caldaigh. You see? I told you you'd gasp in surprise."

Kenneth Greene was more than surprised; he was flabbergasted. "Caldaigh of the Officials? In London? I don't believe it. He'd never take such a chance of being seen."

"There's not much chance of his being recognized. He's changed a good deal from the photos we have of him. He's gone gray. He's bent over. He's not well. He said he has every ailment known to medical science."

Greene was on his feet. "Did you make the pinch? Is he in the building?"

"I let him go in exchange for what he told me. He made me agree to that at the beginning. He appealed to my sense of fairness, which, he said, was why he was approaching me. And I don't know if it's quite proper any longer to refer to him as 'Caldaigh of the Officials.' He's retired due to old age and infirmity. His discharge from active service was honorable, if such a term can be applied to revolutionaries. Now Mr. Greene, please sit down and compose yourself. I don't want the entire staff trooping in here wondering what's up."

"I can't stand the suspense, sir," Inspector Greene said, sitting down quickly on the edge of his chair. "What did he tell you?"

The Chief Inspector drummed his fingers before answering. "A splinter group is planning something in England. He wants us to head it off."

"I knew it! I knew it! I told you as much months ago—"

"Let's be precise, shall we? You didn't *know* it; you *suspected* it. You suspect a good many things. You had a hunch that was convincing only to yourself. It was made up of odd facts and incidents collected from here and there to support a preconceived notion. Following up on every one of your hunches would take fifty thousand men."

Inspector Greene fidgeted in irritation. What was being characterized as a hunch was the result of months of hard thinking and research, most of it done on weekends and evenings. Six months earlier he had marched into this office and unveiled a chain of logic that to his eyes was without a weak link. Penton dismissed it as little more than idle speculation, sending Greene out of the office in a temper. He had slammed the door so hard the entire glass partition had nearly come down. If it had, he would have been fired straightaway. Fortunately, the glass held, and his superior had chosen to overlook the lamentable episode.

As Penton recounted the details of his conversation with Eamonn Caldaigh, Greene reviewed in his mind the hypothesis he had always known in his heart was a splendid piece of detective work. Shortly after he first had the idea of keeping an eye on money the I.R.A. was raising in the United States, the Central Intelligence Agency passed along to the Yard an unconfirmed report that an American arms dealer had placed an order for a planeload of Czech weapons and ammunition to be delivered to an unknown European port. Was Northern Ireland the ultimate destination? Possibly. The dealer had recently visited Dublin and the offices of Sein Fein, the political arm of the I.R.A.

The murder two months later in Amsterdam had removed all

doubt from Greene's mind. Seamus Duggan, thought to be a high-ranking officer in the Provisional Wing's Belfast Brigade, was found bludgeoned to death in an airport men's room, his right hand severed at the wrist. The mutilation intrigued Greene. He tracked down the crew of the British Caledonia Airways flight that had carried the victim from Glasgow. Duggan was a big, impressive man, and they remembered him. He had carried an attaché case on his lap throughout the flight. One of the stewardesses remembered the detail because she had suggested to him that he store it under the seat, which he politely refused to do. He kept a coat over his arm, she said, but she caught a glimpse of a chain attached to the handle. Yes, the case could have been handcuffed to his wrist. The right or left? She couldn't remember.

A phone call to Schiphol Airport had provided another clue. A plane from Prague had arrived the day before the slaying. Its cargo of "cut glass, crystal, and machine tools" was never unloaded. The Czech crew requested and received permission to depart the day of the slaying, though airport police had no reason to connect them with the crime.

In Greene's opinion, Duggan had been in Amsterdam to take possession of a load of Czech arms with a fortune tied to his wrist. His assailants couldn't find the key to the handcuffs, so in desperation shot off his hand. An airport employee who was thought to have blundered onto the scene died of a fractured skull without regaining consciousness. Duggan's murder was not a crime of opportunity. Someone at the highest level of the Provisional I.R.A. had set him up. It could also be assumed that the Provos knew they had a traitor in their midst the instant they learned of the murder.

Inspector Greene had begun monitoring police reports from Belfast and Dublin looking for news of an execution of the type the Provos reserved for traitors: torture, a sack over the head, a bullet in the brain. He didn't have long to wait. A woman named Mary McCabe, wife of Provo Chief of Staff Kevin McCabe, was found on a Londonderry rubbish heap dead of close-range gunshot wounds. Her hands were tied behind her back and there was a cloth flour sack over her head. In her left knee was a quarter-inch hole, probably made with a power drill, a common I.R.A. method of loosening tongues. Mary McCabe was either part of the inner council or overheard its plans, Greene reasoned. Seeing a chance to get rich quick, she tipped someone off. A lover, perhaps? Then why didn't she leave the country before news of the murder got back to Ireland? Sticking around was certain death . . . unless she was double-crossed in turn.

In any event, the trail had grown cold . . . until the breakout at Tobermore, west of Belfast, where four hundred suspected Republican terrorists were under detention by the British Army. Robert Carney and John Maher, both experts in the use of high explosives, had apparently been picked up outside the fence by a helicopter commandeered at gunpoint on the day of the escape. The helicopter, which several times was spotted flying low in an easterly direction in the hours following the breakout, was found a week later on the Irish Channel coast opposite Scotland.

If Carney and Maher had been sprung by the Provos, why were they not taken to a place like Londonderry, where they could have vanished without a trace in the Catholic population? Or why not a few miles farther to the west, to the wild hills of Donegal, where Republican sympathy was strong? Fleeing east didn't make much sense, unless . . . Unless the rescuers of Carney and Maher were the same men who stole the money in Amsterdam. As traitors to the cause they couldn't very well operate in Northern Ireland, and so they were hiding out in Scotland or England. They were planning to blow something up, else why snatch two of the best explosives men in the business?

Greene had watched for reports relating to the theft or illegal purchase of explosives in Britain. He soon became convinced that someone was stockpiling dynamite. A small gang that didn't hesitate to kill uniformed guards was looting the magazines maintained by quarry operators and highway contractors, mainly in the South East. Six incidents in Kent, Sussex, and Hampshire had resulted in a take for the thieves of frightening proportions. The time for theorizing was past. The time had come for action.

The only action Inspector Greene got to take was the slamming of Chief Inspector Penton's office door. Greene was wasting his time, Penton had said. Daydreaming. Fantasizing. Incidents so widely separated in space and time couldn't reasonably be linked, not reasonably enough, at any rate, to justify diverting anyone from his or her regular duties. A man from Northern Ireland stealing explosives in southern England with a fortune in his pocket? More likely he was sunning himself in Australia. Be sensible, Greene.

The incidents were linked nevertheless, and now, thanks to Eamonn Caldaigh, it was obvious that Greene had been right from the start. He listened with satisfaction as Penton reviewed his meeting with the old warrior.

"Don't you recognize me?" Caldaigh had begun. The encounter was fresh in the Chief Inspector's mind, and he related it to Greene as faithfully as he could. "Think back to 1969 and the Civil Rights marches in Derry. We spent an hour together in a parked car trying to come up with a way to head off the bloodshed."

"You are Eamonn Caldaigh? Good Lord . . ."

"I am, and it is your sworn duty as a servant of the Crown to arrest me. But you won't, in exchange for what I'm going to tell you."

Penton nodded his assent. The roar and clatter of the underground train was fearsome, and he had to strain to hear the old man's words.

"We made each other some promises that day," Caldaigh said. "I kept mine, and as near as I could tell you kept yours, even though things went to hell for both of us . . . and for Ireland. That's why I decided to come to you, because you can be trusted, I think. Not like the army officer who rules the roost today in the Six Counties. If I were the Queen of England I'd have him roasted on a spit, in the name of the Father and of the Son and of the Holy Ghost, amen. You are looking at me as if you don't believe your eyes, Inspector. Excuse me, *Chief* Inspector. It's me, all right. You like my new hair color? It matches the purity of my intentions. I've been told it makes me look so distinguished I should stand for public office."

Penton opened his mouth to speak, but the Irishman silenced him by raising a gnarled hand. "Let me finish. There's a young man somewhere in England, I wish I could tell you where, who is planning an atrocity, I wish I could tell you what. He has two and maybe three associates, all armed and dangerous, as you say, which is also true of the British Army. He has plenty of money to carry out his plan, whatever it is. The Officials have men looking for him. The Provos have men looking for him. Maybe it would help if you had men looking for him. Our motives are different, but where's the harm in that? McCabe wants him for personal revenge. You want him to avoid looking helpless. I want him to stop him from further staining the name of Ireland. A big bloody blast with a pile of English dead is the very last thing Ireland needs."

Penton found his voice. "This . . . this young man. Did he murder a man in Amsterdam a year or so ago?"

Caldaigh smiled broadly. He had lost most of his teeth since Penton had seen him last. "Congratulations, Inspector! Scotland Yard deserves its fine reputation. Are you way ahead of me? Am I wasting my time?"

"No, no. It was just a theory we had. We try to keep on top of things, you know. We suspected something was going on, but we didn't know quite what." He would have to tell Greene about this, Penton realized with a sinking feeling, and endure his "I told you so" reaction.

"I was thinking of asking you to meet me in Belfast," Caldaigh said, "but I was afraid you might not want to take the risk, being so close to retirement. I'm retired myself now, you know, so I thought I'd come to you. Time I did a little traveling, before it's too late. This old carcass is finally falling apart. I think I have every ailment known to medical science. A curse, being old. Thank God it happens to your enemies. It's a comfort to know that they get sick and die, too." He made a quick sign of the cross before continuing. "The good Lord did a fine job when he designed me. Every organ in my body is wearing out at the same time. When they put me in the sod nobody will have to worry about spare parts being wasted."

The train lurched to a stop at the end of the line. Penton looked up in surprise. He and Eamonn Caldaigh were the only ones left in the coach. For the first time in his life he had missed his stop and would be late for work.

Penton pushed the photograph Caldaigh had given him across the desk to Greene.

"So this is Jamie Quinn," Greene said, "the Mad Bomber of Belfast. He looks like a schoolboy. A member of the madrigal society."

"The shot is three years old. Caldaigh said he hasn't changed much. The sweet face now shows a touch of meanness, is how he put it. Here are the lad's fingerprints. Here are shots of Maher and Carney from our own files."

"Maher looks thick. His ears are on the large side."

"He's the only one with any education. Worked for a time as an electrical engineer. Tobermore will have his and Carney's prints."

Greene leaned back in his chair and shook his head. "Getting help from the I.R.A. . . . it's unbelievable. I suppose now we owe *them* a favor."

"Not at all. I've already paid a terrible price. I had to stand on an underground platform and listen to a lengthy lecture on the venality of English leadership all the way back to James the First."

"What's Quinn's target?"

"Unknown. Carney called his mother a few months ago and said he was working on something big that would get his picture in the papers. It seems the Provos have a tap on the Carney family home in Dublin and the Officials have a tap on the Provo headquarters in Belfast. Carney mentioned Operation Bluebird."

"Operation Bluebird? What in heaven's name does that refer to?"

"I have no idea. Something in the south of England, apparently. The call came from Maidstone. According to Caldaigh, Provo sympathizers there did some sleuthing of their own, in the pubs and what have you, and found the flat the gang was using . . . two days after they'd moved out."

"The south of England. That ties in with the dynamite thefts. I *told* you those were suspicious."

Chief Inspector Penton pursed his lips and folded his hands on the desk. "Yes, you told me. You saw the markings of a conspiracy. Which is not unusual for you, Inspector Greene. If our roles had been reversed you would have acted as I did. Until this new evidence came along you had little to support your theory beyond a thin tissue of supposition. We still don't have any hard evidence, may I point out. Maybe Caldaigh wants us off beating the bushes for some reason of his own. However, I agree that we must make an effort to find young Quinn and his friends, if they are still in the country. I'm putting you on the case full time. After you've waded in, tell me what help you think you'll need. When I go over this with the Commissioner, he might give it a high priority, in which case you won't be laboring alone."

"Thank you, sir. You can count on me. Did Caldaigh say anything else? Anything at all?"

"No, you have the whole story."

Well, not the whole story, Penton thought as he watched Greene leave. Caldaigh did make a final comment, a joke at Penton's expense, but the Chief Inspector saw no reason to repeat it to a junior member of the department who probably didn't think too highly of him as it was. Respect for one's superiors was an attitude that must be fostered for the good of the entire organization. When the train had reached the end of the line, Penton had made an unthinking comment–a silly comment, he could see in retrospect. Glancing at his watch he had said: “I’m going to be late for work.” The Irishman had grinned, his white eyebrows rising high on his forehead. “Late for work! What a terrible, terrible shame! Would it help if I gave you a note for the Commissioner?” It was a jolly good joke, the Chief Inspector had to admit, and the lion heads on the coat rack, reading his mind, were enjoying it hugely.

Chapter 18

Inspector Greene, whistling happily, spread the travel folders across the top of his desk. He was in a fine mood. The Central Fingerprint Bureau had confirmed that the prints of Quinn, Maher, and Carney matched those taken at the scene of the latest dynamite thefts. So much for the "thin tissue of supposition" unsupported by "hard evidence." Now the chase was on.

He surveyed the holiday locales arrayed in four-color glory before him. "Discover the South East," a headline implored. "Enjoy the splendor and serenity of historic Kent, Surrey, and Sussex." If I were completely bonkers, Green said to himself, setting a challenge, and I thought that blowing something up in serene, historic Kent, Surrey, and Sussex would be good for Ireland, what would I choose? The village clock in Abinger Hammer? The town pump at Faversham, "decoratively painted in pleasing colours, thus adding interest to the local scene"? Why not the Romney, Hythe & Dymchurch Light Railway, Gift Shop and Cafe? He looked at the photo of the narrow-gauge locomotive. The driver waving from the tiny cab looked as big as the Cardiff Giant. Striking when the cars were packed with children, Greene thought, would send reverberations of disgust round the world, if that's what I thought Ireland needed. Just *threatening* to blow it up, maybe that was the plan. No, the train would simply be evacuated. The children would run off into the marsh with their fingers in their ears, looking back over their shoulders hoping to see an explosion. Think of something bigger, Greene chided himself, something more dramatic. The Royal Pavilion in Brighton? Sissinghurst Castle? Canterbury Cathedral? Hmm. Canterbury Cathedral was a possibility. A packet of firecrackers might bring those walls tumbling down . . . tons and tons of high explosives would hardly be needed. I'm on the wrong track. Quinn told Caldaigh he had a target in mind that would divide the country. What could that be? Operation Bluebird . . . there was another clue. He tried to make some sense of it. The bluebird. The Blue Bird. His mother used to read him a story by that name when he was a child. Written by a German, if he recalled correctly. Maybe if he picked up a copy at a bookshop and read it, something would suggest itself. Bluebeard . . . maybe Penton got it wrong. Bluebeard murdered six wives. Quinn was planning to plant a bomb under a group of wives on an outing. But what group? Which wives? The Merry Wives of Windsor. Windsor Castle? Probably not southerly enough.

Inspector Greene rested his chin in his hand and drummed a pencil point on the desk top. Bluebird. The bluebirds over. What were they over? The white cliffs of Dover. He tried to bring to mind the lyrics of the World War II popular song. There'll be bluebirds over the white cliffs of Dover. There'll be tears? love? wives? and laughter, and something he couldn't recall ever after, tomorrow, just you wait and see. When the world is free. Quinn was going to blow up the white cliffs of Dover just as a train was passing by carrying the royal family. Awfully impractical. Dover. Shakespeare Cliff. The ferries. The English Channel Tunnel project. In a few weeks the first bore was due to meet the French coming the other way, according to a piece he had glanced at recently in the *Times*. He thought about the tunnel, and the more he thought about it the better he liked it. He threw his pencil down and touched a button on his intercom. With his other hand he swept the travel folders to one side. "Mrs. Wheeler, would you call British Rail for me? Find me somebody who can give me a report on the status of the Channel Tunnel project."

. . .

The door of Chief Inspector Penton's office swung open, revealing Kenneth Greene. The expression on his face was the one Penton detested most: triumph. Greene took two long strides forward, then dropped to one knee. Spreading his arms wide, he broke into song, an Al Jolson with a British accent:

> There'll be bluebirds over
> The white cliffs of Dover
> Tomorrow, just you wait and see.
>
> There'll be love and laughter
> And dum-de-dum-de-dum . . .
> Tomorrow, when the world is free.

He sprang to his feet and clapped his hands. "I've got the target. Call it a hunch, a lucky guess, a thin tissue, anything you want, but if I needed a code name for something that passes right under Shakespeare Cliff, I'd use "Bluebird"; at least I would if I were Irish and the blood of lyric poets was in my veins. The Channel Tunnel, Mr. Chief Inspector, that's what the bombers are after. It's big, that's why they need so much dynamite. It's far from beloved, which is why they think wiping it out won't fill the English heart with hate. If I were a terrorist, when would I act? Right about now, just before the British and French sides meet at the center. It's as vulnerable now as it will ever be. If I may make a suggestion, sir, we should move quickly."

Penton, who had risen half out of his chair in astonishment at the young detective's performance, sat down slowly. "In your blind, floundering way," he said, "you may have landed on the needle in the haystack. Get on a train for Dover. I'll call the police there and the project people and let them know you're coming."

"I'm on my way . . ."

"And Greene . . ."

"Sir?"

"The look on your face is entirely too self-satisfied. We may already be too late."

• • •

In the quiet aftermath of lovemaking, they lay before the fire on the mattress they had carried from the bedroom. Anne's eyes were closed, her arms folded lightly over her breasts, her legs crossed at the ankle. Frank was resting on one elbow, arranging her hair, still damp from the bath they had taken together, into patterns on the pillow.

"Are you asleep?" he whispered.

Her eyes opened. "No, I've been thinking. When will the tunnel break through to the French side?"

"Can't say exactly. Depends on how fast we both go. Maybe three weeks."

"The moles will simply be driven forward until they bang together?"

"When we are five or ten feet apart there will be a coin flip. The loser's machine will back off and let the other one have the honors."

"Then there will be a ceremony of some sort, isn't that right?"

"Crosley is trying to get the Prime Minister to reach through and shake hands with the President of France. I doubt if he'll be able to swing that. Those guys aren't exactly daredevils. There's been talk of having a kind of victory banquet. The French would bring champagne and cheese, we'll bring I-don't-know-what . . . fish and chips and Coke, I suppose. Why the interest? I thought you hated everything about the project."

"I want to be there to take pictures. I want to go into the tunnel. I want to go in twice, actually. Once to check the lighting and camera angles and again for the celebration."

"No you don't. You told me you had claustrophobia. You told me people had to be crazy to crawl into holes in the ground."

"I want to go into the tunnel."

"It's gloomy down there. It's wet in some places and dusty in others. The face is almost twelve miles from the adit now. It takes forty-five minutes to get there on a muck train that shakes like a bucking bronco all the way. The noise is almost unbearable. You'll hate it. Besides, women aren't allowed in tunnels."

Anne sat up. "Aha!" she said. "The truth comes out. Who says women are not allowed?"

"It's an old tradition."

"An old male tradition."

"I suppose so. Miners are superstitious. They face sudden death all day long. They carry lucky charms. Some of them think a woman in a tunnel brings bad luck."

"I was on the cliff last week with a three-hundred-millimeter lens and I distinctly saw a woman go in."

"That was probably Mrs. Steigmuller. She's a structural engineer with British Rail."

"Did she bring on bad luck?"

"Of course not. She didn't ride out to the face, though. The miners would have had a fit."

"How do you know? Did you ask them?"

"I don't have to ask them. I know how they think."

"Maybe they aren't the sexists you think they are."

"Maybe not, but if just one of them got upset or nervous, the whole crew would be in danger. Everybody has to concentrate on what he's doing. It's a self-fulfilling situation–if one man thinks bad luck is in the offing, he can bring it about just by worrying about it. By being distracted."

Anne got to her feet. "Don't you think that's an attitude that should be challenged? Are you going to let the most ignorant and superstitious oaf on the job dictate your policy? Tell you who can go into the tunnel and who can't? That makes you worse than he is because you are in a position to do something about it."

She had pulled on her panties and now her hands were behind her back fastening the straps of her bra.

"Look at yourself in the mirror," Frank said with a wave of his hand. "You could almost pass for Miss Universe. You sure as hell aren't Mrs. Steigmuller. If you showed up at the face those goons would howl and paw the ground and salivate all over themselves."

"I'll be hidden under a coat and hardhat and boots. I'll be all business with cameras and lights. Anybody who drools should be locked up as a sex offender."

Frank found his socks and shorts on a chair. "What if you couldn't stand it after you got there?" he asked. "What if it gave you the creeps and scared you half to death and you begged me to take you out? Feminism would be set back fifty years."

"What kind of woman do you think I am? When I see a mouse I don't jump on a chair and say, 'Eek!' "

"Now, Anne, simmer down. Look at it from my point of view. I've got the safety of the men to consider. It would be stupid of me to risk getting somebody hurt just to score a tiny victory for women's rights."

Anne walked across the room to him and took him by the shoulders. She looked up into his eyes. "Do you think I'm a good photographer?"

"The best."

"Don't you think I would do a superb job of covering your historic picnic?"

"Yes."

"Then hire me for the job."

Frank sighed. He was going to lose another argument. Not that he lost every one. He had shown her wrong a gratifying number of times. Intellectually, theirs was a painful but stimulating relationship. "Will you accept a compromise?" he asked.

"No."

"Here's what I'll do. I'll take you in on Sunday when only the equipment maintenance crews are on duty. You can see the place and measure the light and so on. I'll post a notice in the changing room where all the miners will see it that you are going to cover the holing-through. Anybody who doesn't like it can speak up or transfer to another shift."

He wasn't making such a big concession, Frank decided. Times had changed. It wasn't so much *women* that tunnel crews objected to now as it was incompetence. All visitors were resented as threats to safety. A professional woman with a job to do would probably be accepted without too much resistance even in such a formidable bastion of male supremacy as the heading of the English Channel Tunnel. And on the day of the holing-through there would probably be more than one female member of the press contingent.

"Thank you," Anne said, embracing him. "One of the things I like about you is that when you realize your ship has sprung a leak you jump overboard with dignity."

Chapter 19

Before coming to the point of his visit, Inspector Greene waited until Crosley's secretary, who had rolled in a tea service, was out of the office with the door closed behind her.

"We have reason to believe," he said, "that your project has been picked as a target by a splinter group of the Provisional I.R.A. At least three men are involved. Two are explosives experts. All are veterans of violence and murder."

Crosley and Kenward exchanged glances, then looked at the photographs the young detective laid on the desk. They didn't recognize the sullen faces.

"The young one," Greene said, "is thought to be giving the orders. We're told he has delusions of taking over the entire Republican movement by pulling off something big and flashy. We aren't certain that the Channel Tunnel is what he's after, but the evidence is–how shall I put it–suggestive."

"May I ask," Crosley said, "what the evidence is?"

Greene marshaled his thoughts before replying. "We know they've stolen a large stock of dynamite in the south, Kent mainly. We know they feel that the destruction of the target they've picked will not turn British public opinion against them. The tunnel, you see, fits nicely. It would take a large blast to destroy it, and it is, if you don't mind my saying so, opposed by a certain proportion of the citizens. Since your workmen are now nearing the center of the Channel and are as far from safety as they will ever be, the strike may well be imminent. Finally, they refer to their operation as Bluebird. You will recall the old song about the white cliffs of Dover, the bluebirds over, and so on."

There was a trace of a frown in Crosley's expression. "We will, of course," he said, "do whatever you think we should, even though your evidence is only, as you say, suggestive. I fail to see how . . . that is, the project presents an almost impossible problem for terrorists. It's not invulnerable, exactly, but . . ."

"Hardly," Greene said.

Frank finished Crosley's thought. "If you sat down and tried to design something that would resist attack, this tunnel is what you'd come up with–a heavily reinforced structure deep underground."

"All the more reason for destroying it, then," Greene said calmly. "The terrorists would seem unstoppable if they succeeded, wouldn't they? The public would be made to feel that nothing is safe from them, not even heavily reinforced structures deep underground. By the same token, if we can thwart the plans we think they've been working on for over a year, then we shall have scored a valuable psychological victory. The other side will look even more futile than usual. Mr. Kenward, permit me to ask you a question. I know you won't like thinking about destroying what you've labored so hard to create, but if you were bent on blowing up the tunnel, how would you go about it?"

Frank looked at Crosley for support. Did he have to apply himself to such a ridiculous–

"How *would* you go about it?" Crosley asked.

Frank made a gesture of hopelessness, then sighed. "Well, let's see. I'd fill a string of muck cars, say twenty of them, with TNT, haul it to the face, and set it off. That might bring the sea in. If not, I'd try *two* trainloads. That's what I'd do if nobody cared. It wouldn't work if people didn't *want* me to blow up the tunnel. A hundred different guys would tap me on the shoulder and say, 'Hey, mister, what the hell are you doing?' "

He walked to the window and looked down at the lower work area. "It might be possible to *flood* the tunnel. Is that good enough? Look at the mouth of the lower access tunnel. It's only a hundred yards from the water. Give me a week and I'll use a couple of trenching machines to cut a slot fifty feet deep between the portal and the shore. I'd dump in the dynamite you say I've stolen and light the fuse at high tide. See what that would do? The sea would pour down the adit to the main bore." He turned from the window and put his forefinger on a profile drawing of the tunnel tacked to the wall. "Down the hill the water would go, past the low point at fifty or a hundred miles an hour, gathering speed, then up the hill to the center of the Channel. The leading edge would probably reach all the way to the face before doubling back on itself." He held his hand flat and slowly raised it. "The tunnel would gradually fill with water, trapping a bubble of air at the far end. The pressure would build as the water continued to come in until the survivors at the face would implode. Well, all right, they wouldn't implode, but they'd get very sick."

"A fascinating scenario, Frank," Crosley said, "if beyond the realm of possibility." He turned to Greene and explained how the job's security system ruled out such direct approaches. The entire perimeter from Old Folkestone Road to the water's edge was lined with a chain-link fence topped by three strands of barbed wire that was checked for breaks twice a day by watchmen. The only entrance to the site was through the main gate, past guards who checked identifications badges. "The job is going twenty-four hours," Crosley added. "No unauthorized person would go unnoticed for long. I suppose a gang could shoot its way in, but what would be accomplished? It would be a suicide mission."

Greene was not to be put off. "Might there not be a way to attack the tunnel without breaching the security line? From the sea? From the air?"

Crosley shook his head.

"Here's an idea," Frank said. "Drive fifty trucks loaded with TNT aboard a car ferry at Dover. Once it's under way to Calais, hijack it, sink it over the tunnel heading, and blow the mother up. I don't know if the tunnel would cave in or not, but it would sure spring a few leaks."

"As you can see, Inspector," Crosley said, "we don't feel there is much chance of losing the tunnel, which will probably survive the next several world wars. However, we will take whatever precautions you feel are necessary. Do you think we should shut the project down?"

"For the moment I'll be satisfied with circulating the photos to your staff and guards. But not to the workmen. If one of the gang is on your payroll, we don't want to tip him off. Depending on how strongly London wants to move on this, we may station a few men here and there posing as surveyors. I'd like a list of every man on the project with an Irish name. We have people very good at checking out backgrounds."

"The list will be in your hands tomorrow," Sir Charles said. He turned to Frank. "Do you suppose we should include men like Malone?"

"The heading boss? No, I'll vouch for Malone. He may have been born Irish, but he doesn't practice it any more."

"Mr. Kenward," Greene said, "you will pardon me for saying that I don't find that sort of remark very amusing. I happen to be Irish myself."

It was Saturday night, and Chief Inspector Penton was at home settling down before the television armed with a mug of bitters and a lapful of reading material. For years he had made it a rule not to turn on the set until he had plowed through all left-over office memos and reports, followed by the *Times,* the *Guardian,* and the *Spectator.* Now with retirement moving ever closer he was beginning to relax a bit. He listened while he read, and his reading fare now included *Country Life* and *The Gardener.*

He groaned when he heard the phone ringing in his study. He couldn't ask his wife to get it . . . the call was on the red line, the number of which was known only to a few department heads and key agents in the field.

"Penton here."

"Ah, Mr. Chief Inspector, top of the evening to you."

The rasping voice, the unmistakable lilt . . . The magazines in his hand slipped to the floor. "Eamonn Caldaigh! What . . . how . . . this is supposed to be a secure line. How did you get this number?"

"I've learned a thing or two in seventy years of war," Caldaigh said, cackling at the policeman's consternation. "We're going to win in the end, you know, the I.R.A. We know all, we see all, we never sleep . . ."

"What in the name of heaven are you blathering about?"

"I have news. Carney got homesick and called his gray-haired Mam again. The gang's in Dover. Are you recording this? Push the little green button."

There was a green button on the desk, but the recorder it was supposed to activate was out of order, stuffed into a lower drawer along with a tangled mass of wire and magnetic tape. Penton grabbed a pencil and began writing on the margin of the *Wedgwood Society Newsletter,* cursing under his breath when the lead broke.

"Yes, yes, go on," he said, trying to project a calm, professional tone.

"He told her to buy a dozen copies of next Wednesday's paper."

"Wednesday, Wednesday, that gives us four days . . ."

"No, three days. To make Wednesday's papers the blast would have to be heard on Tuesday."

"Right you are."

"They're living in a rented house on a quiet street with a dry basement. He's dressing warmly and his mother is not to worry. There are four in the gang, not three. We still don't know what they plan to do. All he said was that it would stun the world. Could it be the big tunnel in Dover they've set their sights on? That would make a lovely disaster."

Penton had found a ballpoint pen and was scribbling furiously.

The pen was dry, but by pressing hard he was leaving a trail of legible grooves.

"Dover . . . rented house . . . tunnel . . . Tuesday . . . yes, yes . . ."

"Here's what you should do, Mr. Chief Inspector. Send fifty men to Dover and start a search. Better act fast because the Provos have about a twelve-hour head start. Shouldn't be too hard to find four strangers with Belfast accents. Easy to tell them from the pasty-faced Englishmen and the illegal Pakistanis. Got to ring off now . . . I hear my wife on the stairs."

It was Civil Servants' Night at Buckingham Palace, and the Commissioner of Metropolitan Police did not want to be called to the phone.

"Penton, this better be good. The Queen is due any minute."

"I'm terribly sorry, Commissioner. Believe me, I spent a good deal of time weighing the need to call you, balancing the pros and the cons–"

"Well, what is it? What is it?"

Penton summarized the call from Caldaigh. The sound of heavy breathing was the only response from the Commissioner. "If we put fifty men on this," Penton ventured, "I dare say we'd pick the blighters up soon enough. Shouldn't be too hard to find four strangers with Belfast accents."

"Caldaigh's word, that's all we have?"

"So far, yes."

"You've got a man there already, haven't you?"

"Inspector Greene, yes, since this morning."

"Has he turned up anything to corroborate the rumor?"

"Not yet."

"Well, we're not going to divert fifty men or even five men just on the word of an enemy of England. We'll divert two men. You and Greene. Get yourself down there immediately. If there's to be a local manhunt, the Dover Police can do it. You can help them."

"You want *me* to go?"

"Yes, *you*. What's the Chief Constable's name in Dover?"

Penton wanted to say that it didn't seem right that *he* should have to go, so close to retirement and all, but one didn't say things like that to the Commissioner no matter how strongly one felt them. What he said was: "Henry Treshnell is his name, sir."

"Treshnell, of course. You tell Treshnell to put fifty men on the case. What else is there for them to do in Dover? Don't call me again until you've got more than speculation."

The Chief Constable of the Dover Police rubbed his chin. It was 10:00 P.M. on Saturday night and he was sitting in the living room of his home talking to Inspector Kenneth Greene of Scotland Yard. "Unusual? Suspicious? No, I can't think of anything that has happened lately that has been . . . well, there was the Hempstead matter . . ."

Greene pressed him for details.

"An old gent named Adam Hempstead," Chief Treshnell said, "a kind of watchman for the railroad, was found a few days ago dead in his lorry. Rolled down an embankment on the road to Dawkinge Wood. Nice fellow. Everybody knew him. Fell asleep at the wheel is what I guessed when I heard the news. Later in the day I heard from the coroner. In his opinion the man had died of heart failure a couple of hours before the accident. There was very little bleeding, you see, despite some rather deep cuts. Doesn't make much sense, does it? Why would anybody take a heart attack victim and try to make it look as though he died in a wreck?"

Neither of them could imagine a reason.

"Could be tied in with the SOS," the Chief added distantly.

"The SOS?"

"A radio message came through from a freighter about 4:00 A.M. Thursday morning. Somebody was flashing a distress signal from the cliff, they said, about a mile or so down the coast from here. Hempstead lives down that way, and if the coroner is right that's about the time he died. The Coast Guard sent a boat by, but there was nothing to be seen."

Greene frowned, trying to put two and two together. "Maybe he was snooping around," he offered, "and saw something that scared him to death. Maybe he stumbled onto the Irishmen and flashed the SOS before they grabbed him. He fell off the cliff, or there was a chase and he fell against some rocks. He was scuffed up, so to avoid having anybody asking questions about how it happened, they put the body in the lorry and rolled it off the road."

Treshnell wrinkled his nose and shook his head. "That's a bit farfetched, Inspector."

"I suppose it is," Greene admitted, his voice trailing off. "Well, let's sleep on it, shall we? Something may turn up in the morning."

But neither of them would get any sleep that night.

Chapter 20

Kevin McCabe stepped off the train at Dover's Priory Station at 10:25 P.M. carrying a single suitcase. He walked across the parking area to the concrete steps leading upward to the street. As planned, a man in a brown mackinaw was waiting for him. He showed signs of too much ale and he was nervous.

"Would you be John Johnson?" the man asked in a heavy brogue.

McCabe nodded.

The man looked around with fearful eyes, then pressed a slip of paper into McCabe's palm. "You'll find the men you're wanting at that address," he said. "Landis Lane, 221. They were easy to find once we had the description. They come into the pub now and again. Stick to themselves. Keep odd hours, I'm told."

"Landis Lane, is it far?"

"You could walk." Gesturing, the man gave directions. When he was sure McCabe understood, he turned and hurried off into the darkness, terrified, it seemed to McCabe, that a policeman would materialize out of the fog and arrest him for the heroic deed he had done for Ireland.

In a small hotel room twenty minutes later, McCabe stood before the dresser mirror adjusting the shoulder holster under his suit coat to minimize the bulge. With the silencer attached, the muzzle of the revolver reached almost to his belt. He smiled slightly at the thought of the turmoil the news of his departure would provoke among the members of the Army Council meeting that night at Ballybay. It would be a disaster if a man who knew as much as he did fell into British hands. Codes, aliases, hideouts, armories, everything would have to be changed all over the Six Counties. Tell them not to worry, McCabe had instructed the officers of the Belfast Brigade before leaving. I'll blow my brains out if I get cornered. The British bastards will get nothing of value from me except the fillings in my teeth. He had to carry out this assignment himself, couldn't they see that? To show he hadn't lost his nerve and to take for himself the pleasure of dealing with Quinn. Maher and Carney he would merely kill; Quinn would be made to suffer.

Chief Constable Treshnell was preparing for bed when the phone rang. It was Inspector Greene again, his voice full of excitement as he relayed the news he had received from Penton in London: The terrorists were in Dover, there were four, they were in a rented house on a quiet street, and their strike was imminent.

"My superior is already on his way," Greene said, "but we don't have to wait for him. We can start the wheels turning. We've got to find these maniacs before–"

"I beg your pardon, Inspector. You want to start looking tonight? Now? For God's sakes, it's almost midnight!"

"Yes, I want to start looking tonight! Speed is critical. How often have we a chance to nip something like this in the bud?"

Treshnell sighed. "All right, I'll meet you at the station in . . . forty minutes."

"Good. London was wondering if you shouldn't put fifty men on this."

"That won't be necessary. Good-bye."

The Chief took his uniform from the closet and laid it on the bed, explaining to his wife that he had to go out for a few hours and supervise a manhunt. "It's that young chap's idea who was here earlier. With him everything is an emergency." He asked her to call the Sergeant on night duty, rattling off the names of half a dozen men he should summon to the station. "Tell him to explain that it's a chance for them to show their stuff for the Yard."

Fifty men, he repeated to himself with a dry laugh as he slipped into his trousers, that's what London thinks is needed? To repel an invasion, yes, but not to find four bloody Irishmen. Six would be sufficient, plus the regular night crew. With luck the job would be done in a matter of hours. Manhunts were something the Dover force were very good at, very good indeed. The port city was a popular point of entry for illegal aliens of all descriptions. Smuggling refugees into Britain on ships and ferries was almost a major industry. Pakistanis, Indians, and Africans were found almost weekly hidden under piles of walnuts and cabbages, crammed into oil drums, and nailed into packing crates. Why, not long ago an entire family of eight was discovered stacked like cordwood under the false bottom of a lorry. Helping Immigration search for them once they slipped past the dock had given the Dover constabulary a great deal of experience. In Chief Treshnell's office was a card file listing every landlord, landlady, desk clerk, cab driver, bartender, and barmaid in town. Greene had photos of the suspects, which would make the search almost routine.

"I'll more than likely be sleeping in the morning instead of going to church," the Chief said to his wife as he kissed her good-bye. "Give my apologies to the parson."

Quinn, Eagan, and Carney left the house an hour after midnight. Maher stayed behind, complaining of a headache and a sore throat. The three drove to the gates of the project, where they dropped off Eagan in plenty of time for him to join the equipment maintenance crews going into the tunnel for the 2:00 A.M.–to–noon Sunday shift.

Eagan didn't mind his job. It was better than sitting around the house all day watching the telly and playing cards and listening to Quinn run on about what he would do to his enemies once he was King of Ireland or whatever the hell it was he had in mind for himself. Besides, he'd much rather work in the big tunnel, which was well ventilated and where every safety precaution in the book was enforced, than in the old Beaumont bore, which could cave in at any minute and where the air smelled like the inside of a sock.

As he walked past the steel legs of the muck surge hopper on the lower work area, he was joined by several of his fellow mechanics and fitters. It gave him a strange feeling to know that buried beneath his feet was a load of dynamite so big it would send the whole goddam place shooting into the air like an erupting volcano. He couldn't help feeling sorry for some of the men he worked with, especially the good-humored ones he sometimes joined for a beer. He had tried not to attract attention by being too friendly, as Quinn had insisted, but when you work with men month after month you can't help getting to know them well. At the bottom of the lower access tunnel, climbing aboard the mine car that would carry him to the heading, Eagan found himself gazing at the faces of the men he liked best, wondering if there were any safe way he could warn them not to come to work on Tuesday.

At Hempstead's cottage, Quinn turned off the pavement onto the dirt road that led down the cliff to the shore. With Hempstead out of the way he didn't have to bother with the precaution of cutting the headlights and engine and coasting to the bottom in the dark. He and Carney had a lot of work to do: go over the electrical connections, seal the explosives off by bringing the roof down with wrecking bars, string wire to the door of the drainage gallery, work on the remote detonating system . . .

Quinn noticed that Carney was getting more and more nervous as the big day approached. He was a natural worrier. Even now in the car he was pressing his hands against his thighs to keep his fingers from quivering. Quinn made a mental note to keep a special eye on Carney when the time came.

Maher was just the opposite. In Quinn's opinion he was *too* calm. Mining the tunnel was a job he went about as if he were repairing a radio or painting a fence. He showed no emotion even when they discussed the things that could go wrong. Did Maher think they could force the Brits to empty the prisons of Irish patriots in exchange for sparing the tunnel and the lives of the hostages? He wouldn't say. If they had to blast the tunnel, were their plans for escape by helicopter to the Irish ghettos of north London good enough? He had no opinion. Quinn wondered what went on behind that long blank face of his and wondered if he would continue taking orders when it was all over and they were in control of the movement. Maybe it was the difference in their ages that kept them from warming up to each other.

Eagan was another problem still. Quick-tempered, a hooligan, a drinker. Keeping him on an even keel and out of trouble for so long had been an exhausting chore for everybody. When the crisis came Eagan was likely to be in a pub singing Irish songs about the Easter Rising of 1916. He was tough and fearless, yes, but not a man you would trust with your life if you had any choice. Quinn wondered if he might be better off leaving Eagan behind when the rough stuff was over, to simplify the escape. There were a thousand like him in Belfast.

The reason John Maher kept his opinions to himself was simple: if he made them known, Quinn would kill him. The escape plans didn't interest him because he didn't intend to be part of them. He moved about the room quickly, opening and closing drawers and throwing his belongings into a canvas seaman's bag. The others wouldn't be back until after dawn, but he wanted to be well on his way by then.

He stopped to blow his nose. His headache was getting worse and so was the soreness in his throat. Christ, he thought, I've got a terrible bug for sure. At least it had provided him with a good excuse for staying at the house. He went to the sink in the corner and turned on the hot water. Gargling with salt might help a little. Quinn . . . he's crazy, that's what he is. The British will never buckle to blackmail. Turn a thousand Republicans loose to save a goddam hole in the ground and a few hostages? Never in a million years. Even with a thousand hostages they wouldn't do it. The whole nation would march to its grave if the reputation of dear old England was at stake, the silly, pompous asses. The tunnel would be blown up . . . that was just a technical problem. They didn't need him any longer for that. Carney could handle the blast while Quinn and Eagan ran around waving guns like a bunch of stupid cowboys. Let the children have their fun . . . he wanted no part of it. He had paid Quinn back with a year of hard work and now he was leaving.

He filled his mouth with hot salt water and tilted his head back. He gargled as long and as deeply as he could without gagging. Whether it helped or not he didn't know, but at least it made him feel he was doing something. He looked at his aging face in the mirror and the bulges in his cheeks as he swished the water from side to side before leaning forward and spitting it out. When he brought his head back up he saw Kevin McCabe in the doorway behind him aiming a gun at the back of his head.

"I want Quinn," McCabe said.

Maher froze, staring into the mirror, one hand on the edge of the sink, the other holding a glass. "He's gone."

"When will he be back?"

"Three, maybe four hours."

"Alone?"

"Carney will be with him."

"Anybody else?"

"Nobody. It's the truth, I swear." His face was sagging in fear as he stared at McCabe in the mirror. "They're crazy, all of them. I was leaving, going back to Belfast. See my bag? My bag is packed on the bed . . ."

When McCabe stiffened his arm and aimed, Maher leaped to one side and whirled, throwing the glass in the same movement. The first bullet hit him in the shoulder, twisting him in the opposite direction and knocking him against the wall. The second, traversing his skull from temple to temple, cut short his cry of pain.

The black sky was showing signs of gray in the southeast when General Otis Jordan, Commander of the Lisburn Army Base south of Belfast, climbed into his limousine for the short ride to the airstrip. So the hideout of the fugitives had been found, had it? Good. Dover, of all the odd places, where they could hardly have hoped to hide forever. He hoped they could be taken alive—he would enjoy personally escorting Maher and Carney back behind the walls where they belonged. That would close the book on one of the most embarrassing incidents of his three-year tour in Northern Ireland: the breakout at Tobermore, escape from which, he had once foolishly boasted to the press, was impossible. "The local police are taking up their positions now," the Commissioner had told him on the phone from London thirty minutes earlier. "Since they're your mad dogs that are cornered, I thought you'd like to be on hand. We'll not wait for you, though, General. When we've got light enough we're going in." The General had thanked the Commissioner and assured him that his instincts were right in ringing him so early in the operation, even though it *was* an ungodly hour.

He turned his face to the window and watched the dark shapes of buildings and trees slip by. A practical thought came into his mind: it might be better if the bombers were taken dead. Alive they would wave their fists in defiance for the cameramen who were sure to be there. Alive they would provoke further atrocities and kidnappings by other fanatics trying to force their release. He picked up the telephone that was recessed into the back of the seat in front of him.

"This is General Jordan," he said to the base switchboard operator. "I want you to locate Lance Corporal Fraser Morris. If he's in this part of the world, I want him flown to Dover. Tell him to bring his tournament weapon."

The limousine stopped and the door was opened. The General stepped out briskly, returning the salutes of his aides. Morris was the finest marksman in a British uniform, the General thought as he strode toward the waiting jet, four times winner of the Commonwealth Games. It might prove very useful to have a man with his talent on hand.

Maher was dead, but a device he left behind put Quinn and Carney on their guards: a car radio tuned to police wavelengths. Carney was driving. Their night's work was over and dawn was spreading quickly across the sky.

"The coppers are busy this morning," Quinn said, turning up the volume. "Listen to them. Usually nothing doing at all at this hour."

"They keep repeating a number," Carney said. "What's that mean?"

"It's a code. It means phone the station instead of using the radio. Something is up they don't want anybody to hear about."

"The 'anybody' meaning us?"

Quinn didn't answer. They had arrived at the intersection of Biggin Street in Dover's downtown district, two blocks from police headquarters on Ladywell Park. A police car crossed in front of them, its warning horn off but its roof light flashing urgently.

"He's turning on Penchester," Carney said uneasily. "I don't like the looks of this . . ."

Quinn raised a hand sharply. "Shh! Listen . . ."

A voice was coming over the radio directing a vehicle to "the schoolyard."

"Jesus, Jamie," Carney said in growing alarm, "that could mean the schoolyard at the end of our street. We could be heading right into their arms."

"Turn right," Quinn snapped. "Go up Castle Hill Road. We can look down on Landis from Connaught."

Five minutes later the two men were standing beside the car, binoculars to their eyes, looking down on the rows of houses several blocks below them. Police cars seemed to be converging on the area from all directions, and in the dawn light they could see uniformed men running, waving, and setting up road blocks. They heard a distant popping sound.

"Is that rifle fire?"

"Sounds like it," Quinn said. "They're either raiding our house or one close to it. What's the name of the old lady that lives across from us? The one who's always asking if we have any laundry she could do? Snead, something like that? Sneath, that's it. Old lady Sneath."

Carney's face was white. He lowered his binoculars and backed toward the car. "We've got to get out of here . . ."

"I want to know what's going on. Where's the nearest public phone?"

From a booth at the entrance of Dover Castle, Quinn dialed his own number and got no answer. Mrs. Sneath's phone rang six times before she picked it up. "This is Mr. Windsor," Quinn said, "the man from across the lane? I was told that something is happening on our street–"

"Mr. Windsor! Saints in heaven, I think it's your house they're after. Police cars parked in front and men crouched down behind, and now there's shooting started . . ."

Her voice was so trembling and broken Quinn could hardly understand her. "I'm at Guston now," Quinn said, naming a town to the north. "Call a constable and tell him I'm on my way and that I can explain everything." He hung up and turned to Carney. "That should confuse them and give us a few extra minutes," he said, getting in the car behind the wheel.

"We've got to get to London," Carney said when they were under way, "they'll never find us in Kilburn or Camden Town."

"We're not running yet," Quinn said firmly, swinging the car toward Shakespeare Cliff, which was now catching the first rays of the sun. "First we're going to do what we've been planning to do."

"Just the two of us? With Maher trapped and Eagan in the tunnel?"

"We don't need them–we can do it ourselves."

"It'll never work . . . we'll need lookouts, the radio detonator isn't ready . . ."

"We don't need a fancy detonator. You can set off the blast by hand, can't you, just by crossing the wires? Then that's what you'll do. We have everything we need. I'll grab a hostage, you go to the beach. We'll keep in touch with our radios."

Carney's voice was almost a whimper: "They'll kill us, Jamie. They're on to us . . ."

"You yellow bastard," Quinn shouted, "you will cross those wires when I give you the signal! We're not going to run out on all the work we've done! They'll not shoot you because you'll have the wires in your lap, and they'll not shoot me because I'll have a gun to somebody's head! If you lose your nerve I'll hunt you down and shoot you myself . . ."

So fully had Quinn lost his temper that the car swerved dangerously, very nearly careening into a drainage ditch as they shot past the entrance to the project. He tightened his hands on the wheel and let up on the accelerator until the car had regained its equilibrium, then floored the pedal again.

The guard at the project gate, startled by the roar of the passing car, picked up his phone and dialed the police to report a reckless driver. All lines were busy.

Chapter 21

Sir Charles Crosley was preparing to do some work in the garden behind the house he had leased on the outskirts of Dover when his wife appeared in an upstairs window. "Telephone," she called, "an Inspector Greene from Scotland Yard." She laughed. "Have you stolen some jewels?"

Awfully early on a Sunday morning for him to be calling, Crosley said to himself, pausing at the back door to knock some dirt from his shoes with a stick. An enthusiastic young fellow, that Greene. We could use a few like him around the office.

He took the call on the kitchen phone. "Yes, Inspector," he said cheerfully, "how is your investigation going?"

As he listened his mouth slowly opened and it stayed open for a full minute. Greene was calling from a house the police had raided on Landis Lane. They had found one of the men they were after, dead, plus another tentatively identified as a high-ranking officer of the Provisional I.R.A. who had apparently killed himself just before the door was kicked in. From what Greene could tell from a pile of papers he was going through, the gang had intended to launch some sort of attack on the Channel Tunnel on Tuesday.

"We've upset that plan," the Inspector said. "Now all we have to do is catch the ones who weren't here, which won't be easy because we've lost the advantage of surprise. The radio stations are already describing the raid. Sir Charles, I need some information. There is a box here full of articles and clippings and maps of something called the Beaumont tunnel. Are you familiar with that?"

"Why, yes . . . it's the remains of work that was done a hundred years ago . . ."

"From what I can gather, it runs along the coast and passes right under your lower yard, is that right?"

"In a manner of speaking, yes, but the last time I visited it, several years ago, it seemed to be blocked and more or less impassable."

"*Seemed* to be blocked. Is there a chance that it could have been opened by men who would stop at nothing, shall we say, as a way to penetrate your security perimeter? To get to the point where your Mr. Kenward said a blast would flood the tunnel?"

"It's possible," Crosley admitted, "but hardly likely. Still . . ."

"Where is the entrance? I'd like to send a couple of men by to check it out."

Crosley told him about the Folkestone Warren Road, the seawall, the old door set into the base of the cliff. "Too bad you can't talk to Adam Hempstead. He was the expert on the old tunnel. He ran his car off the road the other morning and was killed." A silence came on the line. "Inspector, are you still there?"

"The Hempstead accident," Greene said finally. "I learned last night that foul play was involved. Stay close to a phone today. I may want to talk to you again."

Crosley dialed Kenward's number and cursed softly when there was no answer. Probably at his infernal girlfriend's house, he thought, opening a Kent phone book. I'll call him there. I may interrupt a wrestling match, but he must be told what's going on.

No one answered Anne Reed's phone, either. Crosley let it ring seven, eight, nine times before giving up. Damn that Kenward. Lately it seemed as though he was devoting more attention to his love life than he was to his job.

He was returning the phone and the book to the shelf when he heard soft chimes. He crossed the dining room to the front entryway, pausing at the foot of the balustraded staircase to call to his wife that he would see who it was. Two Sunday mornings in a row when the maid was off he had been bothered by gray-haired women armed with Bible tracts. If they want to save my soul, he thought as he opened the front door, I wish they would stay home and pray for me instead of interfering with my gardening.

It was not a gray-haired woman. It was a slender young man with intense blue eyes, skin as white and clear as Irish linen, and a mouth a newspaper writer would later describe as "cruel." He wasn't armed with Bible tracts; he was armed with a gun.

Frank waited with the engine running while Anne ran back inside the cottage to answer the phone. The back seat was filled with cameras, tripods, floodlights, lenses, filters, and film. My God, he thought, with all that gear anybody ought to be able to get good results, even with a subject as difficult as a tunnel.

"Who was it?" he asked when she climbed in beside him, breathless.

"The line was dead when I got to it. Whew! Probably bad news anyway. Let's go."

"So much for the bad news," Frank said, turning onto the motorway, "now tell me the good news you said you had for me."

"The good news is that I'm a failure. That's right! You'll be delighted to hear that at the SKAT meeting last night there were only six people. We lost the main battles to block the tunnel and the link to London and so the members have gradually been drifting off to other things. We've voted to disband. Aren't you thrilled?"

"Not particularly. I thought the outfit did a bang-up job, except for a few excesses in your propaganda. There sure as hell is no reason for you to think of yourself as a failure. Look at your accomplishments! You cost us tens of thousands of pounds when you limited our night muck-haul operation, and you cost us I don't know how many millions when you killed the slurry pumping idea. As far as the London link is concerned, you must have added a hundred million pounds to the pricetag by forcing

British Rail to put so much of it underground. Cheer up! You've driven at least a dozen government engineers into early retirement and possibly even into early graves. And you call yourself a failure!"

She patted his knee. "Thank you. You have a way of looking at the bright side of things."

At the entrance to the project, Frank stopped for a word with the guard. "Morning, Ned! Glad to see you so chipper. Always looks bad when a watchman is sound asleep."

"Never slept on duty in my life, Mr. Kenward, you know that. No, sir! Especially not last night. There was a spot of excitement about an hour ago, I'll say! Two maniacs in a car flew down the road at ninety miles an hour. Tried calling the police on them, but the lines were busy."

Frank laughed. "It's nice to know the police will come to your rescue as soon as they're finished gabbing on the phone. Ned, I'm bringing a visitor in. Anne Reed, a photographer. We'll be going into the tunnel to take some pictures."

"Righto, Mr. Kenward."

Frank drove down the upper access tunnel and parked outside the miners' changing house on the lower yard. "If you've ever wanted to see a men's locker room," he said to Anne, "now is your chance. Come on, I want to fix you up with a hardhat, a coat, and some boots. You'll look adorable."

The next car through the gate was the project manager's, with Sir Charles Crosley himself at the wheel. Ned leaned through the window of his booth for what he expected would be another friendly exchange. Mr. Hendricks of British Rail, Sir Charles, and Mr. Kenward, the three top men on the job, were never too busy to have a word with him.

But Ned was disappointed in Sir Charles that morning. His "Good morning" was answered only by a stiff wave. Straight ahead he looked, with a grim expression on his face. A visitor with him, too, who was supposed to be identified and logged in. Odd. Not like Mr. Crosley. Must have other things on his mind.

He'd give him a minute to get to his office, then he'd ring and ask the visitor's name to keep the log book complete.

One thousand miles south of Dover, an RAF jet carrying a single passenger rose into the morning sky above the British garrison at Gibraltar. Lance Corporal Fraser Morris had been roused from his sleep and rushed aboard with such speed that he hadn't even had time to pack a small bag. He had been told to take only one thing, and he had it cradled in his lap inside a silk-lined carrying case: the highly polished and surgically clean Lee Enfield marksman's rifle with which he had won a trunkful of medals, platters, bowls, and trophies. As the plane banked to the north, Morris, sleep still in his eyes, gazed through the small window at the blue crescent of the Bay of Gibraltar and wondered what the fuss was about.

Carney was puffing heavily when he reached the entrance to the drainage gallery. Quinn had dropped him off at Hempstead's place and he had hiked from there, half-running most of the way . . . two miles at least, he guessed. He set down the sack he had taken from the tool shed and leaned back against the cliff to catch his breath. The sun was well above the horizon now and the sky was clear except for two lines of high clouds in the south. The soaring wall of Abbot's Cliff was on his left; on his right was a long view of the headlands rising and falling as they receded into the distance. A few high-gliding gulls were the only signs of life. The landscape was so remote and peaceful that he had to remind himself that he was in extreme danger. Unless he carried out his assignment without losing his nerve it might be the last beautiful day he would ever see.

He pulled the door open, dragged the sack inside, and dropped to his knees. Where the tunnel wall met the floor he brushed away a layer of powdered chalk to reveal a double strand of twisted wire. With an electrician's pliers he cut off two one-foot lengths and stripped the ends of insulation. Inside the sack were three automobile batteries, which he taped together side by side and connected in series. Several times he stopped, sitting back on his heels and wetting his lips. The detonator he was assembling was childishly simple, but it was still possible to make a mistake. After twenty minutes of work—twice as long as it might have taken if his hands weren't trembling—the job was done. By bringing one end of the double-stranded wire into contact with one of the battery poles he would send a surge of current into the blasting caps a mile away.

Behind the brow of the cliff above him, the two policemen dispatched to take a look at the drainage gallery turned their car down the lane past Hempstead's cottage and headed for the shore. With them was a rifle Chief Treshnell had persuaded them to take along.

Quinn, a black suitcase in one hand and a gun in the other, walked a half-step behind Crosley. "Straight ahead into your office," he ordered. "Make a sudden move and you are finished."

The layout of the building, Quinn noted with relief, conformed well with the sketch Eagan had supplied. From the front door the central corridor ran fifty feet to the door of Crosley's office and a wall ladder leading to the roof. The right-hand wall was lined with private offices, the rest rooms, and a janitor's closet. On the left was a large open area filled with filing cabinets, drafting tables, and desks, deserted on Sunday morning except for two men working at calculating machines in a far corner. The two men exchanged glances when Quinn and Crosley marched by without returning their greetings.

Once inside his office, Crosley felt himself pushed roughly into his chair. He watched his captor kick the door shut and push the locking button on the knob. When the suitcase was swung to the top of the desk and opened, Crosley saw a blood-chilling arsenal of weapons, ammunition, and grenades.

"This is mad," Crosley said without thinking, "you can't possibly get out of here alive. For the love of God, consider what—"

Quinn smashed the side of his gun into Crosley's face, breaking the lenses of his glasses and sending the frames spinning across the floor.

"Keep your mouth shut or I'll blow it off," Quinn shouted, his thin voice cracking. "I'm listening to no bloody advice from no English pig . . ."

Deep stabbing pains from the cracked bridge of his nose flooded Crosley's brain and he lost consciousness for several minutes, his head lolling forward as Quinn bound him to the chair. When he came to he found he had to blink his eyes repeatedly because of blood trickling into them from a cut above his right eyebrow. He was restrained by circles of tape passed around his body and the back of the chair, and his forearms were tied together behind him. The pain in the center of his face pulsed in almost unbearable waves. He fought against it, fought to remain conscious. There was the feel of cold metal against the front of his neck and the soft flesh under his jaw. Tilting his head forward, he saw that a shotgun had been taped to his chest, the trigger side outward, the muzzle jammed into his chin. The man was on one knee threading a loop of cord through the trigger guard.

There was a pounding at the door, and someone was shaking the knob.

"Sir Charles? Sir Charles? Are you all right?"

Quinn grabbed a .45-caliber revolver, a gun that sounded like a cannon when fired indoors, and yanked the door open. "No, he's not all right," he shouted at the two astonished men in the doorway. "He's going to be dead if you don't get the fucking hell out of here."

Impulsively, the man closest to Quinn stepped forward and reached for the gun. "Give me that, you bloody fool—"

The slug that exploded into his chest lifted him off his feet and hurled him to the floor. The second man clamped his hands over his ears and staggered two steps backward, grimacing in shock and terror, his mouth twisting open in a soundless scream.

Quinn gestured with the gun. "Drag him out. Tell everybody

outside that nobody comes into this building unless I tell them to, have you got that? *I said: Have you got that?"*

The man managed to nod, then leaned down and took hold of his companion's wrists. Walking backward with quick, short steps, he dragged the body down the hallway leaving a streaked trail of blood.

While Quinn's back was turned, Crosley managed to carry out the only useful action he could think of. Using his chin he opened the intercom line to the tunnel face. To do it he had to lean far forward, pivoting the chair on its front legs. Just as he heard the click made by the lever moving from "Off" to "Send," he lost his balance and crashed heavily to the floor. At least now, he thought as Quinn bounded toward him, cursing, anybody working in the tunnel had at least a chance of hearing what was going on.

"You stupid bastard," Quinn said, "what are you trying to do, blow your own head off?" He set him upright, then bent his legs back and tied his ankles to the chair struts on each side. With his feet off the floor Crosley was immobilized. "That ought to hold you," Quinn said, straightening up. "I want you in one piece. You're my ticket out of here."

He took a hand-held radio from the pile of equipment and pulled the aerial into full extension. "Carney, are you there?"

A voice crackled back. "All set at this end. You okay?"

"I've got the fucker trussed up like a Christmas goose. You sit tight, nobody even knows where you are. I'm going to make the calls now."

"What if they come looking for me?" The voice sounded plaintive.

"If you get in any trouble, hold out as long as you can, three hours at least. We want to give the press time to get here. Don't lose your nerve . . . I'll pick you up in the helicopter after you set off the blast. The phone's ringing . . . I'll talk to you later."

Ned, the guard at the gate, was calling Sir Charles. On hearing Quinn's voice, he asked if he were by chance speaking to the visitor who had arrived in the project manager's car.

"Yeah, that's right," Quinn said, "I'm just visiting."

"Oh, well, fine, yes, but could I have your name? I keep a register, you see, and–"

"Quinn. James L. Quinn. Get that right."

"Quinn, yes. Q-U-I-N-N, James L., good. And might I ask the purpose of your visit to the project, Mr. Quinn? For my records?"

"The purpose of my visit? To tear your goddam hands from Ireland's throat."

He slammed the receiver down. From his jacket pocket he took a sheet of folded paper and smoothed it on the glass-topped surface of Crosley's desk. On it were written the names and telephone numbers of BBC, ITV, the wire services, and the major London newspapers. This was one blast the bastards weren't going to bury in the back pages. The whole world was going to watch. The whole world was going to hear a new voice speaking in the cause of Irish independence and unity: *his* voice, the voice of James L. Quinn.

Chapter 22

Frank rummaged around in a green metal locker looking for a miner's coat that wouldn't completely engulf Anne. She sat on a bench behind him lacing up her boots.

"This is where the poor fellows change their clothes after a hard day's work?" she asked, wrinkling her nose. "How grim! Doesn't anybody complain?"

"It's just a temporary building, for Christ's sake. Did you expect Spanish tile and cut flowers? Here, try this on." A knee-length coat landed on her lap.

"I don't see why it has to look like one of Her Majesty's prisons. At least put a rug of some kind on this cold cement floor."

Frank took a hardhat from a shelf and went to work resetting the headband. "If this *were* a cement floor," he said, not looking up from the task at hand, "I might put a rug in. What it is, actually, is a *concrete* floor. Anybody who wants to hang around with me has got to learn the difference. Cement is gray, powdery stuff. Concrete is what you get when you mix cement with water, sand, and gravel. A cement sidewalk, for example, would blow away in the first wind. A concrete sidewalk is there to stay."

"All right, all right! Cut my tongue out."

"A contractor in Pennsylvania once got away with putting up a concrete batch plant because a local ordinance banned only 'cement' plants. The State Supreme Court sympathized with the city when it sued, but upheld the contractor on the grounds that to do otherwise would be to commit an act of violence on the English language. 'Cement is to concrete,' the court said, 'as flour is to fruitcake.' "

"You can be a dreadful bore at times."

Frank jammed a hardhat on her head. "A perfect fit." He took her hands and pulled her to her feet. The long coat was grotesquely ill-fitting, but it would do the job of protecting her clothes from water, dust, and oil. "See?" he said, "I told you you'd look adorable. I've got half a notion to throw you down on this so-called cement floor and demonstrate how fond I am of you."

"Don't. I have a loathsome disease."

He had called the heading, so by the time they got to the bottom of the lower access tunnel a locomotive coupled to a personnel carrier was waiting for them. He introduced Anne to the train driver, who seemed refreshed by the spectacle of a female underground and helped her load her photographic gear onto the train, and to a carpenter working on the dispatcher's control booth, who seemed irritated. Frank explained what went on when work was in full swing. The trains were driven over the grating on her left where one after the other the loaded cars were swiveled upside down, which could be done without uncoupling them. The dumped material was carried by a bucket elevator, entirely enclosed to reduce dust, to the conveyor attached to the crown of the access tunnel, which carried it to the surge hopper outside the portal. From there the muck was loaded into trucks for hauling to disposal and fill areas as far away as the Folkestone terminal. The dispatcher controlled the dumping of cars and the speeds of conveyor belts. Before him when he worked was a panel of lights showing the position of every train and crew in the tunnel.

"Enough!" Anne said in self-defense. "I'll forget it all by tomorrow anyway. Come on, give me a ride on your scenic railway."

The rough, rumbling trip to the face was as unlike a ride on a scenic railway as she could imagine. The tunnel was the most depressing thing she had ever seen in her life, and the view ahead was the same as the view behind. It was like a hole bored into a glacier. Everything was white: the curved walls, the overhead lights, the patina of chalk dust that had settled over the pipes, on the train, even on the hat and jacket of the driver. She felt as if she were being drawn into a dimly lit garden hose or drinking straw, and she closed her eyes to stave off vertigo.

At length the train lurched and slowed to a crawl. Anne opened her eyes and saw that a broad structure of some kind was just above their heads. "The trailing conveyor," her escort said. In the distance she could make out the tail end of the mole. Several men dressed in coats like hers were waiting for the train to pull in. Nobody seemed to be doing anything, just like several clusters of men they had passed along the way. She had noticed that about other construction projects as well, and she made a mental note to ask Frank about the logical contradiction involved: nobody did anything, yet things got done.

The train groaned to a stop under the overarching edge of the steel shield. Every sound echoed as it would in a mausoleum. The mole had looked sinister to her when it was brand new and bright in the sunlight; it looked even worse now covered with dust and buried to the hilt. The air smelled stale, like a long-unopened cellar.

In response to her gesture, Frank leaned toward her before climbing down. She placed her lips close to his ear and whispered: "You are out of your fucking mind to work in a place like this." He chuckled all through the introductions.

There were six men in the heading, the foreman and his crew of five mechanics and electricians. No production work was done on Sunday so that the maintenance crews could carefully go over the mole's fittings, hoses, cylinders, motors, and electrical circuits. The Sunday pause in mucking operations also gave the government engineers a chance to record and inspect work already done, setting up transits and measuring instruments in air relatively free of dust and turbulence.

All but one of the men seemed pleased to see Anne—so much

for Frank's fears. The exception was a husky, redheaded young man introduced as Tanner Eagan. He hung back, regarding her with ill-concealed hostility. She dismissed him as a superstitious sexist. He probably thinks my visit is going to bring him bad luck, she thought. I hope it does. As they say in the locker room: Piss on him.

To combat the feeling of claustrophobia that was coming over her, she turned her attention to the technical problems of photography. It was going to be difficult to capture the atmosphere of isolation and undefined danger. For the holing-through ceremony she was going to have to rent some extra lights, that was obvious. For the present, she would try a time-exposure, with someone moving through the mole setting off flashes.

With a shoulder bag full of equipment she walked away from the heading, intending to frame the scene through several different lenses. As she passed the end of the train she heard someone say: "Listen to what's coming over the intercom, Frank. One of the voices is Sir Charles. Sounds like he's in some kind of trouble . . ."

The Commissioner of Metropolitan Police was normally an early riser, but not on this Sunday morning. The sun was high and he was still in bed. He lay rigidly, a soldier at attention, trying not to move. His eyes were closed to the light that was leaking into the room around the curtains, and his eyebrows were drawn together in a deep frown. Buckingham Palace champagne followed by beer in his kitchen, he had discovered to his sorrow, gave him just as severe a hangover as beer in his kitchen alone.

The sound of the telephone struck him with the force of a fire alarm. He groped with one hand, trying not to open his eyes or subject his head to any sudden movements. It was that fool Penton calling from Dover.

"Penton, my God, your timing is impeccable. Remind me on Monday to take away your telephone privileges. Yes, I know how terribly sorry you are for the intrusion . . . Just state your problem and ring off, would you do me that favor, please?"

Penton did him the favor. A dawn raid had netted two dead Irishmen, one of whom appeared to be Kevin McCabe, though the identification was necessarily tentative due to the relatively small percentage of the face remaining to identify. Unfortunately, two and possibly three others were not apprehended. One, a Provo bomber named Quinn, was now holding at gunpoint Sir Charles Crosley, the eminent engineer, and was threatening to kill him and blow up the Channel Tunnel unless a series of demands were met, some of which, in Penton's view, were deucedly awkward.

During the course of the Chief Inspector's recitation, the Commissioner had swung his feet slowly to the floor. He was sitting on the edge of the bed with his head and shoulders sagging like a man who had absorbed a terrible beating. He tried to straighten up and clear his mind. His hangover, he realized, was plainly the least of his concerns.

Penton droned on, listing Quinn's demands in a voice that would have been exactly right for a report on the cost of paper clips and staples. All of the Republican detainees in Northern Ireland were to be released within three hours. A helicopter capable of carrying two passengers was to be brought at once to the parking lot outside the tunnel contractor's headquarters. A direct line was to be set up between Quinn and the Prime Minister for negotiations. A press conference was to be arranged within the hour so that Quinn could talk to the nation live on both television and radio.

The Commissioner forced his mind into gear. Specialists had to be rushed to the scene—the Army's bomb squad, the counterinsurgency unit, his own Special Branch men trained to deal with gunmen holding hostages. Firepower would be needed, armor, perhaps, certainly gas. The more he learned about the situation the worse it got. In a flat, utterly inappropriate tone of voice, Penton piled one horror on another. Crosley was tied to a chair with a shotgun taped to his chest. The bomb was going to be exploded by someone else whose whereabouts, like the whereabouts of the bomb, were unknown.

"Stall for time," the Commissioner said, trying to fill his voice with the sound of authority, "until we can get things organized. Tell the maniac the government is considering his demands."

"Do hurry," said Penton.

The Prime Minister took the call from the Home Secretary on the phone in his limousine. He listened in silent concentration, his lips slowly tightening. When he spoke it was without the elegant accent he used for verbal fencing on the floor of Commons. "Absolutely not! We can't hand over the nation's media to a madman no matter what he threatens." He listened for a moment more. "Yes. I'll leave now and meet you there. Tell the Commissioner to take no action until we've had time to assess the situation."

He broke the connection and said a single word to his driver: "Whitehall." Using the phone again, he called ahead to his personal secretary. "The Prime Minister here. Have you heard the news? On the radio now, is it? I seem to be the last to know. I'm on my way in. I'll want the Secretary of State for Northern Ireland, General Alders . . . everybody in the security cabinet. This may get sticky before it's through."

Chapter 23

Tanner Eagan edged away from the crowd that had gathered around the loudspeaker at the rear of the mole. The dirty, double-crossing sonofabitch, he thought, listening to Quinn's ranting voice, he thinks he can get rid of me just like that, does he? Blow everything up when I'm at the face and take the glory for himself, that's the real plan, is it? Eagan's too stupid, he could imagine Quinn thinking, I'll get him out of the way along with the tunnel. Eagan wanted to shout curses and shake his fists in the air, but to give in to those impulses would be to show he knew more than he should. The others still hadn't figured out what was going on . . . they were the stupid ones. Couldn't they understand what Quinn was saying? Couldn't they see that Crosley was interrupting him simply to make the situation clear? Quinn obviously didn't know the intercom line was open. Quinn obviously thought that his old friend Eagan would be drowned like a mouse in a bottle along with everybody else.

Eagan took his black metal lunch bucket from a shelf, snapped it open, and plunged his hand to the bottom. His fingers closed around the reassuring hardness of his .38 automatic, which was covered with aluminum foil as if it were a pork chop. He unwrapped it, stuck it in his belt, and made his way to the driver's platform of the locomotive. At the mole an argument was swirling, with everyone trying to talk at once.

"We've got to find out what we're up against," the American

said, shouting everybody down. "Hand me the phone . . . Somebody ought to be able to tell us something . . ."

"There'll be nobody to answer it on a Sunday morning," Eagan heard the foreman say. "Nobody at the changing house, nobody at the upper yard . . ."

"The dispatcher's not on duty," the train driver said.

"What about the nurse in the medical trailer?"

"We should get the hell out of here, that's what we should do," somebody said. Others began echoing that sentiment, but the American shouted them down again.

"This might be the safest place right here. If there's a bomb planted down the line we would be riding right into it . . . Hello? Hello?"

"What the bloody hell . . . somebody is taking the train!"

"It's Tanner! Stop him . . ."

Eagan leaned on the throttle and saw the space between him and the rear of the mole widen quickly. He saw the American drop the phone and begin to sprint after him.

"Stay back!" Eagan shouted, waving the gun. The man didn't stop. He kept coming, and in another five seconds he would be on the platform with him. Eagan leveled the gun and prepared to fire.

"Look out!" someone shouted, "he's got a gun . . ."

Just before he pulled the trigger there was a blinding burst of light inches from his eyes. He missed his man, but he knew the shot would put an end to the pursuit. He fired twice more, randomly, to make sure. When he could see again he realized what had happened: the goddam woman, the photographer, had exploded a flashbulb in his face as he went past, risking her fucking neck to save an American. Why would anybody do that? He blinked and peered at the receding mole. He could see the men and the woman standing like so many toy soldiers watching him riding away on the only means of escape. They were doomed and he couldn't care less. He turned his back on them and watched the endless approach of the steel rails that led to daylight. With luck he'd make it before the blast went off. With luck he'd get to Quinn before the cops.

Stripped to the waist, Penton felt ridiculous. His skin hadn't seen the sun in fifteen years and the ghastly pallor proved it. He was sixty-four years old and might be excused the waistline flab and sagging chest on that account, but he knew that a Chief Inspector should have been in much better condition. For a man who was once the very picture of vigor and fitness, it was embarrassing to stand revealed as a physical wreck.

Stripped to the waist and with his hands over his head, that's what Quinn demanded and so that's how he presented himself. Behind him, crouched behind lorries, autos, and construction machines was a mixed and growing army of constables, detectives, and soldiers–it was like the build-up for D-Day, all for a single Irish madman mouthing threats and holding a gun to a hostage's head. He could see the hostage from where he stood, bound to a chair and framed in the doorway at the end of the corridor, his head tilted back by the muzzle of the shotgun under his chin.

Quinn stepped partly into view and waved him forward with his handgun. Penton advanced in slow motion, hoping that the terrorist wasn't as nervous as he was himself. It wasn't just his physical condition that had deteriorated in the last few years, it was his nerves as well. He should never have left London, he told himself bitterly. He should have pleaded an attack of gout or hot flashes, anything . . . his wife would have backed him up. Instead, thanks to a foolish pride and a lifelong habit of doing what he was told, here he was, defenseless and trembling, walking into the very jaws of death.

Ten hours earlier, when he stepped off the train, he had been seized with the reckless idea of checking into an obscure hotel under an assumed name or getting back on board for Ramsgate or Broadstairs. Alibis had spun through his head about falling asleep or throwing a fit–but no, Greene had been there to meet him. Greene, full of pep and anticipation, talking a mile a minute about the developing manhunt and his latest theories about what the plotters were up to. Through the long night at police headquarters he had deferred to the younger man, pushed him forward, in fact, so he could stay out of the limelight himself. Greene was doing a splendid job and he told him so. After the raid at dawn when a call had to be made to the Commissioner, he had urged Greene to make it himself. "Don't be bashful," he told him, "step right up and take credit for what you've done. I'm nearing retirement and don't need the attention."

"Oh, no," the young fool had replied, "you're my superior. It's your place to make the report. If I do it, it will look as if I'm trying to put myself in front of you."

So Penton had called. Carried it off quite well, thank heaven, adopting a tone of such disinterested professionalism that even the Commissioner couldn't have failed to be impressed.

But this! My God, this was something else again! This was a nightmare! He was standing in the doorway of Crosley's office face to face with a snarling dog, trying not to look at the gun that was pointed alternately at Sir Charles's head and his own. Quinn had asked for a conference with the top-ranking Englishman on the scene. Greene had taken the call at the project gate, where a kind of command post had been set up and where all of Quinn's calls were being diverted. "I guess that would be you," Greene had said to Penton, covering the mouthpiece with his hand.

"General Jordan is here," Penton said hurriedly, "that was his helicopter that just touched down."

But the suggestion of the General's name brought nothing but a stream of foul language from Quinn, who refused under any circumstances to deal with the man he called one of the foremost enemies of the Irish people. A Chief Inspector of Scotland Yard? That would be fine. Send him in stripped to the waist and with his hands up.

Pointing with his gun, Quinn explained how he was keeping hold of the loop of cord that was hanging from the shotgun triggers. "See this? Tell anybody with ideas of shooting his way in that if anything happens to me, this Englishman's head goes up in smoke. Why haven't I heard from the Prime Minister? I'm not going to wait much longer."

Penton's mouth had gone completely dry. He had the feeling that if the impulse to swallow came over him he would gag. "The . . . the Prime Minister is considering the matter. He has summoned the cabinet. These things take time . . ."

"Fuck the time! Call him yourself and tell him there is no time. I want the gates of Irish prisons opened and I want them opened *now!*"

"Yes, well, I'll certainly try to reach the Prime Minister and convey your wishes to him in the strongest—"

"Where are the reporters and television crews? Aren't they here yet?"

Newspaper and wire service reporters had arrived minutes earlier and were being held at the command post. A BBC mobile television unit was due shortly. "Not that I know of," Penton managed to say. "They are on their way, I would imagine." The lie hung on him like a flag.

"I want to know the minute they get here. I have a few things to say to the English people." He turned to Crosley and prodded him with the point of his gun. "All right, time to speak your piece."

Penton could tell that Sir Charles was in pain. He had difficulty maintaining a steady gaze. There was a cut on his eyebrow and dried blood on his nose and chin.

"Assure the Prime Minister," Crosley said slowly in a thin voice, "that the threat to the tunnel is real. A large . . . a very large quantity of dynamite has been planted in the old—"

"Don't tell him too much," Quinn snapped, cutting off the attempt to locate the bomb.

Crosley tightened his lips, then began again. "Dynamite has been planted in a way that will admit the sea. Mr. Quinn need only give a signal."

Penton became aware of a new problem: he was in imminent

danger of losing control of his urinary tract. He hadn't been incontinent since he was a small child . . . now, if he was reading correctly the faint feeling of warmth on his upper leg, several drops had already escaped, with a torrent threatening to follow. He closed his hands into fists and curled his toes inside his shoes in an effort to avoid becoming the victim of an overwhelming humiliation.

"Tell them it can be done," Sir Charles said weakly. "It's not a bluff."

"Did you hear what he said? All right, turn around and march out of here. Tell them all exactly what you heard and saw. Move!"

"I'll have to stop at the gents' room," Penton stammered as he turned his back. "I seem to have had a small accident . . ."

"You go straight down that hall and out the front door. If you so much as look either way I'll blast you."

"Blast me if you feel you must," Penton said, "I am going into the gents' nevertheless. I simply cannot rejoin my subordinates in this condition. There is a personal matter I must attend to . . . an indiscretion . . ."

His hands raised, he walked rigidly down the hallway. When he came to the door of the lavatory he stopped, turned, and lowered one hand to the knob. Behind him he heard Quinn's curses but not gunfire. Thank heaven, he thought as he pushed his way inside, the man possesses at least a shred of human decency.

A second military helicopter landed. Lance Corporal Fraser Morris hopped to the ground with his rifle case. Ducking down reflexively he ran clear of the rotors, then stood and looked around uncertainly. The wind raised by the landing had sent gray dust billowing away in all directions, obscuring his view of the surroundings. The air cleared when the pilot cut the engine, and beside a piece of construction equipment a short distance away Morris saw General Jordan waving to him. He also saw a dozen crouching policemen and soldiers with drawn weapons taking cover behind lorries and buildings. On the other side of a fence police cars were arriving with sirens wailing and emergency lights flashing. Men, women, and children dotted the side of a nearby hill.

"General Jordan, sir, what's this all about–"

The General ignored his salute, grabbing him instead by the arm and pulling him behind the machine. "Is that it?" he asked, nodding toward the carrying case.

"Yes, sir."

"Is it ready to fire?"

"It's not loaded."

"Load it."

On one knee, the Corporal placed the case on the ground and lifted the lid. The rifle was displayed in a formed recess like a musical instrument. "Will I need the telescopic sight?"

"Not unless you want to hit the bastard over the head with it. I'm going to put you at point-blank range."

The rifle in his hands, Morris rose and followed the General's gaze across a paved parking area to a low structure on the edge of the cliff. The sun was high and the shadows were sharp. "May I ask what the target is?" Without looking he snapped a clip of ammunition into place and released the safety catch.

"In that building," Jordan said, jabbing the air with a forefinger, "is a Provo renegade with a hostage. See where the other helicopter is? That's where he told us to put it. He'll be boarding that sooner or later to make his escape, and that's where you come in. If he turns his gun away from the hostage for even a split second, shoot him. In the head."

The Corporal nodded. "From here? That's pretty far . . ."

"Not from here," General Jordan said, patting the five-foot-high rubber tire of the machine they were standing behind, "from the bucket of this loader. We're going to lift you about ten feet off the ground and park you next to the door of the building. I don't see how you can miss from there."

Morris lightly touched the trigger with his fingertip. "I won't miss."

Inspector Greene kept his binoculars trained on Penton as he emerged after his meeting with Quinn. The Chief Inspector seemed completely exhausted, like a man tottering off a life raft after a month at sea. He was trying to hold his hands aloft, but his elbows had sunk almost to his sides.

"What the devil's the matter with him?" Greene muttered.

Ten feet from the door, Penton's knees buckled and he would have fallen if two policemen hadn't rushed to his aid. Supporting him from each side, they eased him into a waiting car that sped off with wheels spinning before its doors had closed.

"Are you all right?" Greene asked when the car arrived at the police van inside the front gate. "Did he hit you?"

"No, no," Penton said with a weak wave of his hand. "Nothing like that. I just . . . well, I don't know, a spot of dizziness . . . I . . . the sun . . ."

"What did Quinn say?"

"Nothing much new, really." Penton was short of breath and his color was that of the chalk cliffs. Speaking in short, disjointed phrases, he recounted what he had seen and heard, forgetting only the detail of how the gunman had attached himself with a loop of cord to the triggers of the shotgun. He was having trouble enunciating, and from the look in his eyes seemed on the verge of passing out.

"Take him to the medical trailer," Greene said to the driver. "The nurse should have a look at him. Maybe there's a doctor there by now."

"A wise decision," Penton said in a small voice. "I don't seem well. Not well at all . . ."

Shock, Greene thought as he watched the car leave, he's suffering from some sort of shock.

"Chief Treshnell is calling you from Dover, Inspector Greene." A policeman at the rear of the van was extending to him the receiver of the radiotelephone.

"Penton just came out," Greene reported to the Chief. "Quinn is demanding some reaction from the government. Can you get through to Whitehall and see if there is somebody who will talk to him? And get some more men out here; it's beginning to look like a circus. There must be five hundred people milling about outside the gate."

"Every available officer is on his way from here and from Folkestone, too. Inspector, I've just heard from the two men we sent to check the old tunnel at Abbot's Cliff. They say they've got a gunman cornered inside one of the drainage galleries. He's raving about setting off a bomb."

"What took them so long? They must have left an hour ago . . ."

"There was a locked gate. They went hunting for a key."

"Couldn't they have crashed through with their car? Didn't they think of that?"

"Well, government property, you know."

"Are you still in touch with them?"

"Yes, by radio."

"There's an extra helicopter here now. Tell them I'm on my way."

Chapter 24

Greene pointed at a photo of Robert Carney.

"Yes, yes," said Constable Hale excitedly, "that's him, all right. When we first saw him he was standing on the tracks with a gun in one hand and a radio in the other. After taking a shot at us he disappeared into the old tunnel, pulling the door shut behind him. Neither Constable Carlson nor I was armed. We had to go back to the car to get the rifle from the boot."

Greene signaled the helicopter pilot to wait, then followed the policeman up the ladder and along the seawall. They found Constable Carlson lying at the top of the railroad embankment, the barrel of the rifle resting on a rail and aimed at a shadowed recess at the foot of the abruptly rising slope. The sunlight reflecting off the white palisades was so bright it was impossible to distinguish the wooden planking of the door.

"I'd keep my head down if I were you," one of the policemen said to Greene. "Twice the blighter's popped out of his hole and sent a bullet in this direction. He's a sorry shot, lucky for us."

"Has he been threatening to set off a bomb?"

"Not for a while now. There was a good deal of shouting back and forth at the beginning. He said if we got any closer he'd blow the whole . . . he said he'd blow the whole fucking place up, you should excuse me, sir. He hasn't answered our calls for the last fifteen or twenty minutes, but we know he's just behind the door. If you listen you can hear him trying to raise somebody on his radio."

The men fell silent. Despite the splashing of the water against the base of the wall behind them, it was possible to make out the muffled noice of Robert Carney. "Quinn?" he was saying. "Can you hear me? Quinn? Quinn?"

"The problem he's having," Constable Hale said, "is that his radio won't work inside the hill. He's close to panic, it seems to me."

"Yes," Greene said, "he's cut off and doesn't like it. I'm going to see if I can trick him into giving up. Cover me while I work myself closer. If he sticks his head out, take a shot at him."

At the policeman's nod, Greene straightened up and sprinted across the tracks to the strip of low growth at the edge of the embankment. With his hands on the face of the cliff, he sidestepped carefully toward the door.

When Carney heard Greene's voice he sank to his knees with a sigh of despair. Slowly he sat on his heels and leaned forward until his forehead was touching the cold, damp earth. As a small boy he had sometimes tried to sleep in that position, curling up into as small a ball as possible and burrowing under the quilts on his bed until the air became too stale to breathe. The air enclosing him now was worse–stagnant, foul, and heavy with the odor of the rotting timber supports.

"The game is over, Carney. We've taken Quinn. He was trying to run out alone, playing you for a sucker."

The bastard's lying, Carney thought, Quinn wouldn't abandon me . . . or would he? He had turned his back on Eagan without a second thought.

The darkness at the mouth of the tunnel was cut only by a veil of light slicing downward from a crack in the door. Carney put down his radio and picked up his gun, but his hand was shaking so badly he laid it down again, fearful that he might shoot himself by accident before deciding what he should do.

"You've got two choices. Either come out of there with your hands up, or we'll force you out with gas."

Carney thought of two other choices. He could blow up the

Channel Tunnel or he could not. He found the loose end of the wire and held the pad of his forefinger against the copper point, bringing it close to the bare pole of the battery.

Frank looked at the circle of faces around him. "By the time we could go twelve miles on foot to the portal, they'll either have captured the bastard or sent a train for us. The safest place for us is right where we are."

"Could the tunnel be flooded?" one of the mechanics asked. "You heard Crosley say it was no bluff."

"If the beach is mined. It's the only way I can imagine it. A big enough blast could let the sea into the access tunnel."

"It must be a bluff," the foreman said. "Crosley had a gun to his head, what else could he say?"

Another man agreed. "How could anybody mine the beach in secret?"

Frank raised his hands for attention. "Listen to me. We've got to assume the worst. Let's say the sea comes in. The first rush of water could reach all the way to the heading. We've got to think of a way to protect ourselves against that first wave."

"And if we do?" the mechanic said. "The low reach of the tunnel will fill up and we'll be trapped twelve miles from daylight."

"We can hold out here as long as our food lasts–"

"Fuck that . . . I say we should make a run for it."

Anne held up the telephone. "I've got the nurse! She says she's been too busy to answer . . ."

Frank took it. "What the hell's going on up there? We've been trying to get through to somebody for ten minutes . . ."

"I've had my hands full," the nurse said sharply. "A man dead, two policemen hit by a sniper. Can't talk, I'm trying to save a life–"

"And I'm trying to save seven lives! Goddammit, you've got to get a message to one of the job engineers. Have you got a pencil?"

"Yes . . ."

"A flood will trap us in a bubble of air at the heading. There'll only be one chance in hell of getting us out . . ."

"Not so fast . . ."

"Just take down five words. Hendricks will know what I mean. Ready? First word: Seville. S-e-v-i-l-l-e. Got it? Second word . . ."

"Don't be a fool," Greene shouted. "Give yourself up."

Carney crouched in the darkness. He had told his mother to watch television and read the papers because her son was going to be in the news. How did he want to appear, as a man who didn't have the nerve to carry through what he had spent over a year preparing for, or as a man who dealt the British the worst blow in the history of the Irish resistance? He was cornered and was going to be captured, there was no longer any doubt of that.

He closed his eyes tightly and tried to think logically. He could put a bullet in his brain. No, he would never have the nerve to end his own life, not unless he was in pain and maybe not even then. He scratched the battery pole with a thumbnail to make sure the metal surface was free of dirt.

There was no point in arguing with himself. He would blow up the tunnel and he would not surrender until they drove him out with gas. That would make him a hero in the eyes of the only people he loved–a live hero who could possibly be rescued or traded for.

"What's your answer?" he heard the Englishman shout from outside. "Can you hear me?"

"I can hear you, you bloody pig!" His voice was so hoarse and cracked he hardly recognized it. It didn't sound like the voice of a man who was covered with sweat and whose hands were trembling so violently he could hardly make them obey his commands. "Here's your answer . . ."

Carney hunched forward, jamming the wire against the battery. Sparks snapped and flashed as the circuit was closed. Instantly, the shock wave from the distant explosion passed beneath him, followed by a shuddering motion that made him drop his hands to the ground to keep his balance. Four seconds passed before he heard the sound. Even though the vast bulk of Abbot's Cliff was between him and the blast, the roar was stunningly loud—a great clap of thunder that made him wince. He became aware then of another sound, an ominous groan from somewhere above him that steadily gathered strength and volume. He sensed a vibration as well, as if a dozen trains were rumbling by outside, and he felt a fine rain of sand on his head and shoulders. Specks of chalk popped from the walls on either side, and in the slanting ray of light he could see a cloud of dust welling upward. From behind him came the sound of splitting timbers and the crash of cave-ins as the ancient supports, already overloaded by the weight of tons of earth saturated by winter rains, gave way under the new stresses set up by the concussion. Robert Carney, born in 1939 in Dundalk, Ireland, scuttled wildly toward the door as the ground beneath him heaved like rolling surf. In his final lunge he was carried upward and to the left as the walls and roof burst in upon him. The men who would uncover his body later would find his eyes bulging and his mouth open for a scream he never had time to make.

Chapter 25

The explosion split the beach from the mouth of the lower access tunnel to a point beyond the water's edge and threw up a wall of debris and smoke four hundred feet high. Every window within a mile was shattered, and as far away as Paris and Antwerp needles jumped on seismographs. The project headquarters of Channel Tunnel Constructors, perched on the brow of Shakespeare Cliff, was lifted a foot off its foundations. The imploding windows showered Quinn and Crosley with slivers of glass. For a few seconds it seemed to Crosley that the building would break apart and slip over the edge. Taped to his chair, he could do nothing but listen helplessly to the rolling echoes of the blast and the sound of hail on the roof made by descending rocks. One large stone crashed through to the floor of the hallway.

Quinn, blood trickling from small cuts on his face, grabbed his radio. "Carney! Carney! Why couldn't you wait? Goddammit . . ."

By twisting his head to the right, Crosley was able to see through the jagged remains of the window to the lower yard. A strong offshore wind was moving the towering mass of smoke off the beach and over the headlands, revealing a scene of devastation that made Sir Charles gasp in despair. A canal had been torn open and a boiling river of gray water was surging into the mouth of the access tunnel. The sea had been given a way into the cavity that had been drilled beneath it and was rushing to fill it with massive force. Nausea and dizziness came over Crosley as he thought of the men trapped underground. He hoped his attempt to warn them by opening the intercom had been successful, and he hoped they had stayed at the face, where there would be at least a chance of survival, instead of running for the portal, where they would now be hit by a wall of water racing downhill with the speed and power of a runaway freight train. Despite the way the muzzle of the shotgun was digging into the flesh under his chin, he couldn't tear his eyes away from the nightmare below him. The great tunnel that had been a motivating force throughout his life was rapidly filling with water; the historic project that was a symbol of England's resurgence as an industrial power was being destroyed before his eyes. He felt hatred then, hatred more intense than any he had ever known. He twisted and strained against his bonds, and if he could have burst them he would have hurled himself on Quinn and tried to tear him limb from limb.

Eagan had jumped from the locomotive and was running up the slope of the lower access tunnel when the blast knocked him off his feet and rolled him backward. He was momentarily stunned, and when he lifted his head he saw that he had narrowly missed being crushed under a concrete liner section that had fallen from the tunnel wall. Two workmen he had held at bay with his gun a minute earlier were nearby, picking themselves up off the ground and wondering what hit them. Eagan knew, and he also knew that he would be drowned along with them unless he acted fast. At the far, high end of the access tunnel he could see the patch of light that was the portal. As he watched, the lower half turned black. The sea was in and would be on him in seconds.

He scrambled to the ladder of the bucket elevator and climbed to the top. As he stepped onto the conveyor belt he was struck by a wind of hurricane force. Beneath him a sheet of water covering the floor of the tunnel raced downhill followed by a torrent twenty feet deep. Eagan struggled up the belt toward the portal, every ten feet having to drop to all fours to squeeze under the steel mounting brackets that anchored the conveyor housing to the crown. The rising spray was so thick it cut off his view and made the belt so slippery he could hardly keep his balance. Twice he was submerged in turbulent surges of water and needed all his strength to resist the drag of the waves washing over him.

At the end of the belt, Eagan swung his legs over a railing and dropped to the top of the muck hopper that stood at the mouth of the tunnel, pausing to gaze in awe at the deadly river that was pouring across the beach. Beneath his feet the steel structure shuddered as it stood against the current surging against it. Eagan ran along a catwalk, climbed halfway down a ladder, and jumped several feet to the ramp that led into the upper access tunnel. The pounding roar of the flood and the drenching spray made it hard to think, but he was able to keep his mind on the goal of killing Quinn. He turned and began running up the slope of the upper tunnel. He knew the escape route Quinn planned across the roof of the office building, and he would be waiting for him.

Behind him, the muck hopper, its foundations undercut, slowly sagged sideways into the water and was swept underground.

Three hundred meters beneath the center of the English Channel, the sound of the blast came over the intercom loudspeaker as a rising roar that dissolved into static. The ground shock was felt as a barely perceptible tremor. The lights blinked once, then went out. Frank, Anne, and the five men switched on flashlights.

"Let's go," Frank said. "If water is on its way it might get here in as little as five minutes."

Taking Anne's hand, he led a procession through the passageways of the mole, past the silent control booth, through the door in the forward steel bulkhead, and through an access panel to the narrow space between the cutterhead and the raw face of chalk. He had explained to them what he thought would happen in case of flood. The water would gain speed running downhill to Marker Thirteen and would probably build up enough momentum so that some of it would be sent seven kilometers uphill all the way to the heading. After striking the mole it would fold back on itself and subside into the pond that would begin forming at the low point. And if they survived that? It would be up to those on the surface to cut off the inflow. A motor launch could be sent through to rescue them. If enough water came in to fill the tunnel in the low reach, they might have to wait for pumping to draw the level down enough to pass a boat. The idea he had given to the nurse could be tried, too, but he knew that there might not be time enough to make it work. He didn't mention another possibility–so much water might come in that the air in the heading would be compressed to pressure human beings could not withstand.

The bulkhead door was closed and secured and the access panel was swung shut and locked with steel bars. Frank shone his light around. "Everybody here? Okay, nothing to do now but wait." He slapped his palm against the cutterhead between the teeth that dotted its twenty-six-foot-diameter surface. "I don't see how anything could break through this."

The foreman made a suggestion. "If you feel the air getting warm and heavy," he said, "put your hands over your ears. There might be a big jump in pressure."

Frank noticed that Anne's shoulders were crisscrossed with the leather straps of her cameras and equipment bags. "Good God," he said, "did you drag all that stuff in here?"

"Why not?" she said with a small smile. "If I get out of this alive, I'm going to take some prize-winning photographs with me."

The group fell silent, listening. After several minutes they could hear a distant hissing, a faint rushing sound like tires on a wet pavement–slowly louder, relentlessly louder. One man began sobbing. Another fell to his knees and folded his hands. Frank pushed Anne against the wall and tried to shield her with his body. "I love you," she said, "if that helps any."

A racing sheet of water only inches deep arrived first. Pushed by deeper following waves, it stabbed through the length of the mole like a knife, struck the bulkhead with a clap of thunder, and curled up the curving side walls to the crown. The main wall of water was close behind, boiling with the power of a typhoon, carrying with it debris scoured from twelve miles of tunnel—empty muck cars, tool cribs, ventilation pipes, sections of steel rail. Into the mole it smashed, crushing the control station, uprooting the massive electric motors, stripping the walls of every piece of projecting hardware. The bulkhead withstood the assault only briefly before buckling and splitting like cardboard, allowing the wave to hammer directly against the rear surface of the cutterhead. One of the access panels near the top was forced open and a geyser of water burst through to the face, cascading in a torrent onto the figures embracing each other below. To the thunder of the water was added the sound of screaming. The flow stopped suddenly, as if a valve had been closed, and the water, rebounding, surged away in the opposite direction.

Chapter 26

When the arms of the loader were raised to their full extension, the bucket was eleven feet above the ground. Fraser Morris, his rifle resting across one upraised knee, squinted between the ripper teeth that lined the cutting edge of the bucket like crenellations on a fortress wall. He could see that he was even with the roof line of the building and slightly higher than the rotors of the helicopter twenty feet away. He reviewed General Jordan's last-second briefing. With the blast detonated there was nothing left for the terrorist to do but attempt his escape. Keep your sights trained on him, the General had said, and if you get the slightest chance to shoot without costing the hostage his life, take it.

This would be easy, Morris thought, estimating the distances—almost too easy. If they walked straight from the door to the helicopter they would pass almost directly beneath him. Shoot him in the head, the General instructed. At such short range and in such good light he could have been even more specific. Between the eyes? Behind the ear? This wasn't sporting. This was going to make him feel like those fiends who stalk deer in snowmobiles until the poor animals drop from exhaustion and can be killed with a hammer. It seemed hardly necessary for a man of his skills to be roused from sleep and rushed a thousand miles for a job any recruit could handle. Of course, a recruit might get nervous.

. . .

Cyril Jones, his hair combed and his tie straightened in case he had to go on camera immediately, looked with dismay at the policeman who barred his way at the project gate. Behind him was his BBC camera crew, all of them hoping to create a piece of videotape that would be in great demand the world over.

"Do you mean to say," the normally well-composed announcer said in a high-pitched voice his public never heard, "that the blast has already gone off?"

"I'm afraid so. You chaps are too late for that."

Jones threw down his hands in frustration. "Shit!" he said.

The helicopter rose at a steep angle for almost two hundred feet before swooping forward on a level course. The trip from Abbot's Cliff to Shakespeare Cliff would take about a minute. Inspector Greene saw that the slide at the drainage gallery that buried Carney and almost buried him as well was not the only one. The slopes were marked by at least a dozen fresh scars that he could see. So much material had been brought down at one point that the railway tracks were buried for a hundred yards.

On landing inside the gate, Greene sprinted to the police communications van. A desperate debate was under way. Quinn was now demanding that the escape helicopter be transferred immediately to the roof above Crosley's office. General Jordan was opposed to giving in to this latest demand–he wanted Quinn to come out the front door where his executioner was waiting for him. A Detective Inspector from the regional police headquarters in Maidstone, citing recently articulated national policy, insisted that a hard line must be followed. Withdraw the helicopters entirely, he urged. Make no deals at all. Keep Quinn surrounded for weeks if necessary, even if it costs the hostage his life. Giving in merely encouraged further kidnapping.

Crosley's engineering associates strenuously objected to that reasoning. Quinn wasn't bluffing about the explosion and he probably wasn't bluffing about carrying out one more murder. Hendricks of British Rail made a telling point: this was unlike any other case. There were men trapped in the tunnel who could be saved if the water flow were cut off. Bulldozers that tried to push debris into the canal to block it had taken rifle fire from Crosley's office and had had to back off.

"How far can he get in a helicopter?" Hendricks asked, looking from face to face. "Let him go and surround him somewhere else. Get him out of here so we can go to work."

"No! We don't want a mad dog loose in the countryside! We've got him cornered now and we should keep him there . . ."

Greene could see that no one was in command. The crisis had developed so quickly that no clear lines of authority had been established. Top government officials were on their way from London but still had not arrived. Greene picked up the phone that was connected to Crosley's office and shouted for silence.

"Quinn? This is Inspector Greene of Scotland Yard. You can't possibly escape in a helicopter. Every man, woman, and child in England will be following you. Turn the hostage free and give yourself up. It would be an act of mercy that–"

He was cut off by Quinn's furious reply. "I'm giving the orders! If that helicopter isn't on the roof in two minutes, I'm going to start shooting this bastard's fingers off one by one and throw them out to you. There's nothing more to talk about . . ."

"In the name of God, man, hasn't there been enough violence and destruction?"

The police technician at the field switchboard shook his head. "It's no use, Inspector, he's rung off." He pressed several switches, frowning. "I'm showing a short circuit. He might have ripped the instrument from the wall."

The room was silent. The men looked to Greene for a decision. As a mere Inspector he was technically not the man to be in charge of a group that included a General of the Army, a Chief Police Constable, and a Senior Engineer of British Rail, but in the absence of Penton, who continued to languish in the medical trailer, and because Greene had shown great forcefulness in pressing the manhunt and setting up the emergency command post, he was tacitly deferred to now.

"Put the helicopter on the roof," he said.

Chapter 27

Fraser Morris saw a husky, redheaded man clamber over the edge of the flat, graveled roof and crouch behind a water tank with a gun in his hand. Must be a plainclothes policeman, Morris thought, but such a wild-looking fellow, puffing like a racehorse, clothes soaking wet . . .

With a sudden roar, the helicopter that had been idling below him rose vertically, tilted, and swooped to a landing at the far side of the roof. A skylight trapdoor was pushed open from inside the building. Change in the escape route, Morris decided, swinging around and positioning himself as solidly as possible. Yes, that must be it. The General thinks I'm beyond my range and put the other man behind the tank to back me up if I miss. Why should I miss at ninety feet? Ah, here they come through the trapdoor. The grey-haired man in front, that must be Crosley.

Morris centered his sights on Quinn's face. Crosley was in his field of vision, too, along with the handgun that was being held to his temple. He saw the shotgun taped to the hostage's chest, but had not been told that Quinn's left arm, circling Crosley's waist from behind, was attached to the triggers by a loop of twine.

This is more like it, Morris thought. Now I will be able to show what I can do. If that gun leaves Crosley's head for even a second, I'll squeeze off a shot . . .

The sound of pistol fire brought his eyes up. He gasped at what he saw. The other man was running across the roof shooting at the hostage as if to get him out of the way . . . Quinn was shooting back, the man was down, Crosley was down. Morris raised his rifle and tried to put Quinn back in his sights, losing him when he broke for the helicopter. Panic came over the sharpshooter for the first time in his life as he waved the rifle from side to side trying to relocate his target. He had to raise his eyes again —there was Quinn at the helicopter door, struggling to wrench it open while the pilot, leaning across the passenger's seat, tried to hold it closed. Once more Morris raised the rifle and aimed, this time managing to tighten his finger against the trigger.

General Jordan was watching Quinn through binoculars. "Now!" he said through clenched teeth in an unconscious command to his marksman. "Now!" As if in response, there was the crack of a rifle shot. Quinn's head snapped back grotesquely. He fell, his spinal cord severed at the neck.

Sir Charles, his arms tied behind his back, lifted himself to a kneeling position. Blood was spreading across his shirt from wounds in the upper right side of his chest. The helicopter pilot was the first to reach his side.

"I've been hit. Twice, I think . . ."

"I'll get you to a hospital." The pilot worked swiftly with a penknife to free Crosley's hands and slice the tape that held the shotgun.

"The shotgun's empty," Crosley said, grimacing. "I heard the triggers click when Quinn fell . . . He didn't want me blowing my head off prematurely."

Men were pouring onto the roof. Clement Hendricks was among those who helped lift Crosley aboard the helicopter. A doctor climbed in after him. Policemen with drawn revolvers bent over the sprawled and lifeless bodies of Quinn and Eagan.

"The flood must be stopped," Sir Charles said when he saw the British Rail engineer. "There may be men still alive at the face. Can the portal be collapsed? Have we enough explosives on the site to—"

"Frank thought of a faster way," Hendricks said, motioning for Crosley not to talk. "Just before the blast he got a message through from the heading." He repeated the five words the nurse had jotted down: "Seville-OSARV, RAF bomb portal."

"Frank is in the tunnel?" The news seemed to weaken Crosley even further. His body sagged as the pilot and the doctor strapped him into his seat. "Yes, the Air Force . . . that would be fastest." His words were barely audible over the stutter of the helicopter engine. "But what can Seville . . ."

"OSARV is a submarine," Hendricks said, having to shout as the pilot increased the rotor speed. "It must be Frank's idea that a sub could be put in at Folkestone . . ."

Crosley nodded weakly as the doctor pulled the door shut. The helicopter lifted off, then peeled away, setting a level course across the face of Shakespeare Cliff toward Dover.

Chapter 28

In Evanston, Illinois, William Ingram pulled a shirt from a hanger and jabbed at it with his fingers trying to find the sleeve. He dropped it on the floor and stood staring into space. No, he told himself, I don't have time to get dressed and go to the office. I'll have to make the calls from here. I told Hendricks I'd take charge of airlifting the submarine to England, so I better start right now.

"Clara!" he shouted, trying to wake his wife in the next room. "Clara! Get up! Get me some black coffee! Hurry!"

He sat on the bed and picked up the phone. The sub was in La Jolla, Hendricks had said, just back from a research cruise. What the devil was the name of that oceanographic institute? Good God, it would only be five in the morning in California. He'd have to call the La Jolla police and get them to track down the scientists in charge. His Pacific Coast manager could fly down from San Francisco and get things ready at the San Diego Naval Shipyard. His third call would be to the Strategic Air Command in Colorado Springs to see if they had a Galaxy ready to go.

Clara Ingram appeared in the bedroom doorway. "What on earth is the matter?"

He raised his arm to shake it and shout the way he always did when things went wrong and he wanted action. He hesitated. The phone call from Dover meant that he was president, chairman of the board, and sole owner of little more than a punctured balloon.

The Ingram Construction Corporation, he realized, letting his hand fall to his lap, the goliath he had spent a lifetime building, was a dead fish.

"Somebody blew up the tunnel," he said hollowly, "and the sea is pouring in. They think Kenward's down there. Probably drowned by now. Kenward! And I had to plead with the man to take the job!" Were tears coming to his eyes? He turned his head to hide them from his wife. "There are financial consequences of this, my dear, that we'll both have to face. Get me some coffee, please. We'll have a talk later."

A truck crane was parked on the edge of Shakespeare Cliff with its boom lowered to horizontal. Dangling a hundred feet below in a bosun's chair was a man holding a blazing highway flare, pushing himself across the face of the chalk with thrusts of his legs. Clouds of mist rising from the surging water below made him invisible at times to Hendricks, who was supervising the operation by radio from Crosley's office.

"Right there is fine," Hendricks said, holding the microphone close to his mouth. He watched the man at the end of the cable lean to one side, fix the flare in position, then push himself away. "Pull him up, Tom," Hendricks said to the crane operator, "and get your rig out of there. The bomber is on its way."

He studied the cliff above the portal through binoculars. He was satisfied. Three flares had been placed in a large triangle. At least one remained in view no matter what the wind did to the mist. An explosion anywhere close should bring down a massive shoulder of the hill. If it didn't, they could probably abandon any hopes of rescuing the survivors . . . if there were any.

A Hawker Siddeley Buccaneer bearing the markings of the Royal Air Force crossed the coast above the project with four one-thousand-pound bombs in its weapons bay. Hendricks saw it flash overhead a full second before hearing the whistling roar of the twin turbofan jet engines. Once over the water the plane went into a long, right-hand bank, losing altitude and seeming to diminish in size until it was a barely visible speck skimming the surface of the Channel. After being out of sight for fifteen seconds, the plane burst into view from behind Abbot's Cliff only thirty feet above the ground, streaking like an arrow toward the red glow of the flares. When it seemed certain that it would crash into the slope inside the outlined triangle, it veered sharply upward, clearing the cliff edge by what seemed like inches.

None of those watching from the shattered windows of the headquarters building when the plane passed beneath them saw the bombs released, but they couldn't miss the results: four stunning explosions that made the headlands shake. Four plumes of black smoke merged into a single slowly rising column followed by an upward-boiling plume of white dust. The bombs were right on target, bringing so much of the cliff face sliding down that every trace of the portal was obliterated. The ponderous tide of water moving across the beach was carried by its own momentum halfway up the mountain of material that now blocked its way, and in washing back down into its trench it seemed to be making an effort to claw the portal open again. By the time the air cleared the water was quiet and it was obvious that the leak was plugged. To make sure it stayed plugged, an armada of trucks, loaders, and bulldozers advanced on the trench to fill it with earth.

The French tunneling crews made a dramatic offer. They would push themselves and their mole to the ultimate limits. They would dispense with the erection of liner rings and they would distribute excavated material along the length of the tunnel instead of hauling it all the way to the surface. By such extreme measures they could close the gap that remained between the two headings in thirteen days. When they broke through to rescue their brave British colleagues, they pledged, they would present them with a banquet prepared on the spot by the finest chefs in all of France. The offer was refused with thanks. Proceeding without the protection of liner rings would subject the men to cave-in risks that were too great. Those to be rescued, after all, might already be dead.

A proposal from British Petroleum was accepted. An offshore drilling platform on its way from Bristol to Scotland and now opposite Ostend, Belgium, could be diverted to the Strait. Towing it fifty miles and positioning it accurately over the heading in one hundred sixty feet of water would take four days. Sinking a six-inch-diameter well casing through one hundred fifty feet of chalk—allowing for several misses—would take another four days. The hole would serve to establish contact with any possible survivors, relieve the air pressure, and enable food and medical supplies to be lowered while the long process of pumping the tunnel out was under way. BP was told to proceed with all possible speed.

The main hope lay with OSARV—the Ocean Salvage and Research Vessel. Seville in Pittsburgh and Ingram in Evanston, reporting to Hendricks via a transatlantic conference call, estimated that the craft would arrive in Heathrow within thirty hours, would enter the Folkestone portal ten hours later, and, if the tunnel weren't hopelessly blocked, would reach the face fifteen or twenty hours after that. A team of welders from the Seville plant was on its way to California and would modify the sub while it was airborne. The interior would be stripped of unnecessary equipment, and the outriggers would be reshaped to conform to the inside diameter of the tunnel. Hendricks jotted down the dimensions and weight as Seville rattled them off. Call the industrial drayage companies, Ingram instructed, and have the heaviest trailer in England waiting at the airport, preferably one with rear steering. Stiles must go to work at once outfitting it with a wooden cradle that will hold the sub upright during the trip south from London. It'll be a tight squeeze, so make sure that that part of the tunnel that hasn't been flooded, all the way from the Folkestone portal to the water, is free of equipment.

At eleven o'clock Sunday morning, Pacific Daylight Time, a rigging superintendent at the San Diego Naval Shipyard raised his right arm and moved his hand in small circles. The operators of four Ingram Construction Corporation crawler cranes drew back on their load levers. As the lines were drawn in, the diesel engines labored in unison and the OSARV slowly rose above the water at the edge of the dock. Dripping wet and with its grappling arms and outriggers hanging awkwardly, the submarine resembled a lobster being drawn from a pot–a lobster sixty feet long, fifteen feet in diameter, and weighing one hundred and twenty tons. Waiting to receive it was a lowbed trailer normally used for moving outsized power plant components.

The three-mile trip to the airport took three hours and created traffic jams all over the downtown area. Photographs of the caravan en route–the side-by-side truck tractors at the front, the trailer and its ninety pairs of rubber tires, the walking escort of flagmen and highway patrolmen–were beamed by satellite to all parts of the world. Several London newspapers went to work on special editions that would feature photo spreads under such headlines as "A Last Desperate Chance" and "Hang on–Help Is on the Way."

At the end of the main runway at Lindbergh Field in San Diego was the only plane in the world large enough to transport an object as heavy as the OSARV–a Lockheed Galaxy C5A, its nose swung upward to admit its cargo. To save weight it would take off with only half its maximum complement of fuel. To save time during the fifty-three-hundred-mile flight to Heathrow, refueling would be carried out in the air by a Boeing KC135 Stratotanker, once over the Great Lakes and once over Labrador.

Joe Seville, satisfied that the craftsmen who would accompany the OSARV understood the modifications he wanted made, boarded a commercial jet in Pittsburgh bound for London. He knew more about the submarine than any man alive, so he was going to insist that he be allowed to pilot it through the tunnel. The publicity would be worth a fortune. The block of Seville Steel stock he owned himself could easily double in price. Besides, since his doctors told him to quit skiing he hadn't had much real fun.

The Prime Minister spoke with obvious emotion as the television cameras slowly drew closer. "No matter what the cost, no matter what the sacrifice, the tunnel will be completed as designed. To do anything less would be to dishonor the memory of those whose lives have been so senselessly taken from them, of those who have labored so long and so well on a project that has captured the imagination of the world, and of those who will be rescued, with God's help, from the darkness beneath the bottom of the sea. Violent acts against a free society are detestable, are insane, are an outrage against decency and fairness–a completed tunnel will stand as proof that they are futile as well."

Chapter 29

For most of the two days following the explosion, Sir Charles drifted between sleep and a state of drug-diminished consciousness. The bullets had passed through his body, but heart and lung damage and internal bleeding were steadily draining his strength. There were moments of perfect lucidity. Now, as he was being trundled down a corridor on a gurney toward another encounter with the surgeons, his mind seemed as sharp as ever. He had been allowed to watch the Prime Minister's statement to the nation, and the message had buoyed him. He felt the pressure of his wife's hand in his. He looked at her and tried to raise his head.

"You must make certain he honors his pledge . . . the tunnel *must* be pressed to completion . . ."

"I'll do what I can. Lie back . . . conserve your strength. The newspapers are all on our side now."

"It would be a crime to turn away . . . so much accomplished . . . so near success. If only Frank . . . Angela, you must tell me the instant you hear he's safe."

"Yes . . . yes. Please, no more talking . . ."

His mind drifted back to what the men had said the day before when they were allowed to visit him in his room. Not as much water had flowed into the tunnel as was first feared, certainly no more than three hundred million gallons. Land Rovers entering the Folkestone portal advanced fourteen kilometers, seven miles past the intersection with the Shakespeare Cliff adit, before reaching the flood portion of the bore. Hendricks and Stiles climbed aboard a motor launch and were able to push on four kilometers farther before running out of head room. Where they turned back was about nine hundred meters short of the tunnel's low point at Marker Thirteen.

He saw the lights in the ceiling of the operating room and he felt himself being transferred to the table. Numbers tumbled through his mind. The grade of the tunnel as it rose from the low point to the face six kilometers beyond varied between one and two percent, which meant that water was standing six or seven feet deep at the far end. If Frank and Anne and the maintenance men had survived the initial surge, they were now clinging to the upper platforms of the mole like so many wet rats. Thank God the flow was cut off when it was.

When his colleagues were gathered around his bed, they tried to imagine what they would have done if they had been in Frank's place, knowing the tunnel might be flooded. The phone call he made to the nurse showed he knew what could happen. Pull back the cutterhead, yes, and take refuge on the far side. Surely Frank would have seen it was the only chance.

Crosley himself thought of checking the recording graphs on the electrical generators. The phone call was placed from his hospital room to the project powerhouse. Thirty minutes later, just as the doctor was asking the men to leave, the answer they wanted came back: Minutes before the blast there had been a surge of current into the tunnel consistent with drawing back the cutterhead.

The anesthetist placed the mask over his nose and mouth. Sir Charles became aware then that his wife's hand was no longer in his. He lifted his arm, reaching. "Angela," he tried to say, then fell back, realizing that she had probably been stopped at the doorway to the operating room. It's all right, he assured himself, she'll be waiting for me when it's over. He tried to relax. The gas smelled sweet, and he let it draw him toward the darkness. He closed his eyes for the last time.

It was after midnight in Folkestone. The construction yard and the hillside surrounding the black circle of the tunnel portal were ablaze with floodlights. Two hundred newsmen were on hand to record every detail of OSARV's arrival. Communications satellites enabled television viewers the world over to watch the submarine being lifted by cranes from the highway trailer and lowered onto the improvised cradle of wheeled floats that would take it underground. Two ten-wheel truck tractors connected in tandem nosed forward until the front bumper of the lead vehicle touched the rear edge of the submarine carrier. Workmen lashed them together with cable. Seven kilometers into the tunnel, at the point where water pouring down the Shakespeare Cliff adit had scoured a deep trench in the floor of the main bore, a prefabricated Bailey bridge was being positioned and reinforced sufficiently to carry OSARV's weight.

In a corrugated steel building normally used for repairing construction equipment, British Rail engineers took turns explaining the rescue plan to reporters. The truck tractors would push the cradle into the tunnel until the water was deep enough to enable it to float. The trucks would back off then in favor of a flotilla of motor launches that would both push and pull the cradle into water that was at least fifteen feet deep. Ballast tanks would be flooded to sink the cradle, allowing the submarine to float free. The submarine would proceed under its own power until running out of headroom, when it would submerge for the passage through the low reach of the tunnel, which was completely filled with water. On the return trip the sequence would be reversed.

"But how," a reporter demanded, "did the flood happen in the first place? How could so much dynamite be planted right in the middle of a construction project without anybody noticing it?"

That aspect was still under investigation.

"Look at that pile of junk!" Joe Seville said, staring at the television monitor. "Every muck car in the joint must have wound up here. Is that the ass end of an MG sticking out on the left? That's what Kenward drives, isn't it, Barnhardt? I'll have to tell the silly bastard to be more careful where he parks."

"I'm afraid I wouldn't know what Mr. Kenward drives," said

the man next to Seville. "I've never had the pleasure of meeting him." Lawrence Barnhardt, M.D., of the Royal Navy, a specialist in hyperbaric medicine as well as an authority on exposure, shock, and malnutrition, was the man chosen from many volunteers to accompany Seville on the trip through the flooded tunnel. The two men were seated at the controls of OSARV. Before them were the display screens of the forward television cameras. The water in which the craft was submerged was carrying a high percentage of chalk particles in suspension, and despite the intensity of the submarine's searchlights visibility was limited to fifteen or twenty feet. They had arrived at the lowest reach of the tunnel, where most of the debris carried by the flood had settled. On the invert was a layer of sediment four feet thick. Rising in the ghostly gray-white of the water was a tangle of overturned muck cars, lumber, cable, pipe sections, and pieces of broken concrete.

"Watch this, Doc," Seville said, "and you'll see why a work boat designed for deep-sea salvage was needed for this assignment and not some rinky-dink bathtub toy."

The welders on the cargo plane had done their job well. The submarine's outriggers had been lengthened and fitted with shoes that matched the curve of the tunnel walls. Within minutes the craft was anchored solidly. Seville eased two levers forward. On the television monitors two manipulators came into view like the pincers of a crab. A thin, articulated arm appeared as well, on the end of which was a circular saw and a heavy metal shears.

"I'll have this mess torn apart and spread out in an hour," Seville said, pushing buttons and stepping on pedals as if he were a church organist. "Don't believe me, eh? Look there!"

One of the clam buckets had closed on the tongue of a muck car and pulled it loose. It tumbled slowly downward out of view, pulling several others with it and raising a cloud of turbidity.

Angela Crosley, her eyes red from hours of weeping, rose uncertainly to her feet. The look of the surgeon in the doorway

—the grimness of his mouth, the defeated cast of his shoulders—told her that the worst had happened. She sank into her chair and sobbed convulsively.

The rim of OSARV's conning tower broke the surface, followed by the upper portion of the hull. The clank of the hatch swinging open was magnified eerily in the confined space between the water surface and the tunnel crown.

"We've only got about a foot to spare," Barnhardt said, calling down from the top of the ladder.

"See anything ahead?" Seville asked.

"All clear. Looks like the view through a proctoscope. Hold on! I think I hear cheering! Yes, that's definitely cheering!"

"Give them a holler. I'll blink the lights so they'll know we're not a mirage. Keep your eyes open and don't bump your head. I'm going to ease forward on slow till we touch bottom." He kept his eyes on the television screens. The water, which was relatively clear and free of debris, grew steadily shallower as the submarine advanced. When the bottom of the hull scraped against the invert he cut the power and extended the outriggers. They were a hundred feet from the mole's trailing conveyor, three hundred feet from the face. He struggled to his feet, stretched his arms, and rubbed his face. He had been at the controls for nearly eight hours without a break.

"End of the line," Seville said. "This is as close as we can get. Jesus Christ, I must be getting old. Fifty years ago I could have done this and still felt fresh as a daisy. Break out the rubber rafts, Doc. I hope you know how to inflate the goddam things."

Barnhardt, climbing down the ladder, assured him that he had done it many times on camping trips under far worse conditions, namely, with a wife and two children criticizing his every move.

"What took you so long?" Frank asked, helping Seville climb from the boat to the conveyor deck of the mole. "We were beginning to get a little worried."

"All the trouble we've gone to," Seville said, grinning, "and that's the thanks we get?"

"You old bastard! I've never been so glad to see anybody in my whole life."

The two men embraced. Their eyes were wet.

In turn, Seville threw his arms around Anne and each of the five other men.

"Don't mind Mr. Kenward," the foreman told Seville. "He's just mad because he lost a bet." He explained that Frank had been so sure they would be on dry land within thirty-six hours he promised to pay every one of them a quid for every hour beyond that. He now owed a total of seventy-two quid and they weren't out yet.

"The worst part," Frank said while warmly shaking Barnhardt's hand, "is that I don't get paid till Friday."

"Don't mind me," Anne said, addressing the group and raising a camera, "I'm going to take a few pictures."

Barnhardt gave everyone a brief medical inspection. Two days of alternating rest and calisthenics had left the rescued, in some ways, in better condition than the rescuers. Seville, in particular, would need a few hours' sleep before starting the return trip.

Three yellow rubber rafts moved away from the mole and floated toward the lights of the OSARV. In the last one, Frank and Anne knelt side by side dipping paddles into the water. Seville, their only passenger, sat facing them, talking animatedly about what they could expect when they reached the surface.

"I'll lay you three-to-one odds there'll be five thousand people cheering. There was a crowd almost that big when I left. It's amazing–the whole country seems to be behind the project now. Nothing like a disaster to unite people, is there? Why, Hendricks told me even that bunch of birdwatching fanatics that used to give him so much trouble is helping out by giving tea and biscuits to the cleanup and rescue teams . . . an outfit called DRAT or SPLAT, something like that."

Anne's eyes widened. "You mean SKAT?"

"That's it, SKAT. They're carrying signs saying they were against the tunnel but not the workmen."

"Good Lord," Anne said, "it looks as though I still have a part-time job. I'll probably be put right to work washing cups."

Frank laughed. "You know," he said, "I had half a notion to resign after the first bore holed through, try teaching or something that didn't get my shoes dirty. But not after this. I've got to stick it out now. You can understand that, can't you, Anne? Why I can't walk away? Do you mind if I wait a couple of years before becoming a conservationist?"

"I knew you'd never quit."

"I'm looking *forward* to the rest of the job. I'm going to see that this goddam water gets pumped out of here, get drunk with the French crews at the cocktail party, and set some records on the parallel tunnel that'll stand forever."

"Pardon me for staring," Seville said to Anne, "but you are the best-looking sandhog I've ever seen. Would you mind telling me what possessed you to come into such a godforsaken hole? Didn't anybody tell you there's an old superstition about women in tunnels?"

"I wouldn't listen. If I had known what was going to happen, believe me, I would have stayed in the kitchen."

"And I would be numbered among the dead," Frank added. "She saved my life. She fired a flashbulb in Eagan's eyes just as he was taking a shot at me. Now she's responsible for me as long as she lives." He leaned to one side and kissed her tear-stained cheek. "You'll have to marry me, my friend. It's your duty."

"What's wrong with our present arrangement?"

"It's uneconomical. It's indecent."

"He's been through a terrible ordeal," Seville said. "He'll come to his senses when he's had a hot meal and put on some dry clothes."

"I am in full possession of my senses. There is nothing weird about my wanting to marry Miss Reed. It's the perfectly natural result of having sadistic parents who crippled me morally."

"I might marry you," Anne said. "But if I do, it'll only be for a little while."

Epilogue

On November 17, 1973, after one hundred seventy years of speculation, it looked as though the English Channel tunnel would be built at last. On that day, representatives of the British and French governments put their signatures to a treaty calling for construction to begin and describing how financing, construction, and management would be shared. The respective legislatures had until January 1, 1975, to ratify the treaty and authorize the awarding of the final contracts.

In charge of the project were two groups of private firms, the British Channel Tunnel Company, Ltd., and the Société française du tunnel sous la Manche, which would coordinate the design with the state-owned railroads, supervise the construction firms to make sure they adhered to plans and specifications, and share revenues with the governments for the first fifty years of tunnel operation, after which total ownership would be assumed by Britain and France. Money for construction was to be borrowed by the private firms on the international market; connecting links were to be paid for by the governments. The French, as they had been for over a hundred years, were much in favor of a physical link with Britain and anxious to begin work.

The plan was to drive two parallel railroad tunnels twenty-two-and-a-half feet in diameter and ninety-nine feet apart, with a fifteen-foot-diameter service tunnel between them. The tunnels would be thirty-two miles long, of which twenty-three miles would be under Dover Strait. All three would be driven at once from both ends toward the middle. It was projected that trains carrying vehicles, passengers, and freight could begin their round-the-clock shuttle by 1980.

Following the signing of the treaty, preliminary contracts were awarded for excavating access tunnels, preparing work sites, and driving one mile of service tunnel on both sides of the Channel. The contractor chosen by the British was a joint venture of Balfour Beatty Co., Ltd., Edmund Nuttall, Ltd., and Taylor Woodrow Construction, Ltd., all of Great Britain, and Guy F. Atkinson Co., Inc., of South San Francisco, California. Their work was to be completed by mid-1975, when billion-dollar contracts would be awarded for the rest of the project.

For the service tunnel drive, the British-American contractors ordered a rotary tunnel machine from Robert L. Priestly, Ltd., of Gravesend, Kent; The German-Italian-French group on the other side ordered its mole from the James F. Robbins Co., Inc., of Seattle, Washington.

The euphoria among those who had long advocated the project soon began to fade. In Britain there was a growing chorus of criticism. The national economy was in trouble. It was hard to justify starting a huge capital investment program during an energy crisis and a worsening recession, especially in that part of the country that needed stimulation least. In July of 1975, the Labour government ordered an independent appraisal of economic feasibility in the light of new conditions.

The door began to swing shut on November 27, 1974, when the British government admitted that the cost of the high-speed rail link required between the Folkestone portal and London had risen out of reach, partly because of design changes forced by environmentalists. The January 1, 1975, deadline for ratifying the treaty slipped by. Finally, on January 20, much to the dismay of the French, Environment Secretary Anthony Crosland announced to the members of Parliament that the project would have to be shelved, a victim of politics and inflation.

"A profound dejection gripped the construction sites," reported the *New Civil Engineer,* a British trade journal, "while accusations flew among politicians and tunnel officials in London and Paris. The only agreement was a sadness at the ignoble death of such a noble project."

But the project isn't dead, quite. The British government has pledged to keep the workings in "the best possible state" in case there is a reversal in the country's fortunes. The lower access tunnel has been weatherproofed, and seepage is not being allowed to accumulate. The Priestly mole, after advancing two hundred meters, was left in place, not far from where Colonel Beaumont's machine was abandoned in 1881 and D. Whitaker's in 1923, buried monuments to earlier Channel-crossing dreams. Once a month a British Rail engineer descends the lower access tunnel and walks the length of the service tunnel to check for leaks and settlement and to lubricate the tunnel machine–a ritual of hope carried out in an atmosphere of gloom.

On the French side, where porous ground had to be crossed at the start, it was necessary to let the access tunnel flood. When the British announced that they were withdrawing from the project, water was pouring into the heading near Calais at the rate of one hundred twenty cubic feet per second. Installing a permanent pumping system would have been far too costly. The million-dollar Robbins mole, fortunately, had not been taken underground.

Visitors to the construction site today at Shakespeare Cliff can see the upper yard, the upper access tunnel to the beach, the lower work area, and the lower access tunnel, just as they are described in this book. Everything else is fictional, including especially the characters.

If the project is revived, workers should be assured that the segment of the Beaumont tunnel accessible from the foot of Abbot's Cliff is not connected to the segment that runs under the lower work area and therefore of no use to terrorists, however maniacal they might be.

ACKNOWLEDGMENTS

For technical help I wish to thank Dick Byers, Errol Platt, and Hans Sacrison of the Guy F. Atkinson Company, general contractors; Neville Long of the Bechtel Corporation, engineers; Alan Hardie of Mott, Hay, and Anderson, engineers; S. F. O'Donnell of Scotland Yard; John Dunkley of the British Channel Tunnel Company; Captain B. Robinson, Master Mariner with the Townsend Car Ferry Company on the Dover-Calais run; Derek Burnett, secretary of the Channel Tunnel Opposition Association; and two British Rail engineers, Ron Davis of London and Kenneth Adams of Folkestone. Adams, who guided me along the seawall and into the eerie Beaumont tunnel, is the world's greatest authority on early Channel tunnel schemes; I have relied on an unpublished monograph of his for historical details. For reading the first draft of the manuscript and making many valuable suggestions, I am grateful to Josefa Heifetz, Julia Reisz, and Neville Long. Drawings accompanying the text are the work of Mark Mikulich of Lagunitas, California.

The best of several books on the colorful history of the project is *The Tunnel Under the Channel,* by Thomas Whiteside (Simon & Schuster, 1962), which is an expansion of articles written for *The New Yorker.* The often amazing story of underground construction in general is well told in *Tunnels,* by Gösta Sandström (Holt, Rinehart and Winston, 1963), on which I relied for facts of the Lötschberg disaster.

R. B.
Mill Valley, California